TINY
BLESSINGS

More Mother's Day fiction

Home Sweet Home

In Bloom

A Mother's Love

FERN MICHAELS
CAROLYN BROWN
STACY FINZ

TINY
BLESSINGS

ZEBRA BOOKS
Kensington Publishing Corp.
www.kensingtonbooks.com

ZEBRA BOOKS are published by

Kensington Publishing Corp.
900 Third Avenue
New York, NY 10022

All Kensington titles, imprints, and distributed lines are available at special quantity discounts for bulk purchases for sales promotion, premiums, fund-raising, educational, or institutional use.

Special book excerpts or customized printings can also be created to fit specific needs. For details, write or phone the office of the Kensington Sales Manager: Attn.: Sales Department. Kensington Publishing Corp., 900 Third Avenue, New York, NY 10022. Phone: 1-800-221-2647.

ZEBRA BOOKS and the Z logo Reg US Pat. & TM Off.

First Printing: May 2024
ISBN: 978-1-4201-5582-2
ISBN: 978-1-4201-5583-9 (ebook)

10 9 8 7 6 5 4 3 2 1

Printed in the United States of America

Contents

Tiny Blessings
by Fern Michaels
1

Dogwood Season
by Carolyn Brown
115

Cowboy True
by Stacy Finz
223

TINY BLESSINGS

Fern Michaels

Chapter One

Emma Swan grinned as she poured the remains of her coffee into the shiny white farmhouse sink. Her new condominium, a "smart" condo, had every flashy gadget on the market. She'd immediately downloaded the required apps to her smartphone the day she arrived. With a swipe of her finger, she now controlled the lighting, music, room temperature, security, and smoke detection. A touch screen on her refrigerator told her when her lettuce expired or if she needed milk. She was satisfied that no one could come to her door without her seeing and hearing them first, so the condo was worth every penny she'd paid for it. Not that Emma expected a visitor. She'd only moved in three weeks ago.

Right out of law school, she'd purchased her first condo, which was twenty years old. The bonus: It was on the beach. At the time it was expensive, but worth it for her view of the white sand and water. She hadn't had a dishwasher in her old condo, so now, out of habit, she washed her cup, dried it, and returned it to its hook next to her bright red coffee maker.

Four years ago, when she made her final mortgage payment, her intention was a total condo makeover. But work had gotten in the way—as usual—and it never happened. Nearing thirty-two, Emma knew she didn't want to continue to practice law; no more hustling or working twenty-four-seven. After graduating high school early, she'd gotten a head start on college. She earned a bachelor's degree in education before law school and kept her teaching certificate current. After practicing corporate law in Miami for almost ten years, she now yearned for a slower-paced lifestyle. Harris, her law partner, always teased her about that.

Before Harris could convince her to stay, she'd sold her original condo, hired her replacement, and bought the home she now occupied. The day she placed her condo on the market, she also sent her résumé to several schools in Conch County, where she now lived.

The week before, she'd been called to substitute for a kindergarten class at Orange Grove Elementary. Emma knew she'd made the right decision because she'd smiled all day at the children and their silly questions. The innocence in their pink-cheeked, wide-eyed little grins made her happier than corporate law ever had. She was content to substitute until a full-time position became available, and she made each free day special, taking the opportunity to explore Pink Pearl Cove. Though she hadn't confessed it to anyone, one of the many reasons she'd chosen this small beach town on an island off the Gulf Coast was its name. Low crime and great schools were a bonus.

Her parents had been in their late forties when Emma entered their lives, unplanned. Both attorneys, they'd left her mostly in the care of Lydia, her nanny, who treated her as though she were her daughter. When Emma did spend time with her mom and dad, they doted on her, but only for what seemed like seconds. Then she was returned to Lydia for the remainder of whatever time her parents were at their luxurious home in South Miami Beach. They had spent more time away from her than with her. Sadly, both were now gone, but she did have happy memories of them.

Now it was time for her to make her own memories.

Emma planned to spend a few hours by the pool reading the book she'd picked up at the library. *Who am I kidding?* she asked herself. In the past three weeks, she'd become fascinated by the guy in the condo directly across from hers. So far, she hadn't seen another female enter his apartment. He also defined tall, dark, and handsome, so she'd amused herself by watching him.

"Stalking is more like it," she whispered to no one. It was Saturday, so Emma guessed her neighbor might spend the afternoon at the pool. It was one of the upsides of living in Florida. The pools were heated and the weather warm enough so she could swim throughout the year, even in March.

In the bedroom, she changed into a kelly-green, one-piece swimsuit. It was her favorite color and complemented her olive complexion. Emma tied her dark brown hair in a loose topknot and glanced at herself in the mirror. She was the spitting image of her father, especially her brown, almond-shaped eyes. At five foot nine, she wasn't as tall as his six foot four, but tall enough to want to bring a pair of flats on the few blind dates Harris had managed to finagle her into. Being taller than her dates always bothered her. She thought of her neighbor. He appeared to be as tall as her father had been, maybe taller.

"Come on, Em," she again said to no one. She needed a social life now that she had time. Grabbing her book, beach towel, and sunscreen, she located her keys on the new dolphin-shaped key ring holder she'd hung up near the door just last night. Pink Pearl Cove had dozens of shops she wanted to explore; the key ring holder had been her first purchase at Susie's Sea Stuff. Her cell phone buzzed, reminding her to bring it with her too.

"Hello," she said, using her shoulder to hold the phone to her ear. Closing the door with her foot, she headed to the pool. "I'm fine, Harris. You don't have to call me every day." Her former partner was twenty years her senior. He'd always teased her and treated her like one of his daughters. He had five of them, so what was one more, he would say.

"I'm just checking in—wanted to see how life's treating you in Pinkville," Harris said.

Emma laughed, "It's Pink Pearl Cove. It was the

right decision for me. I taught a bunch of five-year-olds the other day. I hated for the day to end. You know I'm subbing right now." He did know that, but she mentioned it anyway. "It's fun work."

"Yep, I'm sure it is. You sound happy, kid. So on that note, behave yourself. I'll check in soon." He hung up just as Emma located a lounge chair by the pool's deep end.

Unwrapping the towel from her waist, she wished she'd remembered to wear her cover-up. But it was too late now. Arranging the towel on the chaise, she sat down, applied sunscreen, then focused on the book she'd been waiting to read. Emma flipped through the pages of her novel for the next half hour, captivated by the characters trapped in a department store during a tornado.

"Mind if I sit here?" a deep male voice asked.

Emma slammed her book shut, holding it in front of her chest and briefly closing her eyes. It must be *him.*

"Uh . . . no," she sputtered, feeling like a teenager.

She dared a glance at the body next to her. His tanned legs were long and muscular, but no way was he the neighbor she'd had her eye on. He didn't appear tall enough. Should she ask him his name? No, she decided. Even in this age of online dating, with eHarmony, Tinder, and Zoosk—none of which she'd ever used—she wasn't the type to make the first move.

Emma returned to her novel but couldn't focus on the storyline with the stranger lounging beside her. She was hot, but didn't want to draw attention to herself. But if she were going to live here, she'd have to make friends. She might as well start by making a big splash. Literally.

Growing up in Miami, she'd spent hours in the pool and on a diving board. Standing at the edge of the pool, Emma concentrated on her dive. Her toes lifted away from the pool's coping, and she sliced through the aquamarine water like a pro. She swam to the shallow end and back before coming up for air. Wiping the water out of her eyes, Emma lifted herself out of the pool and returned to her chair. Using her towel, she blotted her wet skin. Glancing at the chaise beside her, she saw the guy appeared to be sleeping. Doing her best not to attract attention, she returned to her novel. Again, she became so involved with the story that she forgot about the man in the lounge chair.

Suddenly, a giant wave of pool water hit her book, soaking it. Before she could say anything, a young woman around her age approached the pool's edge. "Hey, I didn't mean to splash you. My nephew double-dared me to do a cannonball. It looks like I win the dare and owe you a book." The woman pushed herself out of the pool. "I'm Marlena. I live here with my husband, Walter. We're babysitting for my sister-in-law today." She motioned to a young boy, who appeared to be eight or nine, splashing in the pool.

"Nice to meet you. I'm Emma Swan, in Four-C." Emma smiled.

"I know," said Marlena. "When there's a new homeowner, everyone knows. We're like a nosy little community among ourselves."

Emma tucked that tidbit of information away

for later. "So, tell me about this nosy little community. Anything special I should know?" She sounded teasing—but she wasn't.

"Provided the weather is cooperative, we have a cookout here at the pool the first Saturday of every month. We have a food fund. Walter and I own Vittles, the local market, so we pick up the food. It's a good time, a get-to-know-your-neighbors kind of thing. Nothing fancy. You should come next month."

"I will."

"So let me know about the book. I'll get you a new, dry one."

"It's a library book," Emma said, lifting her brows and grinning.

Marlena nodded. "I'll buy three copies, then."

Emma laughed. "One is enough. I'm sure the library will understand."

"You don't know Mrs. Whitton. She epitomizes all the negative images of a librarian drilled into me as a kid. She's been around since we moved here. I think she was the town's *first* librarian."

"Surely a damaged book isn't . . ." Emma searched for the right word. ". . . that big a deal?"

"It's not to most folks, but Mrs. Whitton is very serious about her books and their care. I'm surprised you got a library card so soon."

A whiny, high-pitched voice interrupted them. "Aunt Marlena! Are you going to play with me? I'll tell Mommy if you don't hurry up."

"I'm coming, Jeffrey." Marlena rolled her eyes and mouthed to Emma, *He is such a brat.*

"Go on, and I'll let you know Mrs. Whitton's reaction."

"Please do," Marlena called over her shoulder, then made a second giant splash in the pool.

Emma knew she would be friends with this feisty woman. Deciding she'd had enough sun for one day, she scooped up her towel and book, then wrapped her damp towel around her waist.

As she returned to her condo, she planned a cool shower and a salad for dinner while she waited for her book to dry out on the balcony. Plus, she might catch a glimpse of her neighbor across the way. Who knew?

Chapter Two

Nash Kendrick stood on his balcony observing the woman in the green swimsuit. She must be the new resident in the condo directly across from his. Not wanting to spy on her but doing it anyway, he stared at her as she entered her condo. Her drapes were open; she put something on her patio table, then went inside. While he couldn't discern her facial features, he decided that if they matched with the rest of her, she must be a knockout.

He stepped away from the window, a grin on his face. He wondered if Penny would approve of their new neighbor. Probably not, because she was extremely possessive.

Nash had allowed himself to get behind on grading last week's math tests. He planned to spend the remainder of the weekend catching up. He enjoyed teaching math more than he'd thought he would. Numbers came naturally to him. He never imagined he would be teaching math to high school seniors, but he'd also never thought the investment firm he'd spent most of his adult life working at would go bankrupt. After all the lockdowns, New York City became a ghost town. He'd hung around for a few months—he'd never been a quitter—but a year without work sent him to Florida, his home state. Now, two years later, when all the pandemic hoopla had died down, he was glad he'd decided to return to the Cove. He enjoyed his new job way more than he'd thought he would, and he'd learned last week that he'd been accepted as a chaperone for the senior class's spring break trip to Miami Beach. His students didn't give him any trouble for the most part. Though he would wait to form an opinion of how they behaved in Miami.

His grumbling stomach sent him to the kitchen. A salad from Vittles, which was just on the verge of spoiling, was part of his meal for the night. He could've ordered a pizza, but he wasn't one to waste food, so he dug into the salad and added extra dressing to mask the soggy lettuce. He took out a frozen lasagna and put it in the microwave. A few minutes later, he removed the lasagna, took a tentative bite, and decided it wasn't all that bad.

He cleaned up, then took a can of beer from the refrigerator and the stack of math tests out to the lanai. The weather was perfect, and if he just happened to glimpse his new neighbor, he might wave at her. But no—he couldn't do that. She'd think he was a stalker or something. Men had to be very careful around women in today's world. One small mistake could be misconstrued and there would go his career.

Nash popped the tab off his beer can and proceeded to grade the exams. When he finished, he felt a bit let down that he hadn't seen his neighbor. But just as he had the thought, he saw her step out onto her lanai. She wore dark shorts and a green University of Miami T-shirt. He would bet green was her favorite color or that she'd attended the university—or both. He'd say odds were in his favor if he were a betting man, which he had been in his former life. Sort of.

She propped her long legs on the railing, a book in one hand, a glass in the other. She was too far away for him to see the title or what was in her glass. He continued to observe her. *Taller than most women*, he thought. Maybe she was a fashion model. If she wasn't, she could've been. Though he hadn't seen her up close. She might be homely, with missing teeth. He laughed aloud at his thoughts.

His laugh was loud enough to be heard. His neighbor lowered her book and looked in his direction before returning to her reading. He should probably go inside, but he didn't see any harm in lounging a while longer. Penny wasn't home, so he didn't have to worry about her. He would check in later to see how she was. He hadn't had much alone time since he'd taken responsibility for Penny, so he enjoyed this bit of freedom. He knew that when she came home, he would have his hands full. With four little ones, it would be challenging the first few weeks. He'd read several books on their care, so if he needed help, he'd refer back to those resources. Caring for four dachshund puppies and Penny would be a breeze.

He knew he couldn't keep all the pups. Once they were weaned, he would think about finding homes for them, but Nash would deal with that when he had to. Penny's labor had been progressing nicely when he'd left her at the clinic. He'd made all the arrangements as soon as he found out she'd had a rendezvous with Henry, his mother's doxie. He'd told his mom he would give her one of the pups. She was so excited. Nash wondered whether she would be as enthusiastic if he ever married and had children. Again, he laughed. Of course she would. He was an only child. His dad had passed away while he was in college, so it had been just he and his mom for a while. She'd worked part-time at the local veterinarian's office and became attached to Henry, who'd been a puppy when someone dumped him at the vet's office. She'd volunteered to foster him. That was five years ago. After hanging around Henry, Nash had also acquired a love for the breed and adopted Penny. She was the copper color of her namesake and he adored her. He often brought her to class with him. His students loved her as much as he did. She was a good girl in the classroom. Knowing there would be many extra treats, she cozied up to the kids.

Nash was so lost in his thoughts that he hadn't noticed his neighbor was no longer on her lanai. *She probably has a date*, he thought as he took the stack of papers inside with him. He closed the glass door but kept the blinds open. People around the

condo spent plenty of time outside. He was sure to
see her again.

Deciding to put all thought of his neighbor
aside, Nash called the vet clinic. Penny was still la-
boring and, according to Dr. Mellow, she was doing great. Relieved, he took a hot shower and
settled in for the evening. Penny would be fine.
The math tests were graded. Most of his students
had done very well. He was proud of them, and
Penny too.

He clicked the TV on and scrolled through the
guide, searching for something to watch. Nothing
interested him. Crime shows and reality shows
about women whose lips were the size of small pillows were definitely not his thing. He turned the
TV off and decided he'd go for a run. He'd been a
runner his entire adult life. He was more of a trot-
ter since he had Penny, but tonight he felt like he
needed the endorphins that a good run provided.

He laced up his sneakers and grabbed his cell
phone and keys. He would run on the beach. The
tide was out; the sand would be packed hard enough
for him to run on. With that in mind, he headed
to the beach, his head once again filled with vi-
sions of the woman on the lanai.

Chapter Three

Emma was sure her neighbor was watching her while she pretended to read. He had a stack of papers he kept moving back and forth. She had no clue what that meant, but it didn't matter. She quickly went inside to refill her glass of water, and when she returned, her neighbor was nowhere in sight.

If she continued this crazy spying on her handsome neighbor, and if anyone caught on, she'd be kicked out of the community before she even had a chance to belong. Maybe she'd run into Marlena again. She would use her skills as an attorney to discover just who her sexy neighbor was. Subtlety had been her most potent skill when she'd gone up against corporate giants in the courtroom.

Deciding to get some work done, Emma unpacked the large boxes filled with her most prized artwork. For the next hour, she hung the paintings on the main living room wall. When she finished, she used her smartphone to list a few items she needed from the grocery store. She looked up Vittles' address on a search engine, bookmarking it for tomorrow. Next on her list: She wanted to find a family doctor, just in case. Maybe Marlena could recommend one to her. Emma's car was still under warranty, so she didn't need a mechanic yet, but she noted it anyway. What if she had a flat tire? Emma knew she had a lot to learn about her new town. She would find a church of the faith she'd always practiced in Miami and continue here in Pink Pearl Cove. She made friends fast; what better place to make more friends? Tomorrow was Sunday. She clicked through a few websites before finding a branch of her church. She would attend the second service, as she'd done most of her life.

Emma dismantled the large boxes that had contained her artwork, placing them beside the door so she would remember to bring them to the recycling bin. Without anything further that required her attention, she returned to her book, which was now completely dry. The pages had puffed up and she knew a replacement was in order, but it wasn't so damaged that she couldn't read it.

Before settling back into her story, she made a cup of mint tea and took it to the living room. She sat in her favorite chair, a small table beside her, and started reading. She reread the parts she'd pretended to read earlier, while she'd watched her neighbor. She was so engrossed in her novel that she knocked over her tea when she heard the doorbell. It was odd, because no one had rung it before, or knocked on her door.

"Dang," Emma said as she blotted the tea on her shorts with the hem of her shirt. She knew she looked untidy, but she didn't care. This was who she was now, her true self. No longer the sleek, dressed-to-the-nines attorney.

"Coming," Emma called a few seconds before opening the door.

"You left this at the pool," said Marlena, holding out a bottle of sunscreen. "I hope I didn't interrupt anything."

For a second, Emma didn't recognize her new friend. She had shoulder-length blond hair and a smile that lit up her hazel eyes. Emma towered over her.

"No, nothing to interrupt. Thanks for returning this." She held up the bottle before tossing it on the counter behind her. "Do you have time for a glass of wine? I have a bottle I've been waiting to share with someone." She laughed. "I'm not much of a drinker."

"Wine? You bet," Marlena said as she came inside. "I love what you've done with the place. Very modern."

Emma searched through the kitchen drawers for her corkscrew. Finding it, she turned to face Marlena, who'd made herself comfortable on one of the three barstools.

"It is, but it wasn't my doing. I bought it this way. Sight unseen. No, that's not true. I just didn't see it in person before I bought it. Did see photos from the real estate agent. So I had a good idea of what I was getting. I believe the previous owner was in some tech business."

"I think so, though I never met him. He wasn't here very long. Maybe six months?" Marlena said.

Emma uncorked the wine and poured a glass for both of them.

Marlena raised her glass. "Let's make a toast."

"Absolutely," Emma agreed. "To new beginnings and new friends."

Marlena repeated her words, and they clinked their glasses together.

"Let's sit on the lanai; the sun is about to set," Emma suggested to her guest.

Marlena trailed behind her. "You have one of the best views, being on this side of the condo."

"I do?" Emma asked.

"Of course, the building opposite you has beachfront views. It's strange, because their lanais face away from the beach. I believe the master bedrooms have floor-to-ceiling windows."

"I guess waking up with a view of the Gulf of Mexico is appealing. I don't mind taking a short walk to the beach. I grew up in Miami, so maybe I'm burned out on that part. Our house was actually on the beach." She gave a short laugh. It was more like a castle than a house, but she wouldn't reveal that. She didn't want to come off as a braggart.

"I understand. I grew up in Maine and we also lived on the waterfront. I could never understand what the tourists got all worked up about. I do now, but when you're a kid, you never really appreciate what you have until it's gone."

Emma detected a trace of sadness in her voice. "I agree. I've never been to Maine. I hear it's gorgeous in the fall." Her comment sounded lame, but it was all she could come up with. She didn't want Marlena to think she was nosy. Even though she was, at least when it came to her neighbor across the way.

"It is. Walt and I go back in October every year. His family still lives there."

Emma sipped her wine. "You don't have family there?" So much for not being nosy.

"Not anymore," Marlena said. "I have a step-brother. He lives in town. We're close, but that's it."

"So, I take it you were an only child for a while?" Emma realized she was asking questions the way she had in the courtroom. "I'm sorry—it's none of my business. My excuse is that I am—*was*—an attorney. I gave it up to move here. I want to teach school."

Marlena busted out laughing. "You did what?" She held up her hand to stop Emma. "You don't have to explain."

Emma set her wineglass on the table between them. "I should. I was in corporate law for ten years. I traveled the world fighting for corporations that wanted more of whatever they could get their hands on. One day—it was just a couple of months ago—I quit. I sold my old condo, hired my replacement, bought this place, and sent out my teaching résumé to several schools. I've subbed at the elementary school and fell in love with the kids. I think teaching is my true calling. My parents were attorneys and I just followed in their footsteps."

"You're too young to have a second career."

"I started college at sixteen. I was a nerd, I

admit. It was tough the first couple of years in college, but it was a breeze after that."

"I take it your family approves?"

Emma shook her head. "They wouldn't if they were alive. An only child, older parents—that's me."

"I see." Marlena paused, as though she were contemplating her next words. "I had a sister once. She was two years older. We were best friends, even when she was in high school and I was in middle school. She always included me when she hung out with her friends. I was never that bratty little sister to her. She passed away during her first year of college."

Emma didn't know what to say. All the usual words meant nothing. She'd been a recipient of them when her mom and dad died.

"It's okay, Emma. Nothing anyone says can change what happened."

"I would tell you I'm sorry, but I know that doesn't mean diddly-squat. But I am sad you lost your best friend. I never had a sister or a best friend. I was too busy either studying or working."

"Yeah, well, for whatever it's worth, I'm glad you moved here. I think you and I are going to be terrific friends."

"Then let's have another glass of wine to celebrate our new friendship," Emma said. She hurried to the kitchen, returning with the bottle of wine. She refilled their glasses.

After her third glass of wine, Emma felt the false courage alcohol sometimes gave her. She pointed to the dark condo directly across from hers. "What about that guy?"

Marlena saw where Emma directed her gaze. "You won't believe it, but he's a teacher. Math, of all things. His little Penny is in labor right now. I guess that's why he hasn't been home all night. He usually sits on the lanai in the evening. I'm not sure if he's scoping out the women at the pool or what. He's very easy on the eyes."

All Emma took from Marlena's words was that Penny was in labor. "He was here. Before you came over."

"So you two met?' Marlena prompted.

"No. He was here. Not here, *here,* but on his lanai. I saw him. I think he was watching me."

"I wonder if Penny delivered early? He promised he would let Walt and me see the puppies as soon as he brought them home."

"What are you talking about?" Emma tried to clear her head. *Penny was in labor. The neighbor promised puppies.*

Once again, Marlena laughed. "Penny is Nash's dachshund. She's in labor at the vet clinic. He took her there so they could monitor the delivery because he was terrified at the prospect of caring for her alone."

All Emma could do was nod. *Nash.* What kind of name was that?

"Tell me about him," Emma said. She was half lit and didn't care what she said at this stage. It was one of the reasons she rarely had more than one glass of wine.

"As I said, he's a math teacher at the high school. As far as I know, he isn't married and loves dogs."

Emma pondered this. "How long has he lived there?" She nodded toward the condo.

"Maybe two years? He's from around here, so I don't think he will pick up and leave anytime soon," Marlena said. "As much as I regret it, I need to go home. I have that little stinker to look after. He was asleep when I left, but my husband will need a break regardless."

Emma stood up, a bit unsteady after three glasses of wine, but she managed to walk Marlena to the door and say good night.

As soon as she locked up, Emma changed into her pajamas and got ready for bed. She fell asleep as soon as her head hit the pillow.

Chapter Four

Emma stepped out of the shower, her head pounding from too much wine the night before. She knew better. She made a cup of coffee in the kitchen, returning to her bedroom so she could get ready for church. She dried her hair, put on mascara and lip gloss, then slipped into a yellow sheath dress with matching flats. Checking herself in the full-length mirror inside her closet, she looked presentable, despite how she felt.

She clicked the map bookmarked on her phone, grabbed her keys from the dolphin hook, and headed to her car. The church was only five minutes away, so she had plenty of time.

Guiding her sleek white Mercedes-Benz from her tiny garage wasn't easy. Emma considered purchasing a smaller vehicle sometime soon. Once she was clear, she hit the automatic garage door opener so it would close behind her.

Taking the scenic route down Flamingo Boulevard, she saw a few shops open and planned to stop in on her way home. It would be another way she would get to know the folks in Pink Pearl Cove, though she'd learned from Marlena that most referred to the town simply as the Cove.

The lot was packed when she reached the Chapel by the Sea's parking area. Emma had to parallel park across the street. She wouldn't lallygag next Sunday. The early service was either running late or she was too soon for the second service.

It turned out her first assumption was correct. As soon as she crossed the street, the church doors opened and folks spilled out like a bouquet of colorful flowers. Emma couldn't help but smile as she stood to the side, waiting for the church to empty for the next service. Some people lingered in groups, while others went quickly to their vehicles. Five minutes passed before she went inside. Unsure if the locals had specific seats, she chose a pew next to the last row, where she sat in the middle to view the pastor as he spoke.

While she waited for the organist to finish the opening hymn, Emma thought the second service didn't appear as crowded as the first. She listened intently as Pastor Ellison spoke to his congregation. He was younger than most clergy, but spoke with such passion that Emma felt she'd lucked out when she chose Chapel by the Sea. When the service wrapped up, Emma took her time exiting the church, hoping she might run into Marlena or someone she'd met before at the school or library.

A figure blocked the sun as she entered the main aisle. As she made her way toward the exit, Emma stopped so suddenly that somebody bumped into her. A toddler had appeared out of nowhere. Emma almost stepped on the child.

"Miss?" a voice from behind her said. "Are you all right?"

"Uh, sorry, yes, I'm fine," Emma said, searching for the child. A woman scooped him up, disappearing before she could say anything. *As long as the kid is okay*, she thought.

"I don't believe I've seen you here before," the woman commented.

Emma wanted to escape, but a man was blocking the exit, speaking to someone. He didn't appear to have a clue that he was causing a human pileup inside.

"No, today is my first visit," Emma said distractedly to the woman behind her.

"Let's not make it your last," the woman said kindly.

"I'll do my best," Emma said, finally turning around to face the woman. She was tiny, with a head full of white curly hair and sparkly blue eyes.

"Are you married?" the woman asked out of the blue.

Emma swallowed, her throat dry. "Uh, no."

"That's wonderful. You don't have a boyfriend or someone you're interested in?"

Nosy, Emma thought. "What did you say your name was?"

"I'm Mrs. Whitton. I work at the library."

If this was the same woman Marlena had described, she must have two personalities—one for the library and another for the church.

"It's nice to meet you. I was just in the library last week," Emma said, still not giving her name. Could the old gal have an aging son? Maybe she was looking for a fix-up. *No*, Emma thought, *that's too awkward to contemplate.*

"Did you check out a book?"

Beyond nosy. Whoever that was blocking the flow to the exit would get a dirty look from her. Church or not. "Isn't that what the library is for?" Emma said, her voice not as kind as before.

"Now, listen up. If you want to borrow books from *my* library, it's best not to get an attitude with me. Especially here in a house of worship."

Now Emma understood what Marlena had referred to. "I have already checked a book out, and yesterday it got soaked at the pool. The pages are so thick now, I can't close the cover." Emma turned away so Mrs. Whitton wouldn't see the grin on her face.

"Then you will be fined and marked as a book offender. You will not be allowed to borrow books for thirty days. Those are my rules. I will expect a replacement Monday morning."

"A book offender? Are you serious?" Emma asked, trying her best not to laugh.

"It's not something I take lightly, young lady."

Finally, the man running his mouth stepped away from the exit. Emma couldn't get away from old Mrs. Whitton fast enough. She practically flew down the steps and crossed the street to her car.

She gave herself a few minutes to calm down while waiting for the air-conditioning to cool the hot car.

Looking across the street, she spied the guy who'd been running his mouth.

It was her neighbor.

Nash.

Chapter Five

As Emma drove away from the church, she had second thoughts about attending next week's late service. She had no problem getting up to attend the earlier one.

As planned, she drove around downtown, deciding which shop to visit first. Remembering her list from last night, she headed to Vittles Market. Maybe she'd see Marlena. She would tell her about meeting the librarian.

The Cove had more traffic than she thought as she inched the Mercedes between a pickup truck and a van. Parking space was limited. She was unsure if there were too many people living here or if it was because it was Sunday and most people had the day off. Whatever, Emma hoped the parking situation was just a Sunday thing.

Inside, Vittles was packed. Searching for a shopping cart, Emma spotted the last one by the door.

Strolling down the aisles, she was surprised at the variety of the food. Most everything in a box or can was labeled as organic. She tossed a box of steel-cut oats and a jar of strawberry jam into her cart. The scent of fresh bread baking drew her to the bakery at the back of the store. A few people were in line waiting. She'd stand there all day for a loaf of fresh-baked bread herself.

"Hey," Marlena called out. "I see you found us," she said as she came out from behind the counter. She had a white apron on, her hair covered with a bandana, and a smudge of flour on her nose.

"Do you make the bread?" It was all Emma could think to ask.

"I help Walt. He's the baker. We only have fresh bread on Sunday." Marlena nodded at the few people who were waiting. "Most folks place their orders beforehand, so we know how many loaves we'll need. I'll get a couple of loaves for you." She ran behind the counter, returning with two loaves. "Here. Put the extra one in your freezer. It's sourdough this week. Walt's best."

Emma glanced at the people in line. They didn't seem to be bothered by Marlena giving her the bread. "Thanks. I'll spread this jam on the toast I'm having for lunch."

"Good! Let me know if you like it; I make the jam. The strawberries are handpicked from Plant City."

"Wow! I think I hit the grocery jackpot today, though I can't say the same about church this morning."

Marlena laughed. "I'm almost afraid to hear what happened."

"I met Mrs. Whitton. According to her, I've been labeled a 'book offender.'" Emma smiled. "I couldn't help myself; I had to tell her about the ruined book. I'm suspended from checking out any more books for thirty days."

Marlena rolled her eyes. "I wouldn't worry about it. I ordered three copies last night. You can hand-deliver them yourself if you want."

"I'll pass. She kept asking me if I was married or had a boyfriend. It scared me," Emma said jokingly.

"And rightfully so. She has two sons. Lyle and Leland. Neither is married. They're both in their early fifties. And they're bald and still live at home."

"Got it."

"Every new single female in town gets asked the same questions. She'll never get rid of them because they're both lazy goofballs that she enables. That's why she's such a hard-ass at the library. It's the only place she has any control."

Emma nodded, appreciating Marlena's simple honesty. Yet she also felt a touch of sympathy for Mrs. Whitton. "That's sad. Maybe you should invite them to the monthly cookout you have at the condo. Surely there is someone there they might be interested in." She laughed. "I'm joking, sort of."

"I hope so. No one at the condo, at least that I know of, would date either one of them. They missed the love boat a long time ago," Marlena said. "Maybe if they cleaned up a bit . . . who knows?"

Emma just listened; there wasn't much she could say.

"Speaking of dates . . ." Marlena turned her attention away from Emma. "*He* hasn't missed the boat."

Emma followed her new friend's gaze. It was her neighbor again. Nash. "I'd better go. I wanted to stop at a couple of shops on my way home," Emma said.

Marlena reached for the cart, preventing her from moving. "Wait. I want you to meet him."

"Uh, sure," Emma said. He was her neighbor, after all. They might as well get to know each other.

"Nash," Marlena called out. "I have someone I'd like you to meet."

"Hey, what's up, Mar?" he asked as he approached them, his eyes entirely focused on Emma.

Emma took a deep breath, then exhaled when he stood beside her. Yes, he was taller than she. Easily six-five. His skin was tanned and his hair wasn't as dark as she'd thought the first time she saw him, more like a deep, rusty brown. He wore a pair of faded jeans with a light blue collared shirt, the sleeves rolled up to his elbows, revealing muscular forearms.

"Emma Swan," she said, using her attorney voice to introduce herself. His eyes were as green as emerald stones. She held out her hand. As soon as he clasped her hand in his, she felt a vaguely sensuous vibe between them.

"Nash Kendrick. You're my new neighbor," he said, stating the obvious. "I saw you last night on your lanai while you were reading. Book any good?"

It took Emma a few seconds to shake off the sensation of his hand on hers. She gripped the grocery cart harder than necessary and said, "Actually, it's excellent. I plan on finishing it today." She didn't know whether to admire him for noticing her or fear him for spying on her—even though she was guilty of the same offense. If you could call watching your sexy neighbor an offense.

"I'll leave you two to get acquainted. Nash, I have your mom's order. Are you here for that or just grocery shopping?" Marlena asked, breaking the silence.

"Both. I'm in a bit of a rush. Penny had the pups. The vet called me on my way here. I can't wait to see them. Four females! Can you believe that?"

Emma couldn't help but smile. "Congratulations."

"When will you bring them home? I've got dibs on one, remember?" Marlena said.

"I do. I think I'll let the doc decide how long they should stay, but as soon as I have them, I'll let you know so you can pop over and look," Nash said, then turned to Emma. "Do you like puppies?"

She relaxed her grip on the shopping cart. "Of course. Who doesn't like puppies?"

"You'd be surprised. I need to grab a few groceries, so I'll catch you two ladies later."

"The bread," Marlena called out. She reached over the counter, grabbed two loaves, and tossed them.

Nash caught one in each hand. "Thanks," he said before heading down the aisle.

Emma stood there and just watched. For such a small town, she'd experienced more excitement in one morning than in a week in Miami. She was unsure if Nash's words were an invitation to her or just the usual slough-off people used when they needed to make a hasty exit. It didn't matter. She would see him at the condo eventually.

"I'll see you later," Emma said to Marlena.

"Sure thing," she replied. "I'll bring the wine next time."

Emma laughed. "Okay. Another weekend?" she asked. Wine was off the schedule for her for the rest of this weekend. She still had a tinge of a headache and needed a few more cups of coffee to take the edge off.

Emma thought Vittles was a unique little store, far friendlier toward customers than the larger chains where she used to shop. And she'd found all the items on her list as well as some that weren't available in the big-box stores. Even more reasons she was glad she'd left Miami.

Emma had purchased a few frozen items, so she went home and unloaded her groceries first. Later that afternoon she would drive downtown to peruse the shops, as planned. If she was lucky, she might catch a glimpse of Nash again later as well. As soon as she changed out of her dress, she put on a pair of khaki shorts and a red shirt. She also put on her red sneakers. Emma thought her shoes should always match her clothes. That kind of thinking validated every shoe purchase she made. For now, her guest bedroom housed her immense shoe collection. She planned to have a custom closet built in the room just for her shoes. It wasn't as if she needed the extra room for an office. She had all the space she needed.

She was the most content she'd been since before she'd lost her parents. Emma practically skipped to the garage, humming a song she'd heard on the radio that morning while driving to church.

Chapter Six

Emma parked in the same spot she'd parked earlier for church. The traffic wasn't nearly as bad as now. Several shops were open. The Tropical Candies Sweet Shop was her first stop. The scent of sugar filled the air. A couple of teenagers were ordering ice cream, and an older man scooped jellybeans into a clear bag before weighing them on a scale. Behind a counter were several types of fudge. She'd never had a weight issue; she would order a half-pound of peanut butter fudge, along with the peppermint bark, and eat every bit herself without any guilt.

"What can I get for you?" the young girl behind the counter asked after the elderly man paid for his jellybeans.

Emma gave the girl her order.

"Please give me a couple of minutes," she said. "I just got here. Mom went home early with a migraine." The girl was rail thin with brown eyes and a blond braid reaching down to her waist. Emma thought she looked unhappy.

"I'm sorry. That's not a fun way to spend the day." Emma didn't know what else to say. Folks were so friendly here, telling her bits and pieces of their personal lives. She didn't know if she'd ever get used to that. "Mum's the word" was the rule in her old world. She was a great keeper of secrets—not that she had any herself. As an attorney, she'd lived with stories that her clients told her in confidence. Many had no relation to their cases, but Emma was a good listener, and her clients knew she could be trusted.

"Here you go, ma'am," said the young girl.

Emma returned her attention to the register. She handed the girl her debit card.

"If your purchase is less than fifty dollars, we charge fifty cents for using your card."

"Sure, that's fine." Many businesses were doing that now to cover their banking fees.

"Most of the time I don't have to tell that to customers. They spend way over that amount. It's kind of embarrassing," the girl said, returning the card.

Emma tucked her card inside her wallet, then took the bag of fudge and peppermint bark. "It's okay, really. You do what you have to do to stay in business."

"Yeah, well, I guess. I just hate asking people for extra money." The girl really did look distraught.

"I understand, but that's part of being a business owner. You have to make a profit," Emma explained. "I used to be . . ." She trailed off, uncertain if she should tell this girl anything personal. She decided to go ahead. Maybe it would help the teen in some strange way. "I used to be an attorney. Actually, I'm still one. I just quit practicing. In my office, we had to bill our clients for almost everything, even a five-minute telephone call. I didn't like that part, but it's just how the world works. There are little things you can do. Many times I would call clients from home, never charging them. Take them to lunch, my treat."

"My mom would croak if I gave anything away for free."

"Can I ask your name?" Emma queried. She felt the girl needed to talk and knowing her name made the conversation seem more personal.

"Amanda. I'm sorry. I should have my name tag on, but I forgot it again."

"I like that name. I'm Emma. So, you and your mom run the store on your own?"

"Yeah. My dad passed away last year. A boating accident. It's been hard for Mom and me to handle the shop. She always worries about money. When Dad was alive they had help on the weekends. She didn't care about money then."

Emma didn't know any adult who didn't care about money in some sense. You had to have it to survive. The choice to survive in luxury or squalor depended on the individual.

"I'm sorry. I lost both of my parents a few years ago, too."

"Did you have to work when they died?" Amanda asked.

"I did, but I was much older than you." She

wouldn't tell her she'd been left a small fortune. That was tucked away for the future.

"I'm fifteen," Amanda offered.

Emma had thought she was much younger. Maybe she hadn't had much of a chance to mature, given her family circumstances. "So you're in high school?"

"Ninth grade."

Emma knew where this conversation was going and, for a moment, she felt ashamed of herself. But she convinced herself that her question was for the greater good.

"Is your teacher Mr. . . ." She could not recall his last name.

"Mr. Kendrick?"

"Yes, the math teacher."

"He's the only male teacher. Yeah, I have him for third period. He's the coolest teacher I've ever had. He brings his dog to class sometimes."

"I heard he's expecting some puppies," Emma said. "Or rather his dog is."

"I know. Penny hooked up with Henry, his mom's wiener dog. The entire town wants one of his pups, but I don't think he'll give them up."

"What makes you think that?"

"He's just that way. Super sweet. He tells us stories about Penny. You can tell if a person is decent according to a dog's reaction."

Emma had heard this, too. Never having had a pet of her own, she thought it was time for her to consider getting one. Maybe she could adopt a rescue animal. "I guess you'll find out soon enough." She could've told Amanda she knew the pups had arrived, but it wasn't her news to share. The more she learned about her neighbor, the more she liked him. She also considered that all she'd heard about him could be too good to be true.

"I hope so," Amanda said. "He isn't married, just so you know."

"I see," Emma said, wondering why the conversation had shifted to this topic.

"You aren't married, right?" Amanda asked.

Emma had to laugh. "No, I'm not."

"So why don't you hook up with Mr. Kendrick?" Amanda asked.

Emma was used to answering questions on the fly, but no one had ever questioned her marital status besides Harris and that librarian. Words failed her for a second, and then she spoke. "For starters, I don't know him; he doesn't know me. I don't date guys I don't know." She gave Amanda an awkward smile. "Women have to be very careful." She was sure that Nash wasn't a danger to women, but she didn't want to give the impression that knowing someone necessarily gave them a free pass. She hoped Amanda understood the point she was trying to make.

"I think you guys would look cool together. You're both tall. You're pretty." Amanda paused. "Mr. Kendrick is . . ." She laughed, then turned her face to the side.

"He's a nice-looking man," Emma offered so Amanda wouldn't be embarrassed. She remembered when she was fifteen. It had been an awkward age for her too, as she'd just begun her senior year in high school.

Emma was saved when a lady with three small children made a noisy entrance. "I'll see you soon," she said before leaving.

Amanda waved, then turned her attention to her new customers.

Emma was no longer in the mood to shop, so she headed home, along with her bag of fudge, with much to think about.

Once she was back home, with nothing left to do, she finished her ruined library book. Despite what she'd said that morning, she would return the book and those new copies Marlena had purchased. Never one to shuck off responsibilities, she hoped this simple act would remove her from the "book offenders" list. Small-town life—it was what she wanted. Emma had received her first full serving. She couldn't wait to see what tomorrow would bring.

Chapter Seven

Emma got up early Monday morning. She dressed and did her hair and makeup just in case she was called in to substitute at one of the local schools. After nine, she knew all the schools were in session, so unless a teacher had an emergency, she had another free day. Changing to jeans and a chambray shirt, she decided she would work in the spare room today. Which reminded her to call a local carpenter who had been recommended to her by the real estate agent who sold her the condo. After spending twenty minutes on the phone with the contractor, she got his agreement to stop by after lunch to measure her guest room so she could have her custom-made closet.

Emma kept some of her shoes in clear containers she'd purchased from the Container Store. She felt ashamed when she saw that half of the room was covered with expensive shoes. Amanda's words came back to her: Her mother always worried about money. If she added up the cost of just her high heels—the Christian Louboutins, Jimmy Choos, and the Manolo Blahniks—they were worth several thousand dollars. Emma hadn't given much thought to the cost of her shoes before because she'd wanted them and could easily afford them. But not everyone had a choice.

She wanted to help Amanda and her mother. The key was doing it without making them feel like a charity case. A GoFundMe page was out of the question. Discovering a bag of money in the store would never pass; the thought was silly. How to help? She didn't have a clue, but Emma wouldn't give up. She wasn't a quitter.

Maybe a fundraiser through the school? She could ask Marlena or Nash. Emma thought Nash would know because he worked at the school. She would swallow her pride and ask him as soon as she saw him out on the lanai. If she didn't see him, she'd knock on his door. With a temporary fix to Amanda's family's problem, at least in her mind, Emma went through her shoeboxes, discarding several pairs she knew she wouldn't wear anymore. Five-inch heels didn't have a place in her life at this point.

The doorbell rang. "Coming," she called, making her way to the door. She looked at the mess she'd made and hoped to have organized before the contractor, Jack Alan, arrived. But she hadn't.

Upon opening the door and seeing the man waiting on the other side, Emma said, "Jack? I'm

Emma Swan. Thanks for stopping over today." She stood aside, allowing him to enter. He was older than he'd sounded on the phone, but she didn't care as long as he knew what he was doing.

"Nice to meet you, Emma. I didn't have much on my schedule today, so this worked out perfectly." He held out his hand and she shook it, waiting for a reaction like the one she'd had with Nash. She felt nothing other than the strength in his grip.

She guessed him to be in his early forties. He wasn't much taller than she, but he was powerfully built. His arms attested to his ability to swing a hammer and carry heavy-duty supplies. He was handsome in an old-fashioned way. Dark hair combed to the side; friendly brown eyes. A light blue work shirt tucked neatly into a pair of dark jeans. He wore work boots with paper covers over them, like surgeons wore in hospitals.

"If you'll follow me," she said. Emma led him to the guest room.

Jack walked the perimeter of the room, opening the door to the small closet. He took a measuring tape from his carpenter's belt. Emma stayed out of his way while he worked. He wasn't writing down measurements and she didn't want to distract him from the numbers as he memorized them.

"Tell me exactly what you want and where you want it," Jack said. "I'll draw up a set of plans, have you review them, then give you an estimate. If you approve, I'll look at my schedule and give you a start date."

"These," she motioned to all the boxes on the floor, "need a home."

Jack smiled at her. "I can see that. My wife is a shoe lover as well. I built a custom closet just for her shoes a few years ago. Lisa would love it if you came by the house to take a look and see if it's something you'd like."

People are so friendly here, Emma thought, not for the first time. "I would if it's not an inconvenience. I'm going to give away or donate some of these." She pointed to the pile of shoes she'd taken out of their boxes. "Not sure I'll need as much shoe space as I thought."

Jack laughed. "Let me call her now. She should be home," he said, then took his cell phone from his shirt pocket.

Emma left the room to give Jack some privacy. In the kitchen, she took two glasses, added ice, and filled them with sweet tea. Carrying both drinks back to the guest room, she paused to ensure Jack had finished his phone call.

"Sweet tea," she said once Jack had hung up, handing him one of the glasses.

"Thanks. Lisa said she would love to show off her closet. Anytime today works for her."

Emma swallowed a sip of her tea. "I can go now if that also works for you."

"Sure thing. My truck is parked across the street if you want to follow me," Jack said, "My house isn't too far." He guzzled down the tea and then returned the glass.

"I should change."

"No, you're fine."

"Then let's go," she said, smiling. Emma loved the folks in Pink Pearl Cove more every day.

When she pulled out of the garage, she saw Jack's bright red truck with *Jack Alan's Carpentry* painted in white letters on the door panel. He drove slowly as she trailed behind.

Ten minutes later, they arrived at a stunning house at the opposite end of the island, facing the Gulf of Mexico. At least three stories high, it had tall windows that reflected the afternoon sun. That surprised her. She parked behind Jack.

"Your home is beautiful," she said. "Did you build it yourself?"

He smiled at her. "I wish, but no. We bought this from the same real estate agent who referred you to me. We've been here almost five years now."

Jack didn't have a Southern accent, but that didn't mean anything in Florida because most folks were from elsewhere. "Come on, meet Lisa. You two have a lot in common," he said, grinning.

They walked upstairs, which led to a large deck. Glass doors opened as soon as they reached the deck. A gorgeous woman, barely five feet tall, came to welcome them. Emma never expected Jack's Lisa to be so stunning. "I'm so thrilled to meet you," the woman said in a British accent. "I'm Lisa. Please come inside."

"Lisa, I appreciate your allowing me to barge in like this. Jack was nice enough to offer."

Lisa's eyes were the most unusual color, a silvery gray. Her black hair was straight, reaching down to her tiny waist. "It's my pleasure. Jack says you are a shoe lover, too."

"I was—in another lifetime. Really, I still am;

I'm just downsizing. Beach life isn't conducive to Jimmy Choos."

"Now I know we're going to be best friends. I have many of Jimmy's shoes. I worked with him a few years back when we were in London. He's a sweetheart."

Wow, Emma thought. There was more to this couple than Jack's ability to design closets. Emma's eyes widened. "Then call me impressed."

"That's how I met Jack. He worked with Jimmy."

Now Emma was even more impressed. "You did?"

"I did," Jack said and then laughed. "I'll leave you two girls alone. Lisa can tell you all about it and show you her closet. If it's to your liking, I'll start working on designing a closet just for you."

"Please, come inside. I'll show you the closet. Jack's the best. Whatever you want, he'll make sure you have it," said Lisa.

Emma followed Lisa to an elevator. This was beyond extravagant, even for her, and she'd lived in luxury most of her life.

"It's a lot to take in, I know," Lisa said. "Look at the closet first and then I'll tell you the story. Our background is unusual to most folks, but once you get to know us, we're just like everyone else."

Emma believed her.

Lisa's closet was the size of Emma's master bedroom and guest room combined. Shelves with glass doors housed hundreds of shoes, boots, and sandals, any kind of shoe one could imagine. Built-in lights reflected on each pair of shoes.

"This is like shoe fairyland." Emma walked around the space, knowing she wouldn't need nearly as many shelves. She liked the glass doors but could do without the lights. In her small condo, it would appear vain and frankly, silly if she were to display her collection as Lisa had.

"You think it's too much?" Lisa asked.

"Not when you know Jimmy Choo," Emma told her. "How did you meet him?"

"I worked as a shoe model for him and many others."

Emma couldn't help herself—she looked at Lisa's feet. They were tiny. "Lucky you! What a fun career. I'm envious. My size nines feel like boats." She laughed.

"I had a great career; that's how I met Jack. When we moved to the island, for the first six months poor Jack was going stir-crazy. I convinced him to start a carpentry business. Closets are his specialty. He built the displays for many great designers and he wasn't ready to quit when it was time for me to retire."

"You're young; why retire so soon?" Maybe that was too personal, thought Emma. "I'm sorry; I'm nosy." She was embarrassed.

"No need to worry! It's fine because I will ask you the same. I was burned out. Not on the shoes, just the traveling. All the shows, the factory trips—if something wasn't right, I was called at a moment's notice, even though most of the designers I worked with had molds of my feet. It was a great career, but now I enjoy doing what I want. So, what about you? A story lurks behind all those shoes if you need a shoe closet."

"My story is similar to yours. I was born and raised in Miami; I wanted a slower-paced lifestyle. I was a corporate attorney and traveled a lot for clients. I wasn't happy, so I sold my home and found someone to replace me at the firm. I've always wanted to teach school and kept my teaching certificate current. I subbed for a kindergarten class last week. It was the best workday I've had in years."

"You're at the perfect age for it too. Jack and I don't have any children by choice, but we enjoy having plenty of nieces and nephews. They keep us entertained."

"I don't have siblings, so it's up to me." *And I'm not getting any younger*, Emma thought.

"You're not married," Lisa stated.

"No, and no prospects. Not that I'm looking, but someday I hope to marry and have children. I've devoted my life to my career. Time is running out," she said.

"Never give up. I was thirty-five when I married Jack. We've been together ten years now."

"You look fantastic—both of you. So whatever you're doing, it's working. Speaking of which, I need to get back home. I left a mess in the spare room. Shoes I don't want are piled up all over the place."

"Would you be willing to resell your shoes—the fancy ones? We donate the money to charity."

"Of course, I'd be happy to. What charity?"

"We have three. You can choose where your money goes. One goes to a shelter for animals called Pink Pearl Cove Cares. Another is for women needing financial help named Pearl Protects. And then there's the local children's clinic."

"Count me in for all three. Can I make a cash donation as well?"

Lisa laughed. "Of course. I don't know any charity that doesn't accept cash donations. Follow me." Lisa led her to an enormous kitchen with stainless appliances and white marble counters. The cabinets were painted a soothing light gray, reminding Emma of clouds as they gathered before a summer rainstorm.

"Jack built these cabinets?" Emma asked while Lisa scribbled on a slip of paper.

"He did, as soon as we moved in. The counters, too. This is my email and cell number. Text me your info and I'll email the info on the charities. We need all the help we can get. The Cove is small; there aren't many wealthy people here."

Emma would be considered well-to-do by some. It might be time to use the fortune her family had left her. "I'll help you. I need to get involved with the community."

"Good. We'll be friends, just like I thought when Jack told me he was going to meet you today."

"Shoe lovers." Emma laughed. "A breed of our own."

Emma bid the couple goodbye, then hurried down the stairs to her car. As she drove back to her end of the island, the traffic was heavier. Schools were out; Nash would likely be at his condo in an hour. She hoped to catch him and ask him about Amanda. Lisa's charities would cover the financial end of her plan. Nash would know the emotional state of the young girl. Maybe Emma was sticking her nose in places she shouldn't, but she couldn't shake the sadness Amanda unknowingly projected.

She would figure out a way to help her, no matter what.

Chapter Eight

Nash finished the school day and headed to the vet. He was excited to see the new puppies. He knew Penny must miss him as much as he missed her. He parked his old, battered Ford next to a Porsche, not bothering to lock the doors.

"Hey there, Nash," said Tiffany Thompson as soon as he walked through the door. She sprang out of a chair in the waiting room, heading toward him. "I knew I would find you here."

It took Nash a minute to gather himself. *What in the world was* she *doing here, of all places?* he thought. Dread washed over him like a black cloud.

"I'm here to check on Penny," he said.

"I heard she was here with her pups. You know how news travels in the Cove."

He did. "And?" he said, not wanting to prolong the conversation longer than needed.

Tiffany Thompson was the epitome of the girl

next door: blond, blue-eyed, with a perfect figure. Rather, she had been in high school. She hadn't aged well; her blond hair now looked like brittle straw and she wore enough makeup for ten women. She'd been a thorn in Nash's side since he'd returned to the Cove.

"And?" She tossed her long hair over her shoulder. "I thought you might let me have one of the puppies. I wanted to be the first to get one."

"This isn't an ice cream truck, Tiffany." Nash couldn't believe she thought he would give her a puppy. She was exactly as she'd been in high school: a spoiled brat who always got anything she wanted. Always had to be first.

She had the grace to look put off, but he knew her. She was just getting started.

"Nash, sweetie, do you think I don't know the difference between a dog and ice cream?" she asked, her voice dripping with sugary sweetness.

If he were honest with himself—and he was— she probably didn't. "Look, I'm not giving Penny's puppies away now."

"Then when? Because I want one. I would like to see them, so I can pick the one that's best for me."

Nash couldn't stand much more of her childishness. "Even if I were to give you one of the puppies, they can't leave their mother for at least eight weeks." He stopped and cleared his throat. "I won't be giving you a puppy now or anytime soon. Ask your dad. I'm sure he'll be happy to accommodate you."

"You're an ass, Nash Kendrick! This isn't the end of it," she said. "Just wait and see."

She would argue all day if he allowed her to. He

waved her off and headed to the back of the clinic, where the animals were kept.

"Hey, Nash, sorry I wasn't in the reception area. I heard Tiffany and didn't want to interrupt," Naomi, the vet tech, said with a grin. "Weren't you two a thing back in the day?" she teased.

"No."

Naomi rolled her eyes. "You want to see your new family?"

"I do," he told her. "How's Penny holding up?"

"Like a good mommy should. Follow me."

The clinic had two private whelping areas suited for a dog's specific needs. Penny and her four girls were sleeping when Nash tiptoed into the room. Naomi left him alone with the dachshunds. When Penny saw Nash, she wagged her tail but didn't move away from her pups.

"So, how's it feel to be a mom?" he asked, leaning down to pet her. She growled at him. "I know you're just protecting the girls. It's okay." He spoke softly. The four little puppies were reddish brown, just like Penny. Henry's black and brown genetics were nowhere to be seen. Nash couldn't help but laugh. His mom would surely get a kick out of this when she saw them.

He sat on the floor beside the dogs, letting Penny know he was there and wouldn't hurt her puppies. They were the cutest, with their closed eyes, tiny ears poking out, and chunky paws with sharp, tiny nails. He couldn't wait to bring them home. He'd fixed up a whelping area in the spare room for them, plus a space for Penny to eat and drink. He knew she would need much more food than usual. He'd prepped just as the vet had told him to. He'd planned to take a few days off when he brought them home to establish a routine. When Penny started to doze, Nash quietly left the room, knowing sleep was essential to her new mommy life.

He saw Naomi was still in the back. "She still out there?" he asked.

"She left as soon as you went into the back room."

"Good. So, what has Doc said about me bringing the pups home?"

"Another twenty-four hours and they're all yours. You're sure you have everything? I can pop over if you need me to."

"I did everything Doc suggested. I may need you to help when I return to work."

"Sure, I'd be happy to. On one condition."

Nash rolled his eyes. Naomi graduated high school last year. She was in his math class. She'd taken this year off to work at the vet clinic before starting college at North Carolina State in Raleigh, where she would study with the best of the best.

"What's that?"

"You'll let me use your pool this summer. I want to get a perfect tan before I have to go up north. I don't want to look all pasty, being from Florida, you know?"

"Of course. That was the first thing I thought of when I left for college." He laughed. "You can use the pool anytime, kiddo."

"I appreciate it, Mr. *Nash*," she said. He insisted she call him by his first name now that she was no longer his student.

"You have my number," he said before leaving.

"I promise to call if there's a reason," she reassured him.

Nash looked from side-to-side to ensure Tiffany wasn't hiding behind the building. He wouldn't put anything past her. They'd had a couple of dates in high school. On their second date he had her figured out and wanted no more of her. She insisted he take her as his date when he was nominated for prom king during their senior year. He refused and took his best friend, Sarah Lynn. Tiffany's jealousy ruined their evening, and she didn't let up for the rest of that year. He'd been relieved when he was accepted at Columbia University in New York, far enough away so she couldn't stalk him.

It was hard to wrap his head around the fact that he was thirty-four years old and Tiffany still thought she had a chance with him. He wasn't dense, but it was time to tell her enough was enough. Her behavior was juvenile, almost bordering on obsession. He thought about taking out a restraining order if she continued to bother him.

While he was in New York, he'd dated many women. A couple of those relationships had been halfway serious, but not so much so that he'd wanted to spend the rest of his life with either woman. When sparks flew, he would know. Maybe he was destined to be a bachelor. He'd always wanted to have a family, but he wouldn't settle for just anyone.

Sparks. And a handshake. He thought of Emma.

He cranked the engine over on his truck, heading home. He hadn't planned anything for the evening now that he'd caught up on grading pa-

She heard someone calling her name from the pool area. "Emma."

She had to stand up and look to her left to see the pool.

Her stomach did a flip-flop. "Hi," she called to Nash.

"Put your suit on; the water is like hot coffee," he hollered.

She grinned. "I'll pass," she said, immediately regretting it. Then she added, "But I'll come to the pool. You want a glass of iced tea?" she asked.

"I do," he shouted, a bit too loud.

Before anyone noticed them, she hurried to the kitchen, refilled her glass, and poured another for Nash. She couldn't believe he could have seen her on the lanai unless he'd been watching for her.

Three minutes later, she sat on the same chaise longue she'd occupied before. Nash was in the pool, leaning his wet shin against the coping. She'd set the glass down in front of him. She'd thought she would feel awkward hanging out with him like this, but it seemed completely natural.

"Thanks, Emma. You're a lifesaver. I was thirsty." He downed the tea in one giant gulp.

"You could've drunk the coffee you're swimming in," she teased.

"I am one of the few around here who dislikes this heated pool. Especially in the summer months. It's like I said—diving into a hot cup of coffee."

She nodded. "I don't like it either. What's the point? If you're hot, you want to cool off, but the water is like a warm bath."

"We could draw up a petition. Take it to the condo association," he said, smiling.

She shook her head. "You have an answer for everything, don't you?"

He pushed himself out of the pool, water dripping off him. She tried not to stare at him but couldn't turn her eyes away. He was all muscle, with broad shoulders that tapered to a narrow waist. He was tanned all over. It took Emma a few seconds to recover, as it'd been a long time since she'd seen a male specimen in such perfect condition. Actually, she had never seen a guy so *male* before.

Nash sat down on the lounge chair beside her. Emma could feel his eyes on her.

"Tell me about yourself. I've been too busy to be neighborly," he said.

Unusual, she thought. Men, at least the ones she'd dated, always wanted to talk about themselves— their cars, their bank accounts. She had little interest in that type.

"I just moved in. But you already know that," she said.

"Why here? Pink Pearl Cove isn't the most popular beach town in Florida."

"That's part of the reason. I lived in Miami my entire life. I wanted to slow down and get out of the rat race. So I did a bit of online investigating, and here I am."

"Makes sense. Miami's a nice place to visit, but after spending most of my adult life in New York, I understand wanting to escape the city. It can be intoxicating, though it wears off after a while." Nash raised his hands above his head, stretching like a cat sunning itself.

"New York?" she asked, her tone curious.

"I worked in investments."

"I see. That's where it happens. I've been there many times with clients. As you said, it's intoxicating, but only for a while."

She couldn't believe how they were talking, given they'd known each other for barely an hour. But if you added up the time she'd spent spying on him, it would be more than an hour. She wouldn't say that out loud, of course, fearing she would sound childish.

"Clients? What type of work?" Nash asked. She could tell he was sincere and wanted to know more about her.

Laughing, she said, "I was an attorney. Corporate."

He whistled. "I guessed you were top-notch and I was right."

"Why top-notch? Is that good or bad?" she asked.

"Oh, it's perfect. You look professional, a take-no-bull kind of lady."

She wasn't sure she liked his assessment of her. She was professional in her work life, but wasn't a hard-core, do-or-die person.

"I was very professional when I had to be. But I didn't bring work home with me." That wasn't entirely true. She'd told Amanda how she would call clients from home to save them a few dollars here and there. "I also have my teaching certificate. I received my bachelor's in education before law school and kept my license current. Corporate law isn't my calling, so I decided to change my life and career, and here I am."

"You know I teach math, right?"

"Marlena told me when you were at the store."

"Vittles is a one stop shop for food and a bit of local gossip," he said, his green eyes teasing, matching his smile.

"I've only been there once, the same day you were," she said, wanting to clarify that she hadn't been in the store to participate in any gossip.

"I was in a rush on Sunday. Penny was about to give birth. She's my dog, in case you haven't heard. It seems the entire Cove wants one of her puppies. I promised my mother she could have her pick of the litter, but after seeing them, I'm not sure Penny is going to be willing to give them up."

Emma's heart clenched. Nash was everything she'd heard and maybe more. "You want to keep all the dogs?"

"Silly, right? What's a guy like me doing with four puppies and Penny?" He held up his hand. "I know it's crazy, but when I saw those tiny little girls, their little ears, their little feet, I just had such a possessive rush. I don't think I can let even my mom take one."

"So you keep them. Nothing wrong with that." Lots of people had more than one—or four—dogs. She didn't see it as a problem.

"You're serious? You don't think I'm nuts?" Nash asked, his tone serious.

Emma smiled. "No, I don't." Could she tell him that this was yet another trait she found admirable about him? Or was it too soon?

"Go on, tell me what you're thinking. I can tell

raised his hands above his head, stretching like a cat sunning itself.

"New York?" she asked, her tone curious.

"I worked in investments."

"I see. That's where it happens. I've been there many times with clients. As you said, it's intoxicating, but only for a while."

She couldn't believe how they were talking, given they'd known each other for barely an hour. But if you added up the time she'd spent spying on him, it would be more than an hour. She wouldn't say that out loud, of course, fearing she would sound childish.

"Clients? What type of work?" Nash asked. She could tell he was sincere and wanted to know more about her.

Laughing, she said, "I was an attorney. Corporate."

He whistled. "I guessed you were top-notch and I was right."

"Why top-notch? Is that good or bad?" she asked.

"Oh, it's perfect. You look professional, a take-no-bull kind of lady."

She wasn't sure she liked his assessment of her. She was professional in her work life, but wasn't a hard-core, do-or-die person.

"I was very professional when I had to b didn't b one of the few around here who dislikes this heated pool. Especially in the summer months. It's like I said—diving into a hot cup of coffee."

She nodded. "I don't like it either. What's the point? If you're hot, you want to cool off, but the water is like a warm bath."

isn't my calling, so I decided to change my life and career, and here I am."

"You know I teach math, right?"

"Marlena told me when you were at the store."

"Vittles is a one stop shop for food and a bit of local gossip," he said, his green eyes teasing, matching his smile.

"I've only been there once, the same day you were," she said, wanting to clarify that she hadn't been in the store to participate in any gossip.

"I was in a rush on Sunday. Penny was about to give birth. She's my dog, in case you haven't heard. It seems the entire Cove wants one of her puppies. I promised my mother she could have her pick of the litter, but after seeing them, I'm not sure Penny is going to be willing to give them up."

Emma's heart clenched. Nash was everything she'd heard and maybe more. "You want to keep all the dogs?"

"Silly, right? What's a guy like me doing with four puppies and Penny?" He held up his hand. "I know it's crazy, but when I saw those tiny little girls, their little ears, their little feet, I just had such a possessive rush. I don't think I can let even my mom take one."

"So you keep them. Nothing wrong with that." Lots of people had more than one—or four—dogs. She didn't see it as a problem.

"You're serious? You don't think I'm nuts?" Nash asked, his tone serious.

Emma smiled. "No, I don't." Could she tell him that this was yet another trait she found admirable about him? Or was it too soon?

"Go on, tell me what you're thinking. I can tell

there's more you want to say. It's okay if you think I've whacked out." He tipped back his glass, crunching on an ice cube.

He had picked up on her thoughts. Was she that obvious, or was he highly intuitive?

Taking a chance, she decided to be honest. Not that she was a chronic liar, but something was going on between them. He might not admit it yet, but she could feel their chemistry. "I think it's sweet you want to keep the puppies. I hear they're dachshunds, which is the most adorable breed. I had a roommate in college who had a dachshund named Rex. He made us laugh so much. We went through flip-flops like crazy." In her third year of college, when she was of legal age, she'd moved out of the dorm into an apartment with two friends. Rex belonged to Cathryn, though they all took turns caring for him.

"You're not making this up just to make me feel better?" Nash questioned.

"No, I don't work that way," she said, wanting him to know she wasn't the kind of woman to tell him what he wanted to hear to make him feel good. Emma didn't believe he was the type of guy who played games either. At least she hoped not.

"Good," he said.

Nash clearly wasn't one to mince words; she had that much figured out. Emma didn't have a response, so she didn't say anything.

Out of the blue, he asked, "What's your favorite food?"

"In which food group?" she asked, looking at him.

"All of them. For each meal."

Emma laughed. "I like almost anything except anchovies and corn from a can."

"That's pretty specific. No seafood allergies? Peanut allergy? Nothing that would send you to the emergency room? I want to know for when I ask you to go to dinner with me tonight after we stop by the clinic so you can see the pups."

Had he just asked her to dinner?

"You want to have dinner with me?" Emma said to confirm she'd heard him correctly.

"After I show you the pups. Do you like dogs? I hope."

Breaking out into a grin as wide as the sun, she said, "I don't have food allergies and I love dogs."

"That's a relief. I wasn't sure you'd say yes. I've wanted to ask you since I first saw you on your lanai. But the timing has been off. Have you been to Cove's Fish Camp? It's about some of the best seafood around. It's been a while since I was there."

Emma wondered if that was where he took all his dates, but she wouldn't ask.

"No, I haven't been out much since moving here. I've spent most of my time unpacking and getting organized." She didn't feel quite as confident as she had moments before. If this was his go-to date destination, she didn't want to be just another woman he took to his favorite seafood joint. She couldn't help it; those were the vibes she'd picked up on.

"Emma, we can go somewhere else if you want. It's truly the best seafood in town, but there are other restaurants. Heck, I can make dinner if you don't want to be seen in public with me." He stood up and swiped his hands through his hair. "If you say yes, I'm going in to shower and I'll pick you up in an hour. If that's enough time for you?"

"Half an hour. I'll be ready," she said, deciding he wasn't feeding her a line of bull.

"Impressive. See you in thirty," he said before diving into the pool. He swam to the shallow end, then used the steps to get out. Then he went inside his condo via the lanai.

"Okay, I'm flabbergasted." Emma spoke softly to herself as she headed inside. She took their empty glasses with her and put them in the sink. Then she raced to the shower. She shaved her legs and used her favorite gardenia-scented bodywash. After, she hurried to dress. She chose a hot pink, halter-style sundress. In the shoe room, she found the sandals she bought when she purchased her dress online last summer, never having had a chance to wear either. She hoped it wasn't too dressy—or not dressy enough. Honestly, it didn't matter. She was going on a date with a man she had a real thing for. She wasn't going to worry about her clothing.

Emma brushed her hair, letting it hang loose around her shoulders. She added mascara, blush, and clear lip gloss to her face. She whirled around, happier than she'd been in . . . forever. She glanced at the clock; it'd taken her twenty-six minutes to get ready. She stuffed her cell phone, house keys, and wallet in a small clutch purse before returning to her living room to wait for Nash.

At exactly six thirty, the doorbell rang. A guy who was on time—she liked that, too.

Emma ran a hand through her hair, then

smoothed the front of her dress before opening the door. "Hi," she said for lack of anything else to say.

"Hi back," Nash said. "You look stunning, Emma. I'm the luckiest guy in town." He took her hand and closed the door behind them. "Keys?" he asked, and she handed her house keys to him. He locked the door, then returned the keys.

All she could do was stare at him. He wore navy dress slacks, a white shirt with the sleeves rolled up and the top buttons open, and a matching jacket slung over his shoulder. *He could be a male model,* she thought. He wasn't the type, though; she just knew it.

"I had to get my car out of the garage. It's been in there for a while so it needs a bath. I hope you don't mind."

"Not at all," she told him as they walked around her condo to the back of his.

Idling in his driveway was a cherry-red convertible. "This is your car?" Emma asked, stating the obvious. It didn't fit the profile she'd imagined for him—she'd envisioned some sort of SUV, something brand-new. So much for speculating. But she'd been mostly right about him thus far.

He didn't say anything when he saw the expression on her face. He opened the car door for her, making sure she didn't get her dress caught, then went to the driver's side and got in. "Are you okay in a convertible? I didn't want to put you in my old truck."

Emma wondered how old his truck was, but didn't want to ask, fearing it would embarrass him. "Of course. It's the perfect evening for it."

"Good." He shifted the car into first gear, then second as they traveled down Flamingo Boulevard. He didn't drive fast, thankfully. Emma was a careful driver. She never broke the speed limit or ran red lights.

She'd had a date a few years back who'd driven so fast she'd had to call a taxi to take her home. He'd been angry, but there was no way she would have gotten in the car with him again after they'd finished dinner. He'd followed her home and spent thirty minutes doing doughnuts in her parking lot. She'd called the police and they'd issued him a ticket. After that experience, she was careful about whose vehicle she got into.

"This was my dad's car," Nash said as though he could read her mind. "My truck belonged to him, too."

She didn't know what to say, but assumed Nash's father had passed away because he spoke in the past tense. "I love it," she said and meant it.

"He loved old cars. Mom promised him she would give this old T-Bird to me and she did, when I graduated college. I left it here when I moved to New York. You couldn't find a parking spot there unless you were willing to pay big bucks, which I would've, but the car is in mint condition and I wasn't about to let anything happen to it."

"I'm sure your father would appreciate the extra care." She wanted to ask more about him, but she held back. In time they would get to those topics. This was the first date she'd had in over a year. She wasn't going to mess it up by being nosy. If he wanted her to know something, he would tell her.

"Yes, he was a stickler when caring for cars. Heck, I'm named after one. Anything he worked for he treated with kid gloves. My mom too." He slowed down, shifting into first gear, then turned down a side street Emma had yet to discover. "Cove's Fish Camp is a bit out of the way," Nash explained as he turned to the left. "Great for the locals, not so great for the tourists."

"I'm intrigued. And hungry! So, are you really named after a car?" she asked when he pulled into a gravel parking area. Next to it was a small house painted red with all kinds of beach paraphernalia surrounding the walkway. Emma was anxious to try the food.

Nash got out first, then came around to open her door. "Sort of. Charles W. Nash was the president of General Motors in 1912 and later the owner of Nash Motors."

"I love that your name has a history," she said, hoping he was for real. He was almost too good to be true. Emma crossed her fingers. Nash took her hand, helped her out of the car, then closed the door. Before going inside, he turned to her so their faces were mere inches apart. She could feel his breath on her. He smelled of mint. Before she realized what was about to happen, he leaned in, his lips touching her own—just a whisper of a kiss.

When he took his mouth from hers, she wanted him—more than she'd ever wanted a man. Light as air, her heart fluttered like a hummingbird's wings.

"Emma." Nash said her name as though it were a cherished prize.

Hoping he was about to kiss her again, she didn't say anything, just in case.

"There's something I forgot," Nash said as they stood practically nose-to-nose.

Emma hoped he wasn't going to confess his undying love for her. If he did, all of her instincts had been wrong. Nothing good, at least in her experience, happened when a guy told you he was in love on a first date.

She remained still as stone. His next words could be a deal-breaker. She crossed her fingers again for good luck.

"We forgot to stop by the clinic to see the puppies," he said.

She let out a sigh of relief. She nodded, thankful he hadn't said anything worrisome. "What about after dinner?"

Chapter Ten

The food was even better than Nash promised. The waiter suggested Emma try the lobster tower to get a sample of almost everything on the menu.

"They have the best red velvet cake ever," Nash said as the waiter removed their plates.

Emma shook her head. "I don't think I can eat another bite. If the cake is as good as the rest of the food, I'll try it the next time." Did Nash think she was hinting at a second date? She hoped it sounded that way.

"We can have a light lunch here next time, and then you can try the cake. I'll let you choose a time that suits you." Nash reached for his wallet when the waiter returned with the check.

"I'll pay my half," Emma said, as she had with most of her dates in the past.

"You're kidding, I hope," Nash said as he removed several bills from his wallet.

"No, I'm not," she told him, reaching for her purse.

He closed the folder with the money inside, then reached across the table, taking both of her hands in his. "I'm an old-fashioned guy, Emma. If I can't afford to take my date wherever she wants to go, I have no business asking her out in the first place. I don't know how this works in Miami or wherever, but when you're with me, I will always take care of you." He squeezed her hand.

Some women might think him sexist, but she didn't. He was what she desired a man to be. Protective and responsible, without being a control freak.

Dishes clanged in the background and the hum of diners talking filled the small space, but all Emma could focus on was Nash. This felt too good to be true.

"You're thinking about me?" he asked before releasing her hands.

"It's hard not to when you're . . ." She paused. "Saying all the right words." There, that was what she wanted to convey. Emma wanted Nash to know she wasn't threatened by his manliness or paying the check. She could take care of herself, yet it pleased her that Nash wanted to take care of her, even if it was in such a small way. It'd been years since she'd had anyone look out for her. Harris tried in his own way, but this kind of caring was different.

"It's easy when you're with the right person," he said. "You still want to see the pups?"

"Yes, I'm excited," she said, and she indeed was.

The sun was setting, the sky a mixture of orange and pink. The temperature had dropped. Emma wished for a sweater when they stepped outside. As soon as she had the thought, Nash placed his jacket around her. *He's almost a mind reader*, she thought as they walked to the car. Nash opened her door, waited while she got situated, then closed the door.

"I should've put the hard top on; I didn't even think to check the weather," he said as he backed out of the parking lot.

"I love this," Emma said, leaning her head back against the seat and letting her hair blow in every direction.

He shifted gears, then placed his right arm across her shoulders. Emma knew then that she was falling head over heels for this handsome, kind man. She looked at his profile; he was smiling. He squeezed her shoulder, as though he once again knew exactly what she was thinking.

Emma decided he wasn't much of a talker. It didn't bother her because she was pretty comfortable with him. The need to fill the silence with meaningless words that led to nothing wasn't required with Nash.

She closed her eyes, enjoying the cool breeze, the briny scent of the Gulf filling the night air. Seagulls sounded like they were laughing, bringing a smile to her face.

"It's the *Leucophaeus atricilla*, more commonly known as the laughing gull," Nash said.

She turned to him. "How do you always seem to know what I'm thinking?" It was almost scary.

"I snuck a glance and saw you laughing. Those birds sound hysterical, don't they?"

"We had them when I lived on the beach in Miami. They drove my mom crazy, but my dad always got a kick out of it when she was aggravated. Usually, Mom was as cool as a cucumber." Emma realized she missed her family. Lydia had taken care of her most of the time because her parents traveled so much, but they were good parents.

Nash parked the 1956 Thunderbird behind the clinic. He saw Naomi's beat-up car, and Dr. Mellow's van was there too. When he shut down the engine, Emma looked up to see where they were.

"You ready to meet Penny and her brood?" Nash asked her.

Nodding, Emma opened her door before Nash had a chance. It would take time for her to get used to a guy with manners. "I am," she told him.

He took her hand and they went to the back door together. Nash tapped on the window and tried the door, but it was locked. "Let me call Naomi and tell her I'm here," Nash said. He dialed his phone and then said, "Hey, I'm at the back entrance. I've got a friend who wants to see the pups." The expression on his face went from passive to pissed in seconds. Emma hoped nothing had happened to Penny and her puppies.

"Are you serious?" Nash asked, his voice firm, angry. "Let me in and I'll take care of this."

Emma heard the door rattle from the inside, then open. A teenage girl with a pierced nose and short black hair stepped aside, her index finger to her lips, indicating they should be quiet.

"Naomi, you'd better tell me how she managed to get inside here. Aren't you supposed to lock the doors when you close up?"

Emma was surprised Nash was so angry at the girl, that he spoke so harshly to her. Maybe his true colors were finally starting to show.

"I called the doc and he's talking to her now. She won't hurt them, Nash." Naomi sounded frightened.

Emma had kept quiet long enough. "Can someone please explain what's going on?"

Naomi looked at Nash, then back at Emma.

He raked a hand through his windblown hair. "Em, I'm so sorry you have to witness something I should've taken care of long ago."

Now she *was* frightened.

"Should I leave? I can call an Uber," Emma said, remembering the date that went whacko in the parking lot at her old condo.

"No, I want you here with me. Tiffany needs to see this," he said.

Who was Tiffany? Why did she need to see whatever Nash thought she needed to see?

"They're still in the whelping room," Naomi offered.

"Did she drive here?" Nash asked as they followed her down a long hallway.

"I think she was dropped off. I checked and didn't see any cars other than mine and Doc's."

"Naomi, tell Doc I'm here," Nash instructed.

Naomi tapped on the door to their left, stepped inside, then backed out in seconds. "He says okay."

"I don't think I need to be here for whatever this is, Nash. I don't feel comfortable," Emma said. "I'll see the puppies another time." Before he could stop her, she hurried back down the hallway and out the door. She'd brought her cell phone. She'd call for a ride.

Outside in the parking lot, it dawned on Emma that she had no one to call. She didn't have the Uber app on her new phone, or Wi-Fi so she could download it. Scrolling through her contacts, she saw Lisa and Jack's numbers. Would they think she was out of her mind if she called and asked for a ride home? As she'd learned, news in the Cove spread fast. She didn't want to be the subject of gossip, so she debated what to do. Sure that her new friends would help her, Emma decided she would explain how the evening had turned out and why she needed a ride, even though she wasn't quite sure herself.

"Emma, Wait!" Nash called from behind her.

She whirled around, almost afraid to confront him. Emma didn't want to talk to him, though he owed her an explanation. "I am so sorry you had to see . . . this." He waved his long arms around.

"I'm getting a lift home, Nash." She didn't see anything per se. She had just been in a hallway with a girl she didn't know while Nash went from calm to angry in seconds.

"Please, Emma, I can explain. This is beyond weird, I know."

She hadn't hit the green Call button yet. She'd hear him out, then leave. "Go on, tell me whatever it is." She used her courtroom voice. Succinct, to the point.

He shook his head. "This is embarrassing. No, it's more than that. It's disgusting."

She tipped her head to the side, hoping he would pick up on her impatience because he seemed to be able to pick up on so many of her thoughts. "I'm waiting."

"Tiffany, the woman inside. She's got a screw loose. I'm being kind when I say this. I dated her in high school. We went out twice." He paused, shaking his head. "I was prom king; she wanted to go as my date. I took a good friend instead. She's never let me live it down. She was a spoiled brat then. She's a crazy, nut job now."

"I don't see how this has anything to do with your puppies."

"I was here earlier to check on them. As I said, news travels fast around town. She was in the waiting room when I got here. She already knew about the pups and where they were and used them as an excuse to see me. She told me she wanted to be the first in line to get pick of the litter. As I said, the woman has a screw loose. Her family enables her, Emma. She's been obsessed with me for too long. As much as I hate to do it, I'm calling the police. She's refusing to leave the whelping room. She's holding Penny, won't let her nurse the puppies."

"Are you serious?" Emma asked, all thoughts of leaving gone. "Let me inside. I'll tell her the legal ramifications of what could happen to her."

"You'd do that for me?" Nash asked.

"Now that I know you aren't out of your mind, yes. I thought . . . never mind what I thought. Let's get Penny. You can give me the full story later."

Emma followed Nash inside, then down the hallway a second time. It'd been a while since she'd read the Florida statutes, but she knew her state had strict laws where animals were concerned. "Nash, give me a minute. I need to look something up." Now that she was inside she could use the vet office's Wi-Fi to search on her cell for the information she needed. Nash stood next to her.

"I'm ready," Emma said, gripping her cell phone. She kept the browser open in case she needed to refer to it later.

Nash tapped on the door to the whelping room, then pushed it open. "Doc, can you give me a few minutes?"

Doc Mellow was in his late fifties, with curly gray hair and round, wire framed glasses. He was as tall as Nash but skinny. "Are you sure?" Doc Mellow asked, glancing at Tiffany, who sat on the floor holding Penny.

"Yes," Nash said. "Come in, Emma."

"Who is Emma?" Tiffany screeched, sounding like a seagull.

Emma stood next to Nash, shocked when she saw how Tiffany was holding the new mommy. "I'm Emma Swan, Nash's attorney. It would be best if you put the dog down, Tiffany. You're violating several state laws right now. I think Penny needs to feed her pups." She was being too kind. What she wanted to do was take Penny away from the other woman, then yank her up by her overly bleached blond hair and drag her to the police station.

Tiffany gripped Penny closer to her chest. "Nash? She's lying, right? I told you I wanted to see the puppies. I'm just looking," she said in her fake little-girl, high-pitched voice.

He took his cell phone out of his pocket. "I'm calling the police. It would be best if you put down my dog now. I'm sick of your crap. You're a grown woman, Tiffany. You think you can get away with anything. Daddy isn't going to help you now."

"Says who?" Tiffany countered.

Emma couldn't let the woman continue this insane behavior. She glanced at her phone as she recited, "Says Florida Statute 828.12. 'A person who intentionally commits an act to any animal, or a person who owns or has the custody or control of any animal and fails to act, which results in the cruel death or excessive or repeated infliction of unnecessary pain or suffering, or causes the same to be done, commits aggravated animal cruelty. It's a felony of the third degree, punishable by jail time, a fine of not more than $10,000 or both.' I can go on if you'd like."

The puppies started making crying noises, scooting around as they searched for their mother. Nash took three giant steps, grabbed Tiffany's arm, and lifted her into a standing position, taking hold of Penny with his other hand. "Emma, take her to her pups," Nash asked.

Emma took Penny from Nash and carried the new mom over to her babies. "Here you go, precious, right where you belong, with your tiny blessings." As she put Penny in the whelping area, Penny positioned herself so the puppies could nurse.

"Let me go! You're hurting me," Tiffany cried out.

"No. Not until the police arrive." Nash dialed 911 and explained the situation. The Cove had a small police force. He'd gone to school with the chief of police, Roberto Rodriguez. Rob knew Tiffany, knew how erratic her behavior was. Naomi and Dr. Mellow silently slipped out of the room and headed to the reception area to wait for the police to arrive.

Emma stayed beside the animals in case Tiffany broke away from Nash; he didn't have a strong hold on her.

"We're going to walk out of here and you are going with Rob. No questions," Nash ordered.

"You wait, Nash Kendrick. I will see that you lose your job and your teaching license. When I get through with you, you'll wish you'd given me all of those stinky pups."

Emma had to speak up. "If they're so stinky, why in the world would you want one?"

"Shut up, okay?" Tiffany snapped.

Emma did not normally have a temper. But she was so ticked off that she wanted to smack Tiffany across her smug, overly made-up face. "No, I will not shut up. Nash, give me a dollar," she said, fury in her words.

"What?" Nash asked.

"Just give me a dollar," Emma ordered.

Nash reached into his pocket and pulled out a wrinkled one-dollar bill.

"Okay, now I am officially your legal representative. Do you want to file charges against her?"

"You can do that?"

"I can get the ball rolling in a matter of minutes," Emma said, her eyes never leaving Tiffany.

"Then yes, I do. Maybe it will teach her a lesson." Nash wrapped his arm around Tiffany, firmly leading her to the front of the clinic. Emma trailed behind. If Tiffany tried to break loose, she would stop her.

Flashing red and blue lights filled the front room as two police cars pulled up to the entrance. Emma had never had a date end like this. *A first time for everything*, she thought, as Nash walked Tiffany outside while she spewed all kinds of profanities at him.

Naomi spoke up. "She scared me. I didn't know what to do, so I called Doc."

"You did the right thing," Doc Mellow said. "When an animal is in danger in this office, always call me and we'll take care of the matter."

"He's right," Emma said.

"Are you really an attorney?" Naomi asked her.

"Yep, I am," Emma answered.

"That was so cool when you told Tiffany she could go to jail," Naomi said. "Could she really?"

"Yes. Animal abuse of any kind is a crime. Holding Penny hostage and not allowing her to care for the puppies is against the law. Under these circumstances, Tiffany can be prosecuted."

Emma waited while Nash explained the situation to the police. If she were being honest with herself—and she was—another date with Nash probably would not happen.

Chapter Eleven

Nash had never been so mortified in his life. He explained the situation to Rob and told him he wanted to press charges. Maybe if Tiffany were held accountable, she would stop these childish games.

Rob's deputy put her in the back seat of his cruiser, and Nash could still hear Tiffany screaming obscenities as they pulled out of the parking lot. Rob assured Nash that Tiffany wasn't going to be released that night.

Back inside the clinic, Emma, Naomi, and Doc Mellow spoke in his office, their voices hushed. Nash hovered in the doorway, so embarrassed he was at a loss for words.

"Nash, I hope we won't have this problem again. I would hate to have to ban you from the clinic," Doc said, his tone more serious than Nash had ever heard it before.

"As you should. I can't apologize enough. I had no idea she was this . . . insane. How did she manage to get inside afterhours?" Nash asked Doc Mellow and Naomi.

Naomi looked down at her black high-top sneakers. "It's my fault. I forgot to lock the front doors when we closed up."

"What's done is done, but we can't ever let this happen again, Naomi. Let's all leave this as a lesson learned. Nash, I'm not sure what advice to give you regarding this woman, but whatever you decide, I wouldn't wait too long." Doc's words were stern.

"Press charges against her," Emma said. "Sometimes it takes a drastic move to stop obsessive behavior."

Nash nodded. "You're right. There are a dozen instances when she's hung around the condo and the school. I haven't told anyone. It's such odd behavior for a woman her age. I figured she would get the message if I ignored her long enough."

"People like Tiffany play on emotions, especially if they believe the person they're harassing won't take any action. Legally or otherwise." Emma was back in legal mode. "If you can prove she's been stalking you, there are laws against that, Nash. Have you ever documented her behavior? Cell phone pictures? Did you have a friend with you during any of these incidents?" Emma disliked questioning Nash like this, but she didn't want any harm to come to him just because someone else had a mental issue. There were many ways to address this situation.

"I never thought of that. It was just Tiffany

being Tiffany," Nash said. "This is all my fault. I'm sorry. I'll drive you to the condo if you still want to get in the car with me. We can discuss the legalities on the way home."

Emma hated to admit it, but she loved how Nash said, "on the way home," as if they had a shared home.

"I just need to check on Penny first and make sure she's okay," Nash said before heading back to the whelping room.

Doc nodded. Naomi didn't say a word. Emma followed him; she was also concerned about the mommy and her pups.

Inside the whelping room, Penny and her girls were sleeping peacefully.

Emma noticed how Nash's expression softened as he watched his dogs. "I'm bringing them home tomorrow," he told her.

"Good. I can't say I know that much about puppies, but I'm a fast learner. Home is probably the safest place for them. I can help look after them while you're at school," she offered.

"I'm taking a few days off, but thanks. I may need your help. But aren't you signed up for substitute teaching?"

"I am," Emma said as they quietly left the room.

"You may be subbing for me if they can't cover my scheduled days off."

Emma was slightly surprised, but wouldn't mind stepping into his teaching shoes. "That would be okay by me. I've never taught high school."

"Then you're in for a surprise. I have a great group of kids this year."

"Good to know," she said.

Nash spoke to Dr. Mellow and Naomi before they departed, and then he and Emma returned to his car together. Nash opened her door; she leaned against the seatback, staring at the night sky. The stars seemed excessively bright as the clouds drifted away, along with the evening's drama.

Nash drove slowly. When they returned to his condo, he shut the engine down, not bothering to park in the garage. Turning to her, he said, "I don't know if I can make this evening up to you, but I would like the opportunity if you'll let me."

A dozen thoughts swirled through her head. Despite what had happened at the vet clinic, it had been a wonderful evening. She couldn't hold Nash fully responsible for Tiffany's obsession. He was the kind of guy he was, a bit easygoing. Maybe too much so, but that wasn't necessarily a bad thing. "I would," she said, knowing she'd regret it if she didn't.

He let out a deep breath. "Perfect."

He thought I was going to say no! Emma realized.

"Okay, that's settled. So, I'll walk around to my condo and see you tomorrow," she said, putting her hand on the door and then taking it away when Nash got out of the car to open it for her, ever the gentleman.

"Do you mind if I walk you to your door?" he asked when she got out of the car.

"Not at all," she replied. As they walked around the condominiums, she debated inviting him in. Not wanting to give the impression that she wanted the night to have a different ending, she decided not to. There would be other times. She would see him again.

At her door, she automatically handed him her set of keys. He unlocked her door, tucked the keys in her hand, then leaned down, his lips warm against hers. He deepened the kiss, pulling her closer. Emma could feel his heart thudding against her own. She felt as if there was molten lava in the pit of her stomach. Her legs were unsteady. If this continued, she wouldn't have a choice. She would be inviting him in for more than a drink.

He pulled away, his breathing uneven. "I'll see you tomorrow?" he asked.

She just nodded because she wasn't sure she could speak after his kiss.

Chapter Twelve

Nash didn't enjoy what he had to do, but he had no choice. He should've put a stop to Tiffany's obsession when it started. Back then, she'd only been a real pain in the rear. Now he feared she could be dangerous.

"Hey there," said Heather Warren, Rob's secretary. "Tiffany is already gone, if that's what you're here for."

"Rob called me this morning. Said her dad bailed her out earlier. I'm here to sign the papers we discussed."

"They're ready," Heather said, turning away from him and typing on her computer's keyboard. She handed him several sheets of paper. "Sign and date these." She used a yellow highlighter to indicate where he needed to sign.

Nash signed the papers and returned them to Heather. "How long will this take?"

"If she hasn't skipped town, we can handle this today. Judge Anderson is quick with this type of order."

"And if she *has* skipped town?" Nash asked, fearing that in that case, she would only return and this craziness would never end.

"We'll find her, Nash. Tiffany has issues; everyone in the Cove knows that. Let's hope her father doesn't prevent her from getting the help she needs."

He nodded. "You're right. Thanks, Heather. You'll let me know what happens?"

"Of course," she said.

With Emma's advice, Nash had filed a restraining order against Tiffany. Hopefully, she would get the help she needed. Tiffany would react when she was served his complaint. But he didn't want her near Emma, Penny and her pups, or himself.

Today he would bring the puppies and Penny home. Nash had promised his mom she could go to the vet's with him. When he pulled into the driveway of her home, she was already waiting outside with Henry. Nash locked his truck. He'd agreed they would bring the puppies home in his mom's van.

"Good morning, son," Lori Kendrick said. "Did you get any sleep last night?" she asked, grinning.

"Why would you think I wouldn't?" he asked, taking Henry from her.

"You look tired."

"I slept well, just not long enough." He'd spent half the night thinking about Emma. The date they'd had contradicted everything he thought he knew about love. He'd never been so attracted to a woman so quickly. He'd believed all that talk of love at first sight was just gobbledygook. Maybe he was just infatuated because she wasn't jumping all over him, as many of his dates had in the past.

"I put the crates in the back. Nash?" Lori said. "*Hello?*"

"Sorry," he said, stroking Henry's long, floppy ears. "Let's get going. I'll drive if you don't mind." He handed Henry back over to her.

"Fine," Lori said. Nash opened the door for his mother just as he had for Emma. Nash was taught to be respectful to everyone. Being a gentleman wasn't a part-time gig.

As soon as Henry was in his doggy car seat, Nash slowly backed out onto the main road. "I like this, Mom. Smooth ride," he commented, referring to the van she'd recently purchased.

"I do too. I thought of your dad when I was at the dealership. He would've had a fit if he knew I'm driving a van now. He never cared for them."

Nash laughed. "I remember he said they weren't practical. That's what trucks were built for."

Henry barked.

"That's right, Henry," Nash said.

"I can't wait to see Penny and Henry's puppies. Are there any little Henrys?" Lori asked.

Nash laughed again. "I won't ruin the surprise, Mom. Remember, you said you wanted to wait until you could see them for yourself?"

"I was hoping you'd forget, but we're almost there," she said. "I am excited, I admit."

Nash smiled. "You're going to love them." He knew she would, even though Penny had failed to reproduce a Henry look-alike. Or rather, Henry had failed.

As instructed, Nash parked in front of the clinic when they arrived. He clicked the key fob and the passenger door opened automatically. "I think Dad would've had a change of heart about vans if he saw that."

Lori removed Henry from his seat. "Maybe. Now, you've kept me in suspense long enough, Nash. Let's go see Henry's offspring."

Inside the reception area, Nash didn't see Naomi or Dr. Mellow. *After last night, they probably both took the day off,* he thought to himself.

"I'll be right there," Rosemarie, another vet tech, called out.

"No worries," Nash said.

"Sorry about that. I had to remove an IV. Now, what can I do for you?" Rosemarie reached out to pet Henry. He growled.

"Henry, shame on you!" Lori said, turning to Rosemarie. "I didn't realize you were still working here. I thought you retired."

"Doc called me this morning to ask if I could fill in for a few hours. Of course I said yes. I don't think I'll ever fully retire," Rosemarie said to Lori.

"I take it you two know each other," Nash said. "I'm here for Penny, the dachshund with the puppies. We're here to take them home. This is their father," he explained, gesturing toward Henry.

"I remember Henry. Your mom and I were working together when he was first brought in," Rosemarie said. "I think that must be why he's growling. He wants to see his family."

Nash nodded.

"He can smell them. Come on back; we'll get this little family together. Do you have all the supplies Doc requires?" Rosemarie queried.

"Yes, plenty of everything," Nash confirmed.

Henry growled again, his hackles raised.

"Henry," Lori said in a harsh whisper. "You need to settle down."

"He's excited. Aren't you, little fella?" Nash said as he followed Rosemarie down the hallway to the whelping room.

Rosemarie opened the door, letting Nash in first. Henry started whining, almost howling, when he saw Penny. "Here you go," Nash said, lowering the new father so he could see his girls.

"Oh my gosh, they're all brown! Nash, they're beautiful." Lori leaned down beside the whelping area, touching each newborn pup lightly on the head. "How many of each?"

Nash couldn't help himself; he laughed out loud. "Four little girls, Mom. Good fella, Henry. You better man up now—you have a family to look after."

"I just can't pick one; they're so sweet," Lori said. "I want all of them."

"Everyone in town wants one," Nash said, remembering Tiffany.

Rosemarie stood in the doorway. "I'm here if you need my help getting them into the car."

"Thanks, Rosemarie. I'm guessing I'll need a lot of help over the next few weeks," Nash told her. "Mom, see if you can get Henry settled in. Then I'll bring Penny and the pups."

They had three dog crates in the van but only

needed one. Henry could sit with Lori. No way was he going to take his eyes off the new pups.

"Come, Henry. Let's go," Lori said. Hesitant, Henry followed her out the door while Nash took Penny and the puppies in their bed, carrying them to the car.

Penny licked the pups as they slept while Nash eased them into the crate. Once they were in safely, he fastened the seat belt.

"Okay, Mom. Let's go."

Nash drove home so slowly, his mother admonished him. "Nash, this is ridiculous. At this speed, they'll be weaned before they're home."

"I'm just being cautious."

"You're a good man, Nash. I probably don't say it enough. Kent would be so proud of you." Lori's voice faltered when she mentioned her late husband.

"Thanks. I sure hope so. You miss him, don't you?" They rarely had this discussion because it made both of them sad.

"Of course. Our kind of love only happens once, Nash. He was the love of my life. Someday, I hope you experience the kind of love your father and I shared."

The moment was already sentimental, so Nash asked, "How will I know? What's the difference between infatuation and the kind of love you and Dad had? Honestly, I want to know."

"Nash, stop teasing me. Don't give me false hope," Lori said, smiling.

He didn't respond.

"Okay, you're serious." She took a deep breath. "When you meet that special person, you will only notice them, no matter where you are. Life feels almost perfect when you find love. It's all you think about. Every feeling is intensified. Taking out the garbage is exciting when you're doing it with someone you love. It's not something I can explain, other than I can assure you, when you find real lifelong love, you will know."

Nash was beginning to understand. *"It's all you think about."* Since the first time he'd seen his new neighbor, he hadn't stopped thinking about her. At first, it was simple curiosity. After that handshake at Vittles, he felt as if a lightning bolt had struck him.

"Nash, what's going on?"

He carefully turned into the driveway so the dogs didn't shift in their crate. As soon as he shut down the engine, he turned to his mom. "Honestly, I'm not sure." That was all he was willing to say. It was way too early to have these thoughts and feelings. Too early to share them with his mother; he hadn't even hinted how he felt yet to Emma. He wasn't sure what these feelings were or what he would do about them. If anything.

"Let's take these pooches inside," Nash said. "I'm anxious to get them settled in."

Twenty minutes later, Penny was resting in her new whelping area with the girls. Henry was whining to get to her. "Not now, Henry. Later, okay?" Lori smoothed his long ears. "If you're all set, I'll go home," she said to Nash. "Remember, call me if you need anything. I'm good with puppies."

"Thanks, Mom. I'll call if I need to, but I think I can handle this," Nash told her. "Remember, I spend most of my days with a bunch of teenagers. Pups should be a breeze."

"You know where to find me." Lori hugged him before letting herself out.

Nash wished his mom would remarry. She'd been alone too long. He suspected Dr. Mellow had a crush on her. The vet wasn't that much older than she and he, too, had lost his mate. Matchmaking wasn't Nash's best skill, but he thought they would suit each other. His mother had worked at the clinic for years after his dad passed away. Surely there'd been more to her relationship with Doc Mellow than just employee and employer. But it ultimately wasn't his business. He just had relationships on the brain.

With the pups where they should be, he was at loose ends. Nash wasn't used to having very much free time. Emma hadn't shared her plans for the day, other than that she was "on call," so she might be substitute teaching right now. He went out to the lanai on the chance she might be on hers. He hadn't gotten her cell number the night before. That was his bad, but he would see her later.

He would make sure of it.

Chapter Thirteen

Emma peeked through the blinds, hoping to see Nash on his lanai. No luck there. Knowing he had to bring the puppies home, she assumed he was at the vet clinic.

Anxious about her trip to the library, she called Marlena at Vittles. They chatted briefly before Emma asked, "Did the new books come in? I'm dreading it, but I have to return my damaged book to the library today. I'm ready to be removed from the 'book offender' list."

"All three of them. I had them delivered to the store. If you can, pop in and have a cup of coffee with me before you deal with Mrs. Whitton. Or maybe something stronger. She is quite the old battle-ax."

"I feel sorry for her. A little. It's obvious she's unhappy. I'll try to kill her with kindness. Heading your way now," Emma said.

"Good," Marlena replied.

Emma grabbed the clutch purse she'd used the night before, took her keys from the dolphin key ring holder, then set off for Vittles. Much as she dreaded the trip to the library, she would sincerely try to make friends with the librarian. Emma was an avid reader and liked using the library. She could always buy books and often did, but she also believed in supporting libraries.

Arriving at Vittles, Emma was surprised to find that the place was nearly empty. She headed to the bakery, where Marlena waited with two steaming mugs of coffee. "Thanks," Emma said, taking one of the mugs from her. "It's quiet here today."

"Tuesday isn't our busiest day of the week. It's nice sometimes. I love what we do here, but I'm not complaining about a little break now and then," Marlena told her. "Follow me."

Emma followed her to a small yet neatly organized office space.

Marlena gave her a large, padded envelope. "Your gift to Mrs. Whitton."

"You have to let me pay you back for this," Emma said.

"Absolutely not. I ruin the book, I replace the book," Marlena said.

First, Nash hadn't let her pay her share last night and now Marlena refused to take her money. Emma had to get used to how people were on the island. She would eventually adapt to their kindness.

"Okay, I agree. Now let's move on," Emma said, grinning.

"Have a seat." Marlena motioned to a small

table with two chairs hidden in the corner of the office. It was perfect for two people.

"Thank you." Emma took a sip of her coffee.

"Normally, I'm not a gossip, but today, well, I am." Marlena leaned in so close that Emma could see the gold specks in her hazel eyes. "What the heck happened with Tiffany last night? As I said, news travels fast here."

Emma took a deep breath, then eased it out slowly. This wasn't what she had expected her new friend to say. Emma didn't want to be labeled as a busybody. It wasn't her style. However, because Marlena knew about last night's incident already, someone else must have told her. "Tell me what you heard," she asked.

"Tiffany was taken to jail. She tried to take Nash's puppies, or something to that effect."

Emma couldn't help but feel disloyal to Nash when she spoke. "Yes, it was something like that. The situation was resolved last night. I believe the woman had an issue with Nash and was trying to get his attention." She wasn't going into any details. They would come out soon enough.

"Tiffany was released this morning. Her father was spitting mad, according to Heather Warren."

Emma took another sip of coffee. "I see," she said but didn't.

"Heather is the police chief's secretary. She came in this morning after her shift was over. She's a decent girl who likes to share what happens when most folks are tucked away safely at home." Marlena giggled. "Honestly, it's time Tiffany got some help. According to every customer who talks about her, she was raised badly by her dad. They say she was spoiled rotten and continues to act as if she's entitled to anything she desires. I think Nash has been on her list of desires since high school."

Emma knew Nash didn't feel the same. His actions last night proved that.

"I hope she gets the help she needs," Emma replied, and meant what she said. Mental health issues were on the rise and had to be taken seriously.

"I do too. I shouldn't be talking about her. Makes me look as bad as the rest of the town gossipmongers."

Emma finished the rest of her coffee. "I should go and get this over with. Wish me luck."

"Sure thing, Emma. You want to have that bottle of wine later this evening?"

"Can it keep until the weekend? I need to be at the top of my game in case I'm called in to substitute," Emma explained.

"Sorry, I forgot. I sound like a lush. Truly, I'm not," Marlena said.

Feeling guilty for making Marlena feel as if she had to defend herself, Emma said, "One glass. How's that?"

"Perfect. Thanks, Emma. You're a good woman."

"Wait until you see my bad side," Emma joked. "Then you might have a different opinion."

"I doubt that. Now, get out of here. You need to get off that book offender list."

Emma nodded, then hurried out to her car. Emma truly needed a friend, and she planned to spend more time getting to know Marlena. Once she had a permanent teaching job, she'd have a routine. She would invite Marlena and Lisa over for a girls' night out. The three of them had much in common.

The library was a short drive from Vittles. Emma parked in the visitors' only parking area. Wanting to get the delivery over with as quickly as possible, she took the damaged book and the envelope with the new books inside.

As expected, the library was quiet. Emma saw two older women sitting at a table, each with a stack of books. She wondered if they were also on the book offender list and couldn't bring the books home. Smiling at her silly thoughts, she walked to the checkout desk to return her book.

Mrs. Whitton busied herself with a rubber stamp. Emma cleared her throat to get her attention.

"Did you not read the posted sign?" Mrs. Whitton asked as she continued to stamp books.

"No, I didn't. I wanted to return this damaged book and give you three new ones to replace it."

The elderly librarian glanced at her, recognition causing her features to harden even more. "The book offender. Leave them," she said, returning to the pile of books she was stamping.

"You're welcome, Mrs. Whitton. My parents always told me to be polite even when others were rude. So I'll leave these books for you to stamp or whatever. When I'm teaching at Orange Grove Elementary or Skyline Middle or Pink Pearl High School, I'll teach my students what my parents taught me. Kill them with kindness." She plopped the ruined book on the counter along with the padded envelope. "Have a great day," Emma said before she left.

As soon as she was in her car, she thought about what she'd said to Marlena. Some people weren't friendly, no matter how nice you were. Mrs. Whitton was probably one of them. Emma had at least done what she'd set out to do.

When she returned home, Emma didn't have anything on her schedule. She cleaned up the kitchen and wiped down the counters. She felt lost, not having a proper job for the first time since she'd graduated from law school. Not one to watch much television, she touched the TV app on her phone to catch up with the world news. After five minutes, she'd had enough. Swiping the screen on her phone, she downloaded a book from a website she used and took a can of Coke out to the lanai.

She'd just gotten into her book when she heard her name.

"Emma."

Looking up at the lanai across from hers, she waved. "Nash."

"You want to see the puppies?" he asked. "I brought them home this morning."

She closed the app on her phone. "Of course I do. Give me a minute," she called. Inside, she left her cell on the charger and raked a hand through her hair. She didn't bother locking the door because she could see her place from Nash's.

Before she had a chance to knock, Nash swung his door open. "Come in. You look great, Emma," he said.

She widened her eyes. "Thanks, Nash. You look . . ." She paused. "Tired."

"Yeah, that's what my mom said when we were at

the clinic earlier. I had a tough time sleeping last night."

Emma didn't want to bring up the previous evening's craziness, but if it bothered Nash enough to keep him up all night, it must be more important to him than she'd guessed. "You want to talk about it?"

"You're serious?"

"Sure. I'm a good listener if you want to talk."

"I'm afraid I'll scare you off if I tell you what kept me awake half the night."

Emma's heart dropped. Were all the thoughts she'd had about him wrong? She'd been sure he'd felt the spark between them.

"Hey, Emma," he said. "I'm sorry. What did I do?"

He seemed genuinely confused. Maybe it was she who was confused.

She gave a half-hearted laugh. "Nothing, not a thing. So, how are the dogs?"

"They're sleeping. I just checked on them right before I saw you on the lanai. I wanted to see you. I felt I owe you an apology for last night. I shouldn't have let Tiffany get the best of me so that I lost my temper in front of you. I feel like a real piece of garbage."

Is that what kept him awake? Emma thought. "I've witnessed far worse, Nash. I'm an attorney and I lived in Miami. I'm not naive. Last night wasn't a big deal." And it wasn't. At least not in the way he thought.

He crammed his hands in his pockets. He wore faded jeans and a black T-shirt. Emma thought he looked exceptionally sexy. His hair was messy and he hadn't shaved. He wore this look well. Very well.

"Want to sit out on the lanai? I'll get us a drink," Nash said.

"Sure," Emma told him. This wasn't the man she'd gone to dinner with last night. This was a serious Nash, maybe even a troubled one.

She sat in an old wicker rocker while he got their drinks. She hadn't paid much attention to his patio furniture before because she'd been focused on him. Now she took in the rocker, the other chair, and the small table between them. Antiques, she guessed.

"Here you go." Nash placed a glass of ice and a can of Sprite on the table between them.

"Thanks."

He took a deep breath and sat down on the edge of the other chair. "I don't know how to say what I need to say."

Emma cringed as her heart lurched. But she had said she would listen, so she waited for him to get whatever was bothering him off his chest.

Chapter Fourteen

"The beginning is usually the best place," Emma told Nash, unsure if she wanted to hear what he had to say.

Nash opened the soda, pouring it into her glass, the ice tinkling as the carbonated drink fizzled to the top of the glass.

"Right. So, I don't know much about you and vice versa." Nash appeared to struggle for the right words. "But I noticed you right away."

Maybe this wasn't the conversation Emma had been expecting.

Nash took a sip of her soda. "I hope you don't mind."

"It's fine." After all, they'd kissed and swapped germs already.

"I'm having a hard time here. I hope you won't think I'm off my rocker, but what the heck, I'm just going to go for it." He took another drink of soda. "Emma, I think I'm falling in love."

This definitely wasn't what she expected to hear. How did he want her to respond? She'd never been in this situation—a guy she had a thing for telling her he was falling in love.

"Okay." She swallowed, her throat dry. She took a sip from the glass.

"And?" Nash prompted.

Emma felt like she was drowning in emotions and couldn't come up for air. Nash probably didn't realize his words cut into her like a sharp knife. "Maybe I'm not the one you should tell this to, Nash."

Dumbstruck, his face turned a deep red. "Damn. Emma, I thought you and I had a connection. I'm sorry."

"Wait! Say that again."

"I thought we had a connection."

"So, this love thing . . ." Her throat was so dry, she had to take another drink. "Are you saying it's *me*?"

"Of course. Who else would I . . . Emma, I've messed this up." Nash shook his head. "Let me start over. I didn't sleep much last night because I thought about you most of the night. Us, the entire evening. At least the good parts. I've never said this to any woman before, but I believe I'm falling for you. In love, Emma."

"Oh," she said. "I see."

"Are you going to move? Call me a jerk? Please don't keep me in suspense, Emma. If I'm wrong about this connection, please tell me now."

She stood up, walked the short distance over to Nash's chair, and stood in front of him. "Stand up."

Nash did.

"Now kiss me."

He placed his arms around her waist and pulled her close to him. Nash looked at her as if she were the first woman he'd ever kissed. Their kiss was so slow and intimate that when his lips touched hers, their bodies melded into one. Nash traced his hand down the slope of her back, resting on her hip. She raised her arms, placing them around his neck, just barely able to reach him. She toyed with the ends of his hair.

A loud howling forced them apart.

"Penny," Nash said.

Emma followed him into the condo's spare room. Poor little Penny's front paw was caught on the edge of the entrance to her whelping box. "Hey there." Nash spoke softly as he removed her paw. "It's okay." She waddled back to her corner, where the pups slept on a blanket.

"My gosh, they're so tiny," Emma observed. She wanted to pet them, but knew now wasn't the time. "Have you named them yet?"

Nash sat down beside the dogs. "No. I didn't think I would be keeping them. I was going to let the new pet parents make that decision."

"So you are going to keep all four?" Emma asked, a grin a mile wide on her face.

"Yeah, I think I will. Unless you want one?"

"I would love a puppy, but I don't want to take one. If you keep them, I'll help you care for them."

"I'd like that," Nash said. "You want to help me name them?"

"Sure." She scooted closer to their whelping box. Inside, the puppies rested on top of a flowered blanket. "They look like little flower petals."

"Flower girls," Nash mused. "I like that."

"How about Daisy, Rosie, Lily, and Ivy? All flowery names."

"And how will I know which is which?"

"When they're a little bigger, how about collars that match the color of the flower?"

"Good idea."

"Nash, just for the record, I knew we had a connection that morning at Vittles. When we shook hands."

"Yeah, I did too. You made me reconsider everything I ever believed concerning love."

Emma nodded, still a bit unsure of all this. "How?"

"I was one of those guys who never believed in love at first sight, that sort of stuff. I probably shouldn't tell you this, but I don't want to start our relationship without being totally honest. I spoke with my mom this morning. She picked up on my lack of sleep. She told me that when I met someone special, I would know. She didn't mention how, just that I would know."

"She must be a wise woman," Emma said.

"Very. She raised me, after all." He laughed. "Dad passed away my first year of college. It was hard for her. First I left, then Dad. She's a tough cookie. I want you to meet her, if you want to."

"Of course. I'd like that, Nash. I don't have any family." She told him how her parents had died, something she rarely spoke about with others. It had been so tragic. Both had been riding their bicycles. They'd been home in Miami for two days, and Emma had planned to spend a little time with them before they left on their next business trip. Sadly, both of her parents were hit by a van. They didn't suffer, but the shock of their loss lingered for years.

"That's terrible, Emma. I'm so sorry for you," Nash told her when she was done. Then his cell phone rang.

"Answer it," Emma insisted.

Nash went into the hallway, returning a few minutes later with a big grin on his face. "That was Naomi from the vet clinic. She says Tiffany has voluntarily entered Willow House. It's a mental health facility."

"That's great to hear. I'm happy for her."

"According to Naomi, Tiffany's father insisted, and she agreed. Sad, but she's needed help for as long as I can remember. I think having you here in Pink Pearl Cove is changing many lives for the better. Especially mine."

Epilogue

One Year Later

Six months into their relationship, Nash asked Emma to marry him. She wasted no time in accepting. They then had six months to plan a wedding, sell their condominiums, and buy a home together.

Because the puppies had brought them together, Emma thought it only right that they take part in the wedding. For three months, Nash, Lori, Naomi, and she spent hours teaching the pups to walk side by side, to sit, stay, and stand on command.

Emma and Nash were married on the beach, with most of the Cove's residents attending. Lisa and Marlena acted as Emma's bridesmaids, along with Daisy, Rosie, Lily, and Ivy. Each dachshund wore a dress made specifically for her in the flower color she represented. With tiny bonnets on their heads, they received more attention than Emma. She loved them so much that she understood why Nash hadn't wanted to give them up. Henry and Penny and their girls were part of her family now.

"I can't believe how well-behaved they were," Emma Kendrick said to her new mother-in-law. "Perfect little flower girls."

Lori laughed. "I think you and Nash had a big hand in that."

"We loved every minute of teaching them."

Harris showed up at the last minute. He'd been working on a case that was in the headlines, so when Emma saw him at the wedding, her happiness was complete. Lydia had even made the trip, telling her that she wouldn't have missed Emma's special day for a million bucks.

That was six weeks ago. With both of their condos now sold, Lori had invited the newlyweds to stay with her while Jack Alan and a construction crew from Miami built Emma and Nash's dream home.

Emma now had a full-time teaching position at Orange Grove Elementary. She adored her first-grade class. Nash continued to teach high school math.

Emma pondered all of her good fortune while she waited for Nash. He'd started a girls' baseball team and coached three nights a week. She heard

his truck pull up in the long drive that led to
Lori's house. Lori had started working two days a
week at the vet clinic again. Emma and Nash knew
Dr. Mellow and Lori were an item, but they'd decided to leave them alone to do their own thing.
When they were ready, they could tell the folks
they loved.

"You're dusty tonight," Emma said to Nash
when he returned from practice.

"Yeah, I took a few turns batting myself. You'll
never guess who my best pitcher is."

"Tell me," Emma said.

"Amanda Morris. Her mom owns the candy
store."

"Yes, I know her. I worried about her for a long
time. I'm glad she's found a sport she's interested
in. She seemed so lost and sad." Emma remembered the first time she saw Amanda at the candy
store. She and Lisa continued to work with the
three charities that Amanda's family unknowingly
benefitted from.

"She sure as heck isn't lost or sad now. Half the
guys in my math class have the hots for her."

Emma laughed. "That's a surprise. She was so . . .
bashful when I met her."

"She just needed time to grow up a bit. Some
kids take a little longer to mature than others.
She's a good girl. Smart too."

She loved hearing about Nash's students and
their accomplishments. It was so much better than
arguing on behalf of multimillion-dollar corporations. Emma had no regrets about leaving her law

practice. She would always keep her legal license up to date, just as she had her teaching certificate. That was just her way. She'd spent most of her teenage years in school and college. She wanted to be reminded of all the long, hard days and nights she'd spent earning both degrees. She owed it to herself to keep them current.

"Mom at the clinic tonight?" Nash asked.

"Yes. She took an extra night for some reason. Not sure why," Emma said.

"Well, Mrs. Kendrick, you know what that means?" Nash teased her.

"No, I don't. Why don't you tell me."

"Nope, I don't like to tattle. How about I show you?" Nash picked her up and carried her to their temporary bedroom.

Later, Nash and Emma lay snuggled together. The windows were open and a breeze from the Gulf lifted the gauzy curtains. The moon filled the room with a soft glow.

"I like this. Just you and me, alone. Nothing else seems important. I think this is what my mom was trying to tell me when I asked her how I would know when I was in love," Nash said.

"Mm," Emma said, content to let him talk.

"I knew I would marry you the night I took you to dinner. Remember the Cove's Fish Camp? Our first date?"

She smiled. "A first date I'll never forget."

"Any regrets?" Nash asked.

"It's a little too late for that, don't you think?" she teased. "And no, I have no regrets. None. Zilch."

"Good. Because if you did, I'd say tough. You're stuck with me."

"Nash, you are such a romantic. I never pegged you for one when I used to spy on you."

"You spied on me? You're telling me this now? I married a stalker?" he said in mock horror. She'd told Nash this before, and he'd laughed because he'd been doing the same thing.

"Yes, and don't forget, a book offender. That was the book I used to hide my face when I spied on you."

"You've got quite the wicked past. It looks good on you. Have I mentioned that before? I saw you from behind. I liked what I saw, though I remember thinking you could be toothless or just plain old ugly up close. That's why I had to make it my business to see your face."

Emma leaned up on her elbows. "You've never told me that before. Is that true, or are you teasing?"

"True. Scout's honor."

"When you saw my face, I guess I passed your inspection?" She didn't care one way or another. She loved him with all she had to give, and she knew his love for her was true and would last until they were old and feeble.

"Beyond my wildest dreams. You know that. Every morning when I wake up and see you lying next to me, I figure I'm the luckiest guy in the world. I go to sleep with a smile and I wake up with a smile. And I smile in between. So, Em, you've passed my inspection beyond the moon and back."

"That's nice to know."

"Seriously, I'm probably the happiest I've ever been in my life. I owe you for that."

"I understand. I feel the same as you. Now, we need to stop talking like we're two lovesick teenagers. We need to remember we're adults."

"I do that all day. It's fun, but even more fun when we're acting like a couple of kids. I like you when you're being silly."

"I never had much of a sense of humor in my youth. Too much time studying. I'm making up for lost time. Seriously, Nash—are you as happy as you say?"

He rolled onto his side and touched her cheek. "Of course I am. I can't think of anything that would make me any happier than I am right now."

"I'm excited about the house. I can't wait until we make it our own. I've already got a few fabric samples from Lisa."

"Another shoe room?" Nash teased.

"I'll always have a shoe room, maybe not as large as Lisa's, not even as large as the room I had converted in the condo. But I do love shoes, so you will have to get used to that."

"You can have as many rooms of shoes as you want. As long as you're around to wear them, I'm happy."

"Nash, what about tiny shoes? For tiny feet? I'm talking tiny, tiny feet. Like newborn baby feet." Emma couldn't keep her secret any longer.

"Are you trying to tell me what I think you're

trying to tell me? Emma?" He gazed at her, love shining in his eyes.

"What do you think, Nash?"

"I think you're trying to tell me that we are going to have a tiny blessing of our own."

Tears welled up in Emma's eyes. "And I would say, Mr. Kendrick, you're absolutely right."

Nash leaned down and kissed the mother of his child.

DOGWOOD SEASON

Carolyn Brown

Chapter One

"Somebody must have mixed us up at birth," Clara Delaney whispered as she looked into the mirror above the antique dresser in her old bedroom and saw the blond-haired, blue-eyed woman staring back at her. "I'm nothing like Sophia and yet we're twins."

She turned around, threw open the double doors that led out to the balcony, and walked out to inhale the fresh spring air. She figured that she and Sophia had so much to do that they would be working from dawn to dusk for the next ten days. They would both be too tired to even enjoy their honeymoons.

She glanced down at all the dogwood trees just starting to bloom. She would be married right there at the far end of the courtyard, where she would promise to love and cherish Trevor Richmond for the rest of her life. She had always wanted her engagement and wedding to be a special time just for *her*. But oh no! her twin sister Sophia, the social queen of Palestine, Texas, had announced her engagement the day before Clara announced hers, and then Mama Lizzy decided they would have a double ceremony during the Dogwood Festival. Once again, Clara would be standing in the shadow of her sister, just like she did when Sophia was homecoming queen their senior year and when she was chosen prom queen—not to mention all the other accolades.

"Trevor and I could take a little trip to Las Vegas and end all this," she whispered as she turned back into her room. The Dogwood Inn, the second oldest hotel in the area, wasn't actually in Palestine, where the three-week festival was held, but a few miles north in Dogwood, Texas, a little community that consisted of a bar, a hotel, and a couple of antique stores.

The loud ringing of the black, corded phone on the nightstand startled that idea right out of Clara's mind. She grabbed the receiver on the third ring and started across the room to the rocking chair with it in her hand. When she reached the end of the cord the base fell off onto the hardwood floor with a loud thump.

"Hello," she answered as she picked up the heavy thing and set it back on the nightstand.

"What was that noise? Did you think you had a cell phone in your hand?" Mama Lizzy asked.

"Guess I did," Clara answered. "Why don't you put cordless phones in the rooms?"

"This is a vintage hotel, darlin'," her grandmother answered, "and the stipulation when I sell it is that it will stay that way."

"You had air-conditioning installed," Clara countered.

"That didn't change the appearance," Mama Lizzy told her. "Breakfast is ready in five minutes. I can't rouse your sister, so beat on her door on your way down the stairs."

"If she can't hear this noisy phone, she must have her earplugs in," Clara said.

"Oh, here she is now," Mama Lizzy said. "See you in a minute."

Clara replaced the receiver and fell backward on the four-poster bed. She had loved the dogwood wallpaper when she was a child, but today she felt as if it might creep off the walls and smother her. She sat up so fast that the room did a couple of spins before she got her balance and was able to stand. Just a few fast and furious days and then she could move out to the ranch with Trevor, and only see her sister on holidays and the occasional weekend trip she might make to Central Texas. She could endure that, she assured herself as she left the room and headed down the broad staircase.

"And if the going gets too tough, Trevor is willing to fly to Vegas, and Sophia can be the only star in a single wedding during dogwood season," she whispered.

You know very well that you are whistling in the wind, a voice inside her head whispered. *You would never disappoint your grandmother, not after all she's done for you.*

She crossed the lobby, which was set up with four different conversation groups. The desk was located at the back of the large room and still had a sign-in book on a swivel. Way back in the first pages, there were signatures from congressmen, senators, and even a vice president.

"I wonder if the new owners really will keep the whole place vintage, or if there's nothing in the contract about that and they will raze it in a year or two and build an apartment complex or a chain hotel on the ground where it stood," Clara whispered as she made her way through the dining area. White linen cloths covered a dozen tables, and if the hotel was open, a fresh flower arrangement would have graced the center of each of them. For the next little while, only Sophia and Clara would have rooms because Mama Lizzy said they needed the whole time to prepare for the wedding, and the rooms for the guests the day before the event.

Clara went through the swinging doors into the kitchen, where her grandmother was putting her famous banana nut muffins, scrambled eggs and bacon, and thick slices of homemade bread on the table. Sophia was carrying a tray with a coffeepot and three fancy cups across the room.

"Well, well—" Clara's tone was more than a little snarky—"look who is up and around this early."

"Good mornin'," their grandmother said. "You can lose your attitude. Your sister beat you down here by a few minutes. Have a seat, and let's talk about the wedding cake while we eat."

Sophia whipped aside the tail of her long silk robe, which covered a fancy little matching nightgown. Clara felt like a bag lady in her buffalo-plaid flannel robe and faded pajama pants with Betty Boop printed on them.

At least the top and bottom match, the voice in her head said.

"My idea is to have a simple, three-layered traditional cake with dogwoods on top," Clara said.

"Oh, no! If that's what Clara wants, then we'll have to have two separate tables," Sophia argued. "I want a satellite cake with a bride and groom on the top and little crystal figurines of the wedding party scattered on each of the smaller cakes. And each of the satellites should be a different flavor— chocolate and red velvet on the side with the groomsmen and banana, coconut, and pineapple on the brides' side. The wedding cake itself will be vanilla with a touch of almond."

Lizzy sat down at the end of the table. "We're having one table for the cakes—that's the brides' and the grooms' cakes both. If you can't agree by the time our bakery lady gets here, I'll pick out something myself."

"Mama Lizzy," Sophia said in her best whine, "we might be twins, but we have never been alike. We don't even look like sisters. We've agreed to have a double wedding here in the courtyard, but you should let us decide a few individual things."

"I don't care about the cake," Clara said. She was used to giving in to whatever her dark-haired and brown eyed sister wanted. "I don't even care about the wedding. I just want to be married to Trevor."

"You girls don't look a thing alike," Lizzy said. "Trouble is that you don't act like you are even related, much less twins. You never have, not from the time you were sharing a crib, but there's going to be a time coming one of these days when all you will have to depend on is each other. This wedding is going to teach you a little about that."

"I have a good job and credit cards," Sophia said. "I can buy my own cake and pay for my own wedding."

Lizzy stuck her finger close to Sophia's nose. "Little girl," she growled, "I've taken care of your raisin' since you were born. That was the deal I made with your mama when she told me she was pregnant and didn't want to have a baby and didn't even know who the father was. I've never kept a thing about her from you, so I'm just repeating what I told you when you asked me why your mama didn't live with us like other little kids' mothers did." She stopped to take a breath and drop her finger before she went on. "I didn't abide any sassing when you were little and I won't put up with any now. I'm still the boss until you girls put me six feet down or put my ashes in the ground. I told you both at Christmas when you came home with engagement rings that I was going to pay for your weddings, and I will."

"Yes, ma'am," Sophia said in a whisper.

"That's better," Lizzy said, but she didn't even show a hint of a smile.

It was not the first time that a smidgen of smugness had washed over Clara when Sophia got in trouble. That had happened way back when she was about three years old, and it was her first memory. Sophia had gotten sassy with Mama Lizzy and had to sit on the time-out chair. Clara had had the same feeling of self-righteousness back then, followed by the same load of guilt as she had that morning. Today she wasn't a little girl, but a full-grown woman who was looking thirty right in the eyes.

"Now, let's talk about a cake," Lizzy said. "Something as big as Sophia wants is absurd, but we don't want one so small that there's not enough for your guests to all have a slice. So, we're going to compromise. Jill made all your birthday cakes when you were still at home," she said with a smile, "and she will be here in an hour for y'all to taste several kinds of sample cakes. All three of us will write down our top three choices. The one that we all agree on will be your cake. Now, let's talk dresses."

"Please, don't tell me that we have to dress alike," Sophia groaned. "I put the down payment on mine a month ago and will finish paying for it when I pick it up."

"Of course you do not have to dress just alike," Lizzy answered. "A bride should have her own dress, and I've already gone down to the bridal shop and paid the remainder of what you owe. I will reimburse you for the money you paid them already. I told you that I would pay for this wedding and I dang sure intend to keep my word."

"Mine is ready. Trevor's granny will bring it down with her when they come for the rehearsal dinner," Clara said. "I'd planned to have the wedding at the ranch out in the roping arena, so it's just a simple cotton dress. I chose a pair of white lace boots and a cowboy hat with a short veil attached to the back."

Sophia started shaking her head before Clara

had even finished the sentence. "You couldn't wear a white dress in a dirty old arena, and with your curves, I figured you'd have chosen a Cinderella gown."

"Trevor's granny made my dress for me and used some of the lace from his mother's dress for the ruffle around the bottom, and . . ." she raised an eyebrow toward her sister, "it only comes to the top of my boots."

"Well, if that's what you want," Sophia said with one of her superior looks down her perfect nose. "I'll pick my dress up a couple of days before the wedding."

"What does it look like?" Lizzy asked. "Got a picture?"

Sophia pulled her phone from the pocket of her robe, scrolled through the photos, and then handed it to Lizzy. "Isn't it gorgeous?"

Clara leaned over to look at the screen and wasn't a bit surprised at what she saw. With her height and figure, Sophia would look like a runway model in the mermaid dress with its long train. The short veil attached to a tiara would sparkle in her dark hair. And as always, Clara would be walking in the shadow of her gorgeous, exotic-looking sister.

At least she throws a big one, the voice in her head said with a chuckle, *and look on the bright side, you won't get all sweaty if the day turns out to be muggy. Lord knows, she had better apply extra deodorant with those long sleeves.*

"That's not funny," Clara muttered.

"What? That I chose a real wedding dress and you decided to wear something that you can reuse for church on Sunday?" Sophia snapped.

"I was fighting with the voices in my head," Clara explained. "Your dress is lovely, and you will look like royalty in it."

"Thank you," Sophia said with a smile. She didn't get many compliments from her sister, who had always been so practical and yet looked like she could land a part in a movie just on her looks and ability to show every emotion on her face.

She glanced over at Clara's vintage ring, which had been handed down from Trevor's fraternal grandmother. Two small diamonds sat on each side of a larger one. They sparkled when the sunlight from the kitchen window caught them, but there was no way that ring could compare to the two-carat, pear-shaped solitaire set in platinum on Sophia's ring finger. It was proof positive again that she and her sister were twins, but that they were nothing alike.

Lizzy handed the phone back to Sophia. "The dress is exactly what I would have expected you to pick out, and so is yours, Clara. Now, eat your breakfast. Jill will be here with the wedding cake samples pretty soon."

"I'll have some bacon and eggs but no toast or muffins," she said. "I have to watch the carbs. I can't gain a pound before the wedding or my dress won't zip, and I've got a suitcase full of brand-new clothes, including a few bikinis for the beach, that I sure want to fit perfectly. After the wedding, Hunter is taking me to the French Riviera for a week. Where is Trevor taking you, Clara?"

"His folks signed forty acres and the house he's

been living in over to him, so we're just going home after the ceremony," Clara answered.

"Won't that just be old hat, so to speak?" Sophia asked.

"Not to me," Clara answered. "I've never spent the night in the house."

Sophia almost choked on a bite of bacon. "Good lord! Are you still a virgin?"

Clara shook her head. "No, and the rest is none of your business."

Sophia took a sip of coffee, and an image of their mother, Maria, flashed through her mind. The only photograph they had left no doubt that Sophia looked just like her, with her dark hair and eyes. Other than the day they were born, neither of the twins had ever seen their mother. She was eighteen that summer, and from the bits and pieces Sophia had put together from what Mama Lizzy had told them, Maria had been as wild as the old, proverbial March hare. She was on her way to have an abortion when Mama Lizzy found out that she was pregnant.

Their grandmother had talked her out of terminating the pregnancy by offering her a deal. If she would have the baby, Mama Lizzy would raise it, and Maria could go on to the college of her choice and build whatever life she wanted.

Lizzy had sat the girls down when they were eight years old and explained the whole story to them. "You need to know the truth from me, not from some big-mouth gossip," she had said, and then she told them that she still loved their mother. "I miss her every single day, but she hated Texas, and this hotel, and everything about this whole area. She burned her bridges and never looked back. But in my heart, I know that she wanted you girls to have a better life than she could ever give you, so I got to keep you and raise you. I've never regretted a day of my choice, or hers."

Lizzy snapped her fingers. "Sophia, are you sleeping with your eyes open?"

"No, ma'am," she said. "I was thinking about Mother. Both mine and Hunter's mama have both passed away. It's kind of sad that neither of them will get to see us on our special day."

"Mama Lizzy will be there," Clara scolded, "and for all intents and purposes, she's been our mother."

Sophia blushed. "I'm sorry. It's just that . . . well . . ." she stammered.

"I've always been your grandmother and mother all rolled up in one person," Lizzy said. "And I'll be the one walking you both down the aisle at the same time. Thank goodness neither of you has chosen a dress with one of those huge hoop skirts."

"Why's that?" Sophia asked.

"Because I would have gotten lost in the middle of all that foo-foo," Lizzy answered.

"That's the truth," Clara agreed.

Lizzy was about the same height as Clara— which was only a couple of inches over five feet— and she had been a blonde before her hair turned gray. Her green eyes still sparkled, and for someone seventy years old, she had very few wrinkles.

Sophia figured that when her sister was that age she would have the same beautiful skin as their grandmother. And even when they were both past seventy years old she would still feel like a big old weed beside a perfect little rosebud when they were standing next to each other.

Lizzy polished off her bacon and eggs and slathered a muffin with butter. "I suggest you finish up your breakfast and then go get dressed in something other than pajama pants. Take the time to clean up your place and put your dirty dishes in the dishwasher."

Just looking at those muffins made Sophia's mouth water. *Willpower!* That's what she repeated to herself time after time until she polished off the last of her bacon and eggs. She was determined not to gain a single pound between now and her wedding day. She might feel overdressed, but, by golly, her beautiful gown would fit her perfectly.

"Here she is," Lizzy said when the door into the lobby of the hotel opened. "Sophia, you *will* taste the samples. There's no way a few bites will put weight on you."

Clara giggled, and Sophia shot her a dirty look and air slapped her sister on the arm. "It's not funny."

"It is a little bit," Clara declared.

Lizzy waved across the lobby and motioned for Jill to bring her little wagon over to a table she'd set up in the corner. "We've got coffee and sweet tea for our tasting fun."

Fun, Clara thought. *This whole thing is . . .*

Before she could finish the thought, Lizzy stood up and headed over to a round table she had brought in from the dining area. "I couldn't be a part of Maria's wedding. She got married somewhere back East, and I didn't even know about it until after she had passed away. Getting to be a part of all this planning is exciting."

"We owe her more than just this," Clara whispered to her sister.

"Okay, but I really wanted a big event in a fancy venue," Sophia said in a low voice. "After all, I'm marrying a Gamble, and that's a big name in Houston. The Gamble family founded Big Red Oil Company and are like Houston royalty. Hunter's dad is the CEO of the company, and I can't imagine how they're going to feel about coming up here to an old hotel in what's practically a ghost town like Dogwood. I'll feel like a country bumpkin while they're here."

"Well, I wanted a ranch wedding, with a reception in the barn. Someday, when we have daughters, we'll help plan their big day, but let's act excited about this one for Mama Lizzy's sake."

"I'll try," Sophia said with a long sigh.

Clara stood up and walked across the lobby to the table. "These all look too good to eat. You didn't have to decorate them so beautifully."

Sophia followed her, feeling her waistline growing just from looking at the little cakes and cupcakes. "Did you bring pictures of some of your work so we can pick out what we want?"

Jill picked up a thick book from her cart and laid it on the table. "The new trend is to have a small, traditional, three-tiered cake, and then have two-to-four cupcake stands with a different flavor on each one. That's just one idea. I have crystal cupcake stands as well as white, milk glass ones. Most brides match the stands with whatever punch bowl they choose to use. On the grooms' table, there would be a two-tiered chocolate cake, and the cupcakes would be some variation of chocolate—chocolate almond, German chocolate, red velvet, etc. That's just an idea. You are welcome to look through the book and decide what you like best while you sample the cakes. Here's a sheet for each of you to check off your favorite five." She laid three pieces of paper on the table, poured herself a cup of coffee, and sat down.

Clara cut a sliver of the white cake first, put it on a paper plate, and then added a tiny piece of several cupcakes. She had always loved cake of any kind—even those little chocolate and orange cupcakes that were sold in packs of two in convenience stores. When she had marked her favorites from that round she pushed the plate aside and started on the chocolate ones.

"This is going to be a tough decision," she said. "I love all things chocolate."

"You love all things sweet," Sophia grumbled.

"You got that right," Clara agreed with a smile. "What do you think of the cupcake idea, Mama Lizzy?"

"I think it's fabulous," Lizzy answered. "That way, Sophia gets her different flavors and you get your small, three-tiered wedding cake. Have you picked out something from the book?"

"I wanted a crystal bride and groom on the top of my cake and Clara wanted flowers, so how do we compromise on that, Mama Lizzy?" Sophia flipped through a few pages in the book.

"That one," Lizzy pointed. "But I want dogwood blossoms made of sugar, like you did the roses on the anniversary cake for Dillard's, and then that crystal thing I saw two pages back set down in the middle of them."

Sophia flipped back a couple of pages. "Like this?"

"Yep," Lizzy answered. "What do you think, Clara?"

Clara looked down at a picture of a crystal piece that was etched with "Happy Ever After" on top of a cake. "I love it. Are you okay with that idea, Sophia?"

"I can live with it," she said as she ate the last bite of orange cake and made her choices on the sheet. "What about on the grooms' cake? How can we make it represent two very different men?"

"How about putting chocolate-covered strawberries decorated like tuxedos around the bottom and the edge of the top?" Jill suggested.

Lizzy beamed. "I love it. And now, to finish tasting and choosing what we want on the cupcake stands. In my mind, I see crystal stands for the brides' table and the white milk glass ones for the grooms'. And the chocolate cheesecake cupcakes should be on the grooms' side."

"See, that wasn't so hard, was it?" Clara whispered to Sophia.

"It will do, and it is prettier than I thought it would be. I like the sugar dogwood flowers. I was afraid we'd just have a branch with blossoms on it stuck down in the top of the cake," Sophia answered.

"Give me a little more credit than that," Lizzy fussed. "What do you think of the cakes?"

"They are delicious, so the guests will love them," Sophia answered.

Lizzy turned her head to look at Clara. "And you?"

"I love all of it," Clara answered.

Jill pulled out a notebook and a pen. "Okay, now let's talk about how many guests, so I will know how much cake to make."

"Each sister got to invite one hundred, and I sent out fifty," Lizzy answered. "We have RSVPs from two hundred. That will fill the courtyard, and we will have extra tables set up in the lobby for the dinner after the wedding."

Jill wrote that down, and which cupcake stands were to go on each table. "Do you want the cupcakes in gold or silver foil?"

"Silver for the brides' table," Lizzy answered. "Gold for the grooms'. See, I told you girls that we didn't need six months to a year to plan a wedding. We'll get it done, and the courtyard will be beautiful with all the dogwoods in bloom."

"But Mama Lizzy—" Sophia started.

Lizzy held up a palm. "The shorter the planning period, the better. That gives you less time to bicker. You got to pick out your dresses. I decided to have the wedding in the courtyard while the dogwoods are in bloom. That cuts down on the amount we spend on flowers. We can house everyone comfortably right here in the inn. That way guests can come as early as they want and stay as long as they can. I've closed the hotel until after the wedding and hired Luther, my chef, to come back that day to cook for us. That way we'll be ready for the rehearsal dinner and breakfast the next morning. Y'all got to compromise on the cakes. Seems fair enough to me."

"Yes, ma'am," Clara agreed.

"I really do like his shrimp alfredo," Sophia said with a smile.

"Okay, ladies," Jill said, "Have you made your decisions about flavors?"

The only flavor for the wedding cake that they all had on their list was the plain old vanilla with a touch of almond, which was Clara's all-time favorite. She might look really plain beside her gorgeous sister at the ceremony, but she would get the cake she wanted, so that was a win in an otherwise difficult situation.

Chapter Two

Trevor laced his fingers in Clara's as they watched the parade kick off the first day of the Dogwood Trails Festival. "My mama and daddy brought me and all five of my brothers to town for this festival every year. I've probably been coming to it since the spring after I was born."

"Mama Lizzy has pictures of me and Sophia in one of those double strollers," Clara said. "But by that time, you must've been about four years old. Did I ever tell you that I had a crush on you back in high school? Maybe I should say when you were a senior and I was a freshman."

Trevor squeezed her hand. "Honey, I've always worn glasses and had thin hair, and you were so beautiful that I would never have thought about asking you out in those days."

"Why not?" Clara asked.

"Fear of rejection," he answered with a chuckle. "I'm the luckiest man in the whole great state of Texas to have you on my arm today. And I intend to show you just how much I love you for the rest of your life."

"I love you too," Clara said and planted a kiss on his cheek.

"So, how did the wedding cake stuff go yesterday?" Trevor asked.

"Better than I thought it would." Clara went on to tell him what they had decided. "I was afraid that I might have to take you up on that offer to fly to Vegas for the weekend, but Sophia finally came around. She really wanted a big fling-ding wedding that would last a week, something in a fancy venue with golden chandeliers."

"And you wanted a simple ranch wedding. I'm amazed that y'all can agree on anything." Trevor nodded toward a taco vendor. "Let's go get a snack over there when the parade ends."

"Sounds good to me," Clara said, "and then we'll have snow cones for dessert."

"Hey, we located the cutest little handmade jewelry vendor," Sophia said as she and Lizzy joined them. "I bought a pair of earrings for each of my bridesmaids to wear to the wedding. They're different shapes, but all in shades of green like their dresses. Have you bought your gifts yet?"

"I have only one attendant," Clara answered. "I asked Trevor's grandmother to be my maid of honor because you're already taken as a bride. She's going to wear a green floral dress and emerald earrings that her husband gave her on their first anniversary. I thought I might give her a framed picture of me and Trevor as a thank-you gift."

"She would love that," Trevor said. "I've always hated pictures of myself, and being the baby of six boys, there aren't a lot of me. But honey, if you're in the photo, I'll feel like a king."

Sophia rolled her eyes. "How we can be twins is a total mystery."

"Amen to that," Trevor agreed.

"They are named after my sisters," Lizzy explained. "Sophia is the image of my oldest sister, Clara, and Clara looks just like my younger sister, Sophia. I should have switched their names at birth, but they were both bald-headed at that time. And I couldn't tell what color their eyes were. Both of my sisters were gone before the girls were born, but I wanted to honor them by giving them namesakes."

"Did your sisters get along?" Clara asked.

"Lord, no! None of us could go half a day without an argument," Lizzy answered. "Thank goodness for that, because it fitted me for what I was about to go through raising you two. Come on, Sophia. Let's go see about that vendor over there with the purses. I could use a new little clutch bag for the wedding."

"Mama Lizzy!" Clara said as she shook her finger at her grandmother. "You've been on so many committees and were even president of the Chamber of Commerce. I bet you have a dozen bags in your closet that would work for a wedding."

"Probably twenty or more," Lizzy told her. "But

not a one of them matches the dress I have picked out for that day. You and this good-looking fiancé of yours enjoy the day. Have her home by midnight, Trevor."

Trevor tipped his cowboy hat toward her. "Yes, ma'am. See y'all tomorrow morning in church. Reckon it would be all right if I stole her away for a family dinner at the ranch? We'd be glad if you and Sophia could join us."

"Thank you, but I'll have to turn you down, son," Lizzy said "I've promised my friend Marlene that I would go to lunch with her after church, but I'm sure Sophia will be glad to have a good meal rather than eating sandwiches or leftovers."

"Yes, I would," Sophia muttered, and then wondered why she'd said such a thing. She didn't want to go to church, pretend to listen to a boring sermon, or go out to the ranch to smell fresh cow patties. Give her the scent of hot concrete and greasy burger joints any day of the week over cows and hay. "Why don't y'all pick me up at the hotel after church?"

"I'll wake you up in plenty of time to go to the services with us," Lizzy told her. "I'll drive us, and then you can go out to the ranch with Trevor and Clara."

And that's the reason I moved away from this area and vowed to never come back, Sophia thought as she and her grandmother headed toward the vendor with the purses. *Mama Lizzy wants to micromanage every minute of my time.*

"Why don't you call Hunter and see if he wants to come up here and go out to the ranch with you tomorrow?" Lizzy asked.

"Good grief, Mama Lizzy," Sophia gasped. "It's a three-hour drive up here, and then another three for him to get home."

"Doesn't he love you enough to make that effort?" Lizzy asked but didn't wait for an answer before she went on. "Or maybe he could get that little company plane to bring him up here like y'all did at Christmas. You can pick him up at the airport and take him back after supper. That way, you four could spend a little time together. He doesn't even know Trevor."

Sophia didn't roll her eyes, but it took a lot of willpower and effort not to do so. "They can get to know each other later." She couldn't imagine "The Cowboy," as she called him when she talked to Hunter about Trevor, and a man who wore three-piece suits and ties to work having any more in common than she and her sister did.

"He *is* coming a couple of days before the wedding, isn't he?" Lizzy persisted.

"He'll be here on Wednesday before that Friday," Sophia answered, and picked up a cute little navy-blue purse. "What do you think of this one?"

"I know you're changing the subject," Lizzy said, "and that purse looks downright dowdy. Let's go sit at a table with an umbrella over it and enjoy a piña colada."

"It's a little early to start drinking," Sophia said.

"Honey, you ain't in Houston," Lizzy said with a giggle. "And after putting up with you two all morning, I think I'm entitled to a drink."

Sophia pulled out her phone and found the icon that showed her how many of her points a drink would cost. She'd already done some damage to the count with a breakfast the size of the one she'd eaten.

"Maybe you could have something this next couple of weeks without looking up the calories and fat grams," Lizzy said.

"Why are you always fussing at me?" Sophia put the phone back in her pocket. "I just want to be beautiful for my wedding day."

"Does Hunter think you are beautiful?" Lizzy asked.

"Of course he does," Sophia answered.

"Would he love you if you gained twenty pounds or were hugely pregnant?" Lizzy persisted.

Sophia frowned. She couldn't lie, but how could she tell her grandmother that she and Hunter hadn't even talked about children?

"Uh-huh," Lizzy said.

"What does that mean?" Sophia asked.

Lizzy got in the line of people waiting to buy a frozen piña colada. "It means that Clara and Trevor want four kids and have already picked out names for them, and from the expression on your face, you and Hunter haven't even discussed the idea of a family. That scares me. You have your mother's genes, whether I like it or not."

"I want a family," Sophia said, "but not for a couple or three years, and I am *not* my sister. You should know that by now."

"Oh, honey, I may not be real smart, but I've managed a hotel since I was twenty years old, *and* I know you two girls very well," Lizzy said. "You are jealous of Clara because she's small and cute. She envies you because you are tall and beautiful."

Sophia put her phone away. "I'm not so sure that my laid-back sister could ever be jealous of me, but on another note, I've changed my mind. I do want a drink."

"Good girl," Lizzy said. "We'll sit over there and watch the people for a spell. It's been a year since I took time off from work just to enjoy the afternoon. I'm glad you are here to share it with me."

Chapter Three

Sophia would have far rather stayed home and spent time on the phone with Hunter on Sunday morning, but then again, she didn't want an outdoor wedding either.

"What you want and what you get are two different things," she murmured, quoting one of her grandmother's favorite sayings.

The old girl had been tough on Sophia, but not any more so than she'd been on Clara. They had to share a room in the little apartment behind the lobby desk until they were sixteen. Sophia thought about their birthday that year as she applied her makeup. Mama Lizzy had told them that they could have their own room in the hotel for their special birthday present, but it had to be on the second floor. Her reasoning was that the ground floor had to be saved for folks who couldn't climb stairs.

"Yeah, right," Sophia said with a giggle. Her grandmother hadn't fooled her one bit. If her room had been on the ground floor, sneaking out the doors and through the wrought-iron gate at the back of the courtyard would have been easier than on the second floor.

But she had been so excited to have a full bed instead of a twin size, and to put her personal things on a whole dresser without having to split it down the middle and share it with Clara. But that night she had lain awake until almost dawn, feeling as if someone had died and things would never be the same again.

A knock on her door brought her out of the past and into the here and now. "Clara?" she called out.

"Nope, it's me," Lizzy answered, and then peeked into the bedroom. "Do you feel like a teenager again in your very own room with a balcony?"

"Little bit," Sophia answered. "Why did you put us on the second floor when you gave us our own rooms?"

"So you wouldn't sneak out at night," Lizzy answered. "Besides, I thought you'd enjoy having a balcony. Breakfast is on the bar. I've already eaten, and we've had a change of plans. My friend is picking me up here, so you can ride with Clara."

She was gone before Sophia could say that she'd rather drive her own vehicle. She tucked her cell phone into the pocket of her silk pajama bottoms and headed downstairs. When she reached the lobby her phone rang. She fished it out and smiled when she saw that Hunter was calling.

"Good mornin', darlin'," she said. "I miss you so, so much, and I've only been away from you for a few days."

"I miss you too," he said, but there was something in his voice that didn't sound right.

"Is everything okay in the big city?" she asked.

"Not really, but I don't want to discuss it on the phone. I'll be there tomorrow about noon and we'll talk face-to-face," he answered. "Lots has happened since you've been gone."

"Is this about us?" Her heart felt as if it had turned to stone. Hunter was the love of her life, and if he broke up with her now, she would never get over it.

"We are fine, darlin'. I love you, but I've got to go now," he said. "Lots to do today so I can come to Dogwood and spend some time with you."

"Okay, then, I'll see you about noon tomorrow," she told him.

The call ended.

The worrying began.

Five years ago she and Hunter had gone to work at the same time for the Big Red Oil Corporation in Houston. They flirted for a few months, and then he asked her out, and it was all history from then on. They worked together on jobs that involved all kinds of PR work, setting up events, managing travel arrangements, and even supervising the promotional crew for the huge business. For the past two years they had lived together, and right after the new year they had put a down payment on a condo that would be ready when they came home from their honeymoon. Everything had gone exactly according to their plans, except, of course, for the actual wedding. Surely nothing could be wrong, could it?

"Good mornin'," Clara said.

Sophia whipped around at the sound of her sister's voice right behind her. "You shouldn't sneak up on people like that."

"I didn't," Clara protested. "What's got you in a tizz this morning? You look like the weight of the world is on your shoulders. Are you still wishing that you didn't have to share your wedding day with me?"

"Yes, but that's not what's on my mind today," Sophia admitted. "Hunter called and he's coming to Dogwood tomorrow."

Clara started walking toward the kitchen. "And that's a bad thing?"

Sophia followed her across the lobby, through the dining room and into the kitchen. "No, it's wonderful, but he only has enough vacation days for our honeymoon. I had extra days because I haven't taken any time off for the last five years. He talked like he would be here from now until the wedding."

Clara opened the lid of a stainless-steel warmer to find pancakes and bacon. "Maybe he really had more time and he wanted to surprise you."

Sophia picked up a plate, stacked pancakes on it, and then added several strips of bacon. "I've seen his payroll stubs and they show exactly how much time he has accumulated."

Clara poured two cups of coffee, set them on the table, and then fixed her own plate. "You really are nervous, aren't you?"

"Yes, I am, but how can you tell?" Sophia asked.

"Food is our go-to for comfort when we're sad or when we're nervous," Clara reminded her.

Sophia set her plate on the table and eased down into a chair. "I figure stress eats calories."

"If that's the truth, then we should both be five pounds lighter than we are now by the time we get married," Clara teased as she joined her sister.

"Do you ever wonder how our lives would have turned out different if our mother had stuck around?" Sophia asked.

"Not so much now that I'm grown, but I used to think about it a lot," Clara answered. "Especially . . ." She paused and blushed.

"Go on," Sophia said.

"My freshman year in college," Clara said, and then stopped to take a bite of her pancakes.

Sophia pointed her fork at her sister. "You're stalling by putting food in your mouth, because if Mama Lizzy catches us talking with a mouthful, we'll be in big trouble."

Clara finally swallowed and then took a sip of coffee. "How is it that we revert to being kids when we come home to this hotel? I live in my own apartment in Palestine. I'm a loan officer in a really big bank and people respect me, but when I'm here I feel like I have to obey the rules."

"Remember that song that talks about always being seventeen in your hometown?" Sophia asked.

Clara nodded. "Yes, I do, but I believe we're always ten years old in the Dogwood Inn."

"You got that right, sister," Sophia agreed. "Despite the way we feel about it, I hate to see Mama Lizzy sell the place. It's been in the family for decades."

"Yep." Clara nodded again. "It's a sturdy old girl, and I fear that whoever buys it will destroy the vintage feel. I bet the first thing the new owners do is put in an elevator and tear off all the wallpaper."

"And take out the four-poster beds and make everything all modern," Sophia added.

"Oh! My! Sweet! Lord!" Clara gasped.

"What?" Sophia glanced at both of her shoulders. There weren't many things in the world that terrified her, but spiders did, and the look on her sister's face said there might be one about to crawl onto her neck.

"It's nothing to do with you," Clara said quickly. "I just got a vision of new owners ripping all the dogwood trees out of the courtyard."

"No!" Sophia clamped a hand over her mouth. "Those trees have been there longer than the hotel itself. Mama Lizzy said they built this place around the dogwoods to keep from cutting them down. Maybe when she sells the place she could put a condition in the contract that says the trees can't be touched."

"That's a good idea," Clara agreed.

We just agreed on something, Sophia thought. *That's the first in a very long time.*

Clara slid into the pew beside Trevor and kissed him on the cheek. "Good mornin', darlin'."

"It is now that you're here." Trevor smiled and took her hand in his.

Your romance is all sticky-sweet now, but what happens after ten years? the pesky voice in Clara's head asked.

She had never had a single doubt about marrying Trevor—until that moment. Of all the places, it had to happen in church. She remembered the unfinished conversation she had had that morning with her sister, when she had almost confessed to understanding their mother a little better. She was a college freshman when she had a big pregnancy scare herself. She had already broken up with her boyfriend and had to sweat it out alone for a week before she had enough nerve to take a test. She still got queasy when she thought about how she'd felt that day as she waited the few minutes for the results of the test to show up. During that week she came to understand her mother better than she ever had before. When the test showed a negative line she went to the doctor the next day and got birth control pills.

Sophia nudged her on the shoulder and whispered, "You were going to tell me something about our mother at breakfast, and then we got off on a tangent about new owners for the hotel."

"Later," Clara whispered. "Have you figured out why Hunter is coming so soon?"

"Nope, but his tone told me it's not good," Sophia answered.

Lizzy leaned up from the pew behind them and tapped Clara on the shoulder. "Shhh . . . you can talk when you get home."

Clara winked at Sophia, and she held up five fingers. Clara knew what she meant. They might be seventeen in their hometown and ten years old in the hotel, but in church they were only five. Thinking back to when they were that age caused Clara to realize that sitting side by side on a pew was one of the only times that they whispered without arguing. Did that mean there were magic powers in church—in addition to numb bottoms by the time the sermon was finished?

That morning the preacher began by reading the whole twenty-third psalm. Clara listened while he read all the verses, but soon after that she went into la-la land as Sophia had called it when they were kids. That was the place where she blanked out everything around her and sank down deep into her own thoughts. And there was no way her sister could make her believe that *she* hadn't taken trips down the path to that land either.

La-la land that particular Sunday meant pondering whether she was getting cold feet about being married. Was it normal to worry about something that might—or might not—happen ten years down the road? When the preacher asked Trevor to deliver the benediction she still didn't have a clear answer. She needed some time alone to sort it all out.

Everyone stood up and began shaking hands with their neighbors and friends, but before things got too noisy, she whispered to Trevor, "Sophia is having a tough time today and I feel like she needs me. Would it upset the family too much if I took a rain check on dinner?"

"Darlin', you do whatever you need to do," Trevor answered and kissed her on the forehead. "But you have to be there next week because the folks tell me they have a surprise for us that day."

Clara gave him a quick hug. "Do you know what it is?"

"Nope," he replied. "But they say we're going to love it."

"I hope your grandma is making her famous brownies," Clara said. "We both love those. Maybe she's even making an extra pan for us to freeze for the first night in our house."

"Might be, but I get the feeling it's something bigger. Call me later," Trevor said and then disappeared into the crowd with his family.

"Aren't we going out to the ranch?" Sophia asked.

Clara shook her head. "We took a rain check for next Sunday. Let's go into Palestine and eat the buffet at the pizza place, and then go to the ice cream store and have banana splits for dessert. We're both under stress, so that should burn off all the fat grams, and we'll vent for a couple of hours."

"I've got a better idea," Sophia said. "Let's order the pizza for takeout and go back to the hotel. We can eat it out in the courtyard, and you can tell me what you were going to say about our mother."

"I'll agree if we can stop on the way and get a quart of rocky road ice cream," Clara said.

"And a quart of orange sherbet," Sophia added. Clara chuckled.

Sophia rolled her eyes. "We might be friends someday, but honey, we're too old to be the kind of twins who feel pain when the other one hurts."

"We weren't raised to be like that." Clara looped her arm in Sophia's. "Mama Lizzy raised each of us to be our own, independent person."

Sophia patted her sister's hand. "Do you think she raised our mother like that?"

"I don't," Clara answered. "From what little I've learned through the years, Mama Lizzy and our grandfather were superstrict with Mother and she rebelled against it. She must have been about sixteen when he passed away, and that's when she really hit a rebellious streak. I believe that Mama Lizzy felt guilty about the way things turned out, and when she took us to raise she tried a different method."

Sophia put the ice cream and sherbet in the freezer and then joined Clara in the courtyard. Her sister already had the pizza box open and was scarfing down her first piece. She motioned for Sophia to sit down and twisted the tops off the two beers that were sitting on the table.

A soft breeze ruffled the first few blossoms on the dogwood trees that surrounded the courtyard. A cardinal came to rest on the cast-iron gate that led from the back side of the U-shaped yard into the alley. Everything seemed peaceful except in Sophia's heart and mind.

She would be so glad when the wedding was done and over with, so that she could go home to Houston and begin her life as Hunter's wife, but . . .

Why does there have to be a but? she asked herself.

"Do all brides get cold feet and have second thoughts?" Sophia whispered as she sat down across from her sister.

"I don't know about every woman, but this one right here is feeling a little chill on her toes," Clara answered.

"You?" Sophia almost choked on a bite of pizza. "You've always had things so lined up and in order. I can't believe you would have a single second thought in your head."

"What if," Clara said in a low voice, as if she was afraid the cardinal might carry tales, "ten years down the road I have regrets, or worse yet, what if Trevor does? What if, after I have children, I get fat and he doesn't love me anymore? From what I've read, kids change more than just a woman's body. They change relationships. What if Trevor and I don't grow together but we grow apart? I love him too much to cause him that kind of pain."

Sophia could hardly believe her sister was confiding in her, or that Clara was echoing some of her own thoughts and fears. "I saw a meme the other day on the Internet—I can't quote it exactly, but the idea was that in a relationship, true love doesn't happen by accident. It requires deliberate effort and takes work, but in the end it's worth it. You and Trevor won't grow apart. You kind of share one root, and it will just keep getting deeper and deeper."

"That helps," Clara said, "but are you preaching to me or to yourself?"

"Maybe both of us," Sophia admitted. "Until Hunter gets here tomorrow I'll probably keep feeling like the other shoe is about to drop."

"What if the other shoe is that Hunter is about

to call off the wedding because it's too hick town for him?" Clara asked. "Or if one of his old loves has come back into his life and he's figured out that she's his soulmate?"

"Hunter is not that kind of man. I could hear worry in his voice, but he dearly loves Mama Lizzy, so I don't believe he would do something that mean." Sophia took a sip of the beer and then picked up a slice of pizza.

"If you're wrong, I have no problem with you two getting married in some fancy venue," Clara said. "Trevor and I can fly out to Vegas for a weekend and get married."

"Thanks, but the invitations have been sent, and if I'm wrong about him on this, evidently I don't know him at all and maybe we *should* postpone the wedding," Sophia said between bites. "Let's talk about what you said this morning."

"Have you ever been late and sweated it out until you found out you weren't pregnant?" Clara asked.

"Nope," Sophia answered. "I take my pill faithfully. After what happened with our mother and our birth, I'm terrified of having children. What if it's in our genes not to love our children? After all, she gave birth to us and Mama Lizzy says she didn't even want to hold us. As soon as she could, she left town and never came back, not even one time. I wonder if she even asked Mama Lizzy for pictures of us, or if she just pretended that we never happened. Her obituary didn't list any children, just that Elizabeth Delaney was her mother."

Clara finished off her first slice and took several gulps of her beer. "What if she didn't come back because she had regrets and couldn't bear to face us?"

"I never thought of it that way," Sophia answered, "but I will admit that even though we can't complain about our lives, I was really mad at her for a long time. Other kids had a mother to bring cupcakes to school parties, and they lived in houses with yards and neighbors with kids."

The cardinal finally flew away and a blackbird took its place.

Clara finished off her beer and stood up. "We had a Mama Lizzy who brought the fanciest cupcakes, made by her chef here at the hotel, to our parties. We had a courtyard where we pretended that our dolls were princesses and we were queens. And who needed neighborhoods when we had a new group of guests to dote on us every few days?"

"I guess we are twins after all. You are the light side in more ways than just your blond hair and I've got the dark streak. You saw the good in being raised in a hotel and I remember the downside," Sophia said.

Clara patted her sister on the shoulder. "Everyone has two spirits. No one is totally good or totally bad, except maybe for the folks who have severe mental disorders. Kind of like our flavors of ice cream."

"How's that?" Sophia asked.

"Basically, I try to find the good in everything, but sometimes I let doubts and fears creep in. Your dark side has a light side that has hope written on it. I like rocky road, which is dark. You like orange sherbet, which is light. Does that make sense?"

"More than you think," Sophia answered. "Speaking of ice cream?"

"I can agree with you on that." Clara stood up. "I'll bring it out here. One scoop or two?"

"Three," Sophia said, "and you'd better be right about stress destroying calories and fat grams."

Chapter Four

Sophia had always been a night owl. Even as a child, she would read until the wee hours and then hate the wake-up call at seven o'clock the next morning. Adjusting her sleeping pattern when she went to work for the oil company had not been easy, but when the alarm went off each morning, she reminded herself that Starbucks was on the way to her job.

That Monday she was awake when the sun was nothing but a sliver of orange rising over the eastern horizon. She went downstairs, poured herself a cup of coffee, carried it out to the courtyard, and sat down in the same chair she had used the afternoon before. When daylight had fully arrived the streetlights at the four corners of the courtyard went off. That meant it was at least seven o'clock, and if she was in Houston, she would be in line at Starbucks.

"Five more hours," she whispered as she finished the last sip of her coffee.

"Good mornin'," Clara said as she backed out of
the door with a mug in each hand. "I saw you sitting out here when I stepped out on the balcony
and I could tell that your cup was nearly empty. I
can't believe you are up this early."

"I had a rough night," Sophia admitted. "At
least we're going to the florist this morning. I can't
believe Mama Lizzy has had us wait until the last
minute to get everything done."

"She didn't," Clara said, and then handed off
one of the mugs, which had sunflowers printed on
the outside. "The appointment for today has been
on her calendar ever since we announced our engagements. I stopped by one afternoon after work
to check on her and overheard her talking to the
florist."

"Thanks for this," Sophia said. "I shouldn't be
surprised, but I am."

"Speaking of surprises, did I tell you that Trevor's
family is putting together some big, fancy surprise
for us and plans to announce it next Sunday?"
Clara asked.

Sophia took a sip of the hot liquid and glanced
at the flowers. "You didn't tell me that. I'm glad it's
you and not me. I'd worry about what it might be
all week. Where did Mama Lizzy get mugs like
this? Everything around here has always been dogwoods, in keeping with the logo."

"I don't have a single doubt that they've put
their hearts and souls into whatever they've got
planned," Clara said and then took a deep breath
and sat down across from her sister. "I love the

smell of early morning. I'm usually up before dawn, but this morning I slept until the sun had risen. And about the mugs, I gave them to her for Christmas. I'd planned to use sunflowers and daisies in my barn wedding."

"Good morning," Mama Lizzy said as she joined them. "I just got a call from the florist. She says she's got a cancellation and can see us at eight thirty. I thought we'd take care of that and then go have breakfast at Aunt Lucy's Café. Her biscuits and gravy are almost as good as Luther's."

Sophia pushed back her chair and stood up. "That sounds great."

She was happy to have anything to keep her busy until Hunter arrived, and she didn't intend to say a word about a late breakfast that had more carbs in it than she usually ate in a week. "I'll be ready and in the lobby in a few minutes."

"Me too." Clara stood up. "I hope it doesn't take long at the flower shop because just thinking about biscuits and gravy is making my mouth water."

"Then go put something on other than pajama pants," Lizzy said. "You don't have to get all dressed up or put on makeup, but you do need to wear a bra. Especially you, Clara."

"Are you saying that I don't have big enough boobs to need a bra?" Sophia asked.

"Nope, but even a nearsighted bat could tell that Clara could give Dolly Parton some competition with her boobs," Lizzy said with half a giggle. "Now go on and get ready. I've got some great ideas for your bouquets, and for the boutonnieres and corsages."

Sophia followed her sister through the kitchen,

dining room, and lobby, and then up the stairs to the second floor. "I've always envied your boobs and tiny waist," she whispered.

"And I've always been jealous of your height and long legs. You look amazing in a bikini and I look like I've stuffed two cantaloupes into the top of mine," Clara said and then disappeared into her bedroom.

A picture of two cantaloupes stuffed into a bikini top popped into Sophia's mind as she went into her room. She giggled as she grabbed a brush from her dresser and ran it through her hair. She had forgotten that Clara also had more of a sense of humor—and she was jealous of that too.

The dress, the bouquet, the cake, and the venue had seemed so important when Hunter proposed a few months ago, but they had lost their luster that morning as Lizzy led the way into the flower shop.

A lady with a gray bun on top of her head and twinkling blue eyes came from behind the counter. "Good morning, ladies," she greeted them with a smile. "Welcome. I'm Robin, and if you will follow me, we'll talk in the lounge where it's a little more private. I understand dogwoods are the theme of your wedding. Lizzy, your twins grew up to be beautiful women. I haven't seen them since they were tagging along with you when they were little girls."

"And they're still as different as night and day," Lizzy said with a chuckle as she fell in behind Robin.

The small, private room just off what Sophia

thought of as the lobby had a glass-top coffee table surrounded by six light blue, wingback chairs. "Y'all have a seat," Robin said. "Can I get you something to drink? Coffee, tea, maybe a mimosa?"

"We're good," Lizzy answered for all of them and sat down between her granddaughters.

Sophia could have used a mimosa, or two, or maybe half a dozen to calm her nerves, but she didn't speak up.

"Okay, then." Robin sat down and picked up a notebook from the coffee table. She pulled a pen from the bun on top of her head. "I understand the theme for the wedding is dogwoods. We seldom get to do something that unusual, so we're all excited about it here in the shop. Let's start with the brides' bouquets and move forward from there. Big, small, nosegay, trailing?"

"Medium, not nosegay, but not trailing," Clara answered, "and I love sunflowers and daisies. Could you work a few of either of those into the bouquet, and maybe use yellow ribbons?"

"That sounds like a great idea," Lizzy said. "What would you like in yours, Sophia?"

"Red roses and red ribbons," Sophia answered, amazed that her grandmother had even asked.

"Red and yellow?" Lizzy frowned and then smiled. "I love it. The dogwoods need a little bit of color. How about using that same idea for the centerpieces? Maybe some branches with the blossoms on them, and then daisies and roses to brighten them up."

"Yes!" Clara said.

"Sophia?" Lizzy asked.

"Sorry, I was picturing that in my mind," Sophia

answered, "and I do like it a lot. Could I have red roses for the corsages and boutonnieres on my side of the wedding?"

"And I'll have daisies on my side," Clara said. "We'll blend the city wedding and the country one together that way."

"I love it." Lizzy clapped her hands and then handed Robin a piece of the monogrammed stationery from the hotel.

Robin glanced at it for a few seconds. "You *are* organized. The wedding is at six o'clock, so we'll have everything there and set up an hour earlier."

If there is a wedding, Sophia thought, still not sure if the news Hunter was bringing would break her heart.

"That sounds great," Lizzy said. "You will also bring the arch and set it up, along with the two big ferns . . ."

"And the stands to set them on," Robin finished the sentence and nodded. "I'm planning to take pictures of everything to put into my book. I bet next year I'll have a dozen dogwood weddings booked, once the brides see how beautiful it is."

Sophia's thoughts shifted from her own anxiety to using the Dogwood Inn for a wedding venue. As Mama Lizzy said, the hotel provided everything—from rooms, to a dining room for the reception, a lobby for dancing, and a courtyard for the ceremony. She made a mental note to talk to her grandmother about offering to book the hotel for weddings.

"If you have any more questions, just call me," Lizzy said as she stood up. "Girls, are y'all ready to go get some breakfast, and then go home and talk seriously about menus? We need one for the rehearsal dinner and one for the reception. Luther is meeting us this afternoon and would like to see what we've come up with so he can get to organizing what needs to be done. See, I told you that we could get everything ready in a few days."

Robin, Clara, and Sophia all stood up at the same time.

"Thank you for trusting me with such an important event," Robin said. "I wish all brides came in with such a definite opinion about what they want."

She and Lizzy carried on a conversation all the way to the door, while Clara and Sophia followed them.

"That was easier than I thought it would be," Clara whispered. "We each got a little bit of what we wanted."

"Like you said, the city and country are coming together with a whole lot of Elizabeth Delaney thrown in," Sophia said with a smile.

"Well, we Delaneys are known for being opinionated," Clara said with half a giggle. "It's amazing that the three of us can even compromise."

"Do you think changing your name to Clara Richmond is going to help with that attitude?" Sophia asked.

"Nope," Clara answered. "Is going from Delaney to Gamble going to affect your attitude?"

"I doubt it very seriously," Sophia answered.

"What are you two talking about?" Lizzy asked as she held the door open for them.

"Changing our names," Clara answered.

Lizzy got into the back seat of her vintage, baby-blue Cadillac and tossed the keys to Sophia. "It's your turn to drive. I always hoped the two of you would either marry twins or maybe brothers, or even cousins with the same last name, so you'd still share a last name."

Sophia slid in behind the wheel. "I hate driving this big old boat, and parking it is a pain."

"I'm glad it's your turn to drive," Clara whispered.

"This 'big old boat,' as you call Jezebel, was given to me on my sixteenth birthday, and my daddy said I had to treat her like I would the hotel when I inherited it. I've kept both of them in pristine condition and will continue to do so," Lizzy reminded them.

"Does the car go with the hotel when you sell it?" Sophia asked.

"Not just no, but *hell no!*" Lizzy declared. "I'd be buried in Jezebel if I could find a way to do so."

"Why'd you name her Jezebel?" Clara asked.

"Seemed fitting at the time," Lizzy answered. "Suffice it to say the first person I took out for a ride was your grandfather."

Sophia started the engine and pulled away from the curb. "Do I hear a story?"

"I'll tell you someday, maybe on my one hundredth birthday, if y'all are around to give me a big party," Lizzy said.

On the drive to the café, Sophia did the math in her head. Mama Lizzy was seventy years old. She and Clara would be thirty that summer. That meant they would be sixty when their grandmother was a hundred. Would she still be alive, and would she still be married to Hunter? She tried to visualize the two of them at that age, maybe with a couple of children and possibly a grandchild or two, but the pictures wouldn't materialize.

Did that mean she wouldn't be married to Hunter? She blinked back tears at the very idea.

Chapter Five

Sophia's heart almost stopped when Hunter came into the lobby. She stood up on trembling legs and he opened his arms. She walked into them, and he wrapped her up in a fierce hug. She could feel his heart pounding in unison with hers for a moment. Then he took a step back and kissed her. The passion was so hot between them that it eased her fear that he might be coming to tell her that he was backing out of the wedding.

He took another step back, took her hand in his, and led her to the sofa in the corner of the lobby. "We've got a lot to talk about and you need to be sitting. What I've got to tell you has still got my mind going in circles."

Hunter was over six feet tall and broad shouldered, and he carried himself with confidence. His crystal-clear, blue eyes and blond hair made most women take a long look, but it was his brilliant smile that almost made them need drooling bibs. Sophia had been attracted to him from the beginning, but what she'd fallen in love with was his kind heart.

"Spit it out," she said. "Nothing you say can come close to all the scenarios that have played through my mind since you called."

"Big Red Oil has closed its doors. Neither of us has a job anymore. We don't have severance pay or even a payroll check coming in next month. I'm not sure which of the company's assets have been seized and frozen, so we will be putting in job applications instead of going on a fancy honeymoon," he said and then took a breath.

"Seized and frozen?" she whispered as the news swirled around in her mind. She felt as if she was on that old, squeaky merry-go-round at the park where Mama Lizzy took them to play on Sunday afternoons after church.

He ran his fingers through his hair. "They borrowed millions for new ventures that didn't pan out, and the banks foreclosed on the whole business. They've known it was coming since Christmas and have been scrambling to keep afloat, but it wasn't possible. We were told to gather up our stuff and leave by five on Friday. I just couldn't tell you on the phone."

"Our condo?" she asked, hoping that after the wedding they could salvage that part of their plans.

Hunter shook his head. "Our apartment lease is up on the last day of this month, and because we don't have jobs, we can't afford the rent, and we sure can't afford to buy a condo until we are employed and settled. I used part of our savings to have all our things moved to a storage unit. Thank God your grandmother insisted on having our wedding here or we'd have to postpone it. There's no way we could have afforded to pay for a venue and everything else. I am so, so sorry, darlin'."

Sophia couldn't begin to take in all that news. She had worked for the oil company since the week after she graduated from college. She'd always planned to save more money, but somehow, by the end of the month, there wasn't much left after she'd paid the rent on an expensive apartment in Houston and kept up with all her other bills.

Her mind stopped twirling. "I've barely got enough in savings for two months' car payments and another six months of insurance," she gasped.

"Me too," Hunter admitted. "I'd planned to use our Christmas bonuses to pay off the credit card for our honeymoon."

Tears filled her eyes and streamed down her cheeks. Of all the things she had thought he might tell her, a disaster like this had never entered her mind. "What are we going to do?"

"Be glad that we've got skills, and hopefully we will be able to find jobs in our field fairly quickly," Hunter answered. "Please, tell me that you'll still marry me. I love you so much."

"Of course I'll marry you, and I know Mama Lizzy will let us live right here until we find something," Sophia assured herself as much as him. "That's the beauty of having a grandmother who owns a hotel. We'll have a roof over our heads and Luther to cook for us."

"How would you like the idea of putting out

feelers in this area?" Hunter asked. "Living expenses wouldn't be as high as they are in Houston."

"We'll talk about that later," she answered. "I see
Luther parking out front, and we need to talk
menus for the rehearsal and reception with him.
My mind is spinning around so fast that I can't
think about anything for more than five seconds. I
need to catch my breath over this news before we
make plans about where to live. You've known
about it for a couple of days, but I'm just now getting hit with it. Didn't you get any scuttlebutt
about any of this from your dad?"

Hunter shook his head. "Not much. I thought
he was teasing last week when he said he hoped I'd
been saving a chunk of money. I figured he was
just giving me fatherly advice." He pulled her close
and kissed her on the forehead. "I'm so sorry for
having to unload such a mess on you. You shouldn't
be thinking about anything but flowers and wedding cake right now. I haven't slept all weekend for
worrying over what we are going to do and disap-
pointing you about the honeymoon I promised."

"A honeymoon can be anywhere, darlin'," Sophia
told him.

"We'll find jobs and we'll go on that trip for our
tenth anniversary. We'll pay for it in cash because
we're throwing away our credit cards. I'm never,
ever letting us get in this kind of mess again."

"I agree with you," Sophia said. "No more living
beyond our means."

"Hello, Sophia, and hello, Hunter," Luther said
as he came into the hotel. "Is everyone in the
kitchen?"

"Yes, they are," she answered. "We will join you in a few minutes. Don't start without us."

"Wouldn't dream of it," Luther said and waved over his shoulder. A tall, lanky man with a headful of thick, gray hair, he had been the chef at the Dogwood Inn ever since before Sophia and Clara were born. Back then, his hair had been jet black and he'd had fewer wrinkles than he did now. Looking back, Sophia wondered how he'd maintained his patience with her and Clara running around underfoot.

Hunter stood up and pulled Sophia up beside him. "We have to tell your grandmother."

"She will try to fix and micromanage, the way she always does," Sophia whispered.

Hunter dropped her hand and draped his arm around her shoulders. "Maybe that's not such a bad thing."

Clara could tell by the expression on her sister's face that whatever news Hunter had brought, it wasn't good. Sophia had been crying, and Hunter, bless his heart—the meaning of the saying would be determined later—looked like he had seen a ghost or lost his best friend. The man had better hope he hadn't caused her sister pain. Clara might not like Sophia most of the time, but she loved her, and she would not abide anyone hurting her.

She raised her eyebrows, and Sophia barely shook her head. She mouthed the word, *Later,* and then sat down in the chair that Hunter had pulled out for her.

"Okay, we're all here. Glad you could come early, Hunter," Lizzy said. "Y'all start throwing ideas out for the rehearsal dinner. We'll get that all settled and then move on to the reception."

"Shrimp alfredo," Sophia said.

"Chicken parmesan," Clara suggested.

Lizzy nodded in agreement. "How about we do a buffet for the rehearsal dinner with those two choices for the entrée and serve thick slices of Luther's homemade Italian bread and a salad with them? Then we could have a cheesecake dessert bar.

"Do you have any other ideas, Hunter?" Lizzy eyed him.

Elizabeth Delaney had always been able to read people, which made Clara wonder exactly what her grandmother was seeing right at that moment. Was she ready to throw him out, or would she sympathize with whatever problem he had brought up from Houston?

After a pause Hunter shook his head. "That all sounds wonderful."

"Then is it a go?" Luther wrote down what they'd said and then looked up. "I can make the mini cheesecakes a few days ahead of time and freeze them. Is this set in stone, or do we need to think about it? Do we move on to the reception now?"

"I was thinking that your glazed ham and smoked turkey breast might be good for the two entrées, with all the sides that go with what we usually serve up for Easter dinner," Lizzy said. "If y'all have any other ideas, speak now or forever hold your peace."

"Well, Easter is the next day after the wedding, so we could always use the leftovers for dinner that day," Luther said.

"Exactly what I was thinking," Lizzy said. "So, are we all good with that? Hunter?"

"It all sounds delicious," Hunter said.

Clara had forgotten that Easter was the day after the wedding. Surely the Richmond family wouldn't expect her and Trevor to be at a big family gathering. Granted, they were planning to spend their honeymoon in their new home at the ranch, but she had hoped they could have one day all to themselves.

"Clara?" Lizzy's demanding voice jerked her into the present.

"Sorry." She almost blushed. "I was woolgathering about the next day being Easter Sunday. You know how much Trevor and I both love your ham and turkey, Luther. I'll speak for both of us. We are all in with this," she answered.

"Well, I don't expect you girls to race downstairs that morning to see what's in your Easter baskets," Lizzy said with a chuckle. "I imagine you'll drive out of here that evening and I won't see you for weeks or months."

"Hey, now," Clara scolded. "I'll pop in as often as I can."

"Until I sell this place and move into a retirement home, or until I decide to live on a cruise ship. I put the pencil to the paper and found that I can go on one cruise after another and live cheaper than I can in one of those fancy-schmancy retirement villages. Marlene and I've been talking about it for a while now," Lizzy explained.

Clara didn't argue, but a cold chill chased down her spine at the thought of her grandmother being out of the country on a ship all the time, or even moving into a retirement home. Then she thought about the Delaney family *not* owning the Dogwood Inn. Fear settled in her chest when she realized that she wouldn't be able to pull her suitcase into the lobby anytime she wanted and go up to her old bedroom. She refused to let the tears building up behind her eyes tumble down her cheeks.

"Please, don't sell the hotel," she whispered.

"Why would I keep it?" Lizzy asked. "I'm past retirement age. I've devoted my life to this place, raised you girls here, and you've gone on to live your lives. I'm not complaining. The Dogwood Inn has been good to me, and I'll be able to go anywhere I please and do what I want. But I've got to admit I hate to see it go to a corporation that will probably raze it and build a condo complex. They'll cut down the dogwood trees and put a swimming pool in the place where the courtyard is. My grandparents built this place and ran it until they died. My daddy inherited it and raised me here until he passed away. I was twenty when I inherited it, but I picked up the reins and did well enough. Luther's daddy was the chef back then, and we had all kinds of fancy folks coming and going. In those days everyone dressed in their finest cocktail attire for supper, but not so much anymore."

Clara had heard the story dozens of times, but that day the words pricked her heart. She had never even thought of inheriting the hotel someday. She'd gone to college, gotten a business degree in finance, and come home to work for a bank in Palestine.

What if . . . she thought, but stopped the question before it even formed. She couldn't change horses in the middle of the river, as Mama Lizzy had warned her so many times.

And you can't ride a horse with only one butt, Clara remembered hearing too often to count. That meant that she had chosen her path and it was too late to change her course now.

Or was it?

Chapter Six

"**O**kay, time's up," Lizzy said at breakfast the next morning. "Something is going on with you—" she pointed at Sophia and then moved her finger around to Hunter—"and you, so spit it out. Are we having a double wedding or a single one?"

"Double," Sophia whispered, "but . . ."

Hunter laid a hand on her arm. "Let me, darlin'." Then he went on to tell Lizzy what had happened. "We thought we had our whole lives in order, and then . . ." He shrugged. "We are kind of struggling with the question of whether we get our résumés ready to apply for new jobs today, or maybe wait until after the wedding."

Clara got up from the table and gave her sister a hug. "I'm so sorry. Want me to ask if there are any positions open at my bank?"

"I'm still in shock, so I don't even know what I want to do or where to start," Sophia answered.

"Right now, you've got a place to live and food to eat," Lizzy said, "but I've got a better offer than a bank job. Why don't you girls let me give you this hotel? Hunter, you can take over the operations. Clara can do the books and Sophia can do the day-to-day work with Luther and oversee the cleaning crew. I figure it will take at least three people to do what I do, and there's three of you sitting right here at the table with me."

"I don't know what to say," Hunter whispered.

"Nothing," Lizzy said. "You don't say a single word until you've all thought about it for at least twenty-four hours. It's a big decision and you need time to process it. If you look at the books, you'll see that you would all have a generous salary, probably more than any of you make right now. I'll stick around until the end of the summer to help you make the transition, and then I'm out of here. My friends from Sunday school class and I are going to Grand Teton for a few months. I'll see if I . . ."

"Mama Lizzy!" Sophia gasped. "You can't leave for that long!"

"That's what you've got out of what I just offered?" Lizzy finished off a cup of coffee, stood up, and went to the counter for a refill, then came back and sat down. "I've got a buyer on the hook right now. The deal can easily be closed by the end of August. I'd rather give the inn to you than sell it and put the money in trust funds for you. Either way, the place has always been and still is your inheritance, whether you take the hotel itself or the value of it in a retirement fund. Besides, the two of you don't come around for days, or sometimes even months." She glanced over at Clara and then shifted her gaze to Sophia. "You won't really miss me."

Guilt wrapped its cold arms around Sophia and tears flooded her eyes. She couldn't argue with her grandmother because what she'd said was the truth.

"This is the first time ever that I haven't had a full house for the Dogwood Trails Festival weeks, so I'm going to take advantage of the free time these next couple of days. Marlene and two of our other friends and I are going on a little jaunt to Shreveport to hit a casino or two. Wedding guests will start arriving on Thursday and I want to be here to greet them. Luther will be here, and the cleaning staff and the dining room folks will be back on duty that afternoon," Lizzy said.

"But . . ." Clara gasped.

"There are no buts," Lizzy said. "You've got until Thursday night to think about my offer. If you don't want the place to be sold, you'll take over. If you decide you want the place, I'll make an appointment with my lawyer for you to sign the papers I already have drawn up. If you don't, I'll take the bid a corporation has offered me. That's all there is to it."

"What about the rest of the wedding plans?" Sophia's mind was whipping around in circles so fast that everything was a blur.

"I'll be home on Thursday to help with whatever last-minute details need to be done, but I've been working on these plans since you announced your engagements, so everything is pretty well taken care of. Basically, y'all have a couple of days to think about my offer because you have nothing else to do," Lizzy answered. "This will give you some time. Clara, you'll have to talk things over with Trevor, and maybe the two of you can spend some time together on the ranch. Sophia, you and Hunter will be on your own here in the hotel if Clara decides to leave."

Sophia glanced over at Hunter. The poor man looked as bewildered as she felt. Learning that their jobs had been thrown out the back door like trash, then trying to figure out how to tell her the horrible news as he made the drive, must have been agonizing. And now, this offer to consider.

"Mama Lizzy, I've never stayed a night in this place without you being here," Sophia managed to say.

"No time like the present," Lizzy replied and stood up. "My suitcase is packed and in the lobby. I'm taking Jezebel because the Shreveport hotel has valet parking and she won't be sitting out in the weather. She's spent her whole life in the climate-controlled garage just off the courtyard. I would never mistreat her. Got to admit, it does feel strange to be wheeling my brand-new suitcase out of the hotel."

"Have a good time," Clara said, "and call us when you get there so we know you are safe."

Lizzy waved her hand around. "I know. I know. Don't pick up strangers. Never carry all your money in one place. I made up all those rules, so you don't have to recite them to me. See y'all Thursday around noon. If folks arrive earlier than that, y'all can greet them, hand out room keys, and make them welcome," she said as she left the kitchen.

"I can't believe that just happened," Sophia whispered. The quiet in the kitchen was almost deafening. Neither Hunter nor Clara had spoken a word. "Say something, please," she begged. "My mind is going crazy right now."

"So is mine," Clara said. "I thought I had my life all planned out until retirement and now I get thrown this curveball."

Hunter finally said, "That's a lot to consider, and I appreciate the offer, but you never wanted to move back here. This would be a lifetime commitment."

Clara stood up and began to clear the table. "I can't bear to see this place sold out of the family and possibly torn down, but . . ."

"But are we really going to even consider this?" Sophia said as she and Hunter both pushed back their chairs, got to their feet, and carried their plates to the sink. "It's a permanent commitment for years to come, not just a temporary job until we find something better."

"How many rooms does the hotel have?" Hunter asked.

"Forty," Clara answered, "but two of them aren't available to anyone but me and Sophia."

Sophia loaded the dishwasher and poured three more cups of coffee. "Let's take this to the lobby, where it's more comfortable. In addition to the hotel rooms, there's the dining room, which seats fifty, and folks come from all around the area to eat here. Luther's cooking is well-known and liked, and Mama Lizzy told us that he's training his son to take over the kitchen when he retires."

"How far in the future is that?" Hunter asked as he followed the two women out of the kitchen.

"Luther was maybe twenty-five and had just taken his father's place when we were little girls, so he might be here for another five or ten years," Clara answered and then sat down in one of the wingback chairs that faced the sofa. "If we decide to keep the hotel, we will have plenty of time to get settled in before he retires."

"Would we have to live here?" Hunter asked. "At first it would be fine, but what about when we have a family?" He waited for Sophia to take a seat on the sofa and then sat down beside her.

Sophia shrugged. "We were raised in this place. There's a two-bedroom apartment back behind the check-in desk."

"I can't live here," Clara declared. "Trevor and I already have a house on the ranch."

"Were you planning to work after you get married?" Sophia asked.

"Of course," Clara replied. "I don't know jack squat about ranching."

Sophia shot a look across the coffee table at her.

"What?" Clara snapped.

Sophia tapped her forehead in a gesture directing Clara to think. "What's the difference between going to the bank for eight hours a day or coming here for the same amount of time? Your job would involve taking care of books and numbers, taking money to the bank, dealing with finances. Hunter and I would be responsible for the hiring and firing of staff and general management. We would need to live here unless we hired a manager for each shift, which would cut down on profit."

Hunter ran his fingers through his hair, which left no doubt in Sophia's mind that he was nervous even thinking about such a commitment. "At first we could hire a night manager and we'd be responsible for the day shift, but are we seriously even considering this? I love you, Sophia, and I'm willing to do whatever you want. After all, this is your heritage, and it *would* be a shame to see it torn down. But remember, this isn't our only option as far as jobs go."

"I just never saw myself living here, much less running the hotel," Sophia said with a long sigh. "In my mind, Mama Lizzy was going to live forever."

"In mine too." Clara matched her sigh.

"Why do you call her that?" Hunter asked. "She's not your mother."

"Because she told us to," Clara answered. "For all intents and purposes, she is our mother, even if she didn't give birth to us. She wanted us to call her 'mama.' She says we tacked on the Lizzy because we heard everyone in the hotel calling her that, and it just stuck. What do you call your grandparents, and do they even know about the company having to close its doors?"

"My dad's folks are 'Grandmother' and 'Grandfather,' and on the other side they're 'Grandpa' and 'Granny,'" he replied. "Yes, they know about the company. Grandfather was pretty upset about it. He advised my dad on more than one occasion against borrowing more and more money for new ventures that didn't pan out. Dad has always been what they call a big-or-bust man, and he got in over his head."

Sophia snuggled up closer to him and took his hand in hers. "What are they going to think about you running a hotel if we decide to do this?"

"I'm not sure, but it's really not their decision," Hunter answered. "I'm glad we've got some time to think about things, to go over the books and see what kind of salary we would have, and then decide together what we're going to do."

Clara stood up and headed toward the check-in counter. "We might as well see about the finances before we go any further with this conversation."

"Do you know how to go about that?" Sophia asked.

"I know the passwords to get into the accounts," Clara answered.

"Should we ask Lizzy to be sure that she meant for us to go snooping around in the finances?" Hunter asked.

"I helped Mama Lizzy set up the program to put everything on the computer, but she keeps double books because she doesn't trust cyberspace," Clara said and kept walking. "Let's look at what we'd be getting into, what the overhead is, and all that. She told me what passwords to use when I set everything up for her. She offered to give us the place, and she actually encouraged us to look at the books, so I don't think she will mind."

Sophia tucked her hand into Hunter's, and together they followed Clara into the office—the small, "holy sanctuary" that they had never been allowed to enter unless Mama Lizzy was in there with them. Clara switched on the light, and nothing had changed. Metal file cabinets still lined one wall, and Sophia shuddered at the idea of going all through the hard copy folders and ledgers that were housed there. The old oak desk in the middle of the floor faced the door, and the chair behind it should have already been donated to a museum. Mama Lizzy had told them that the desk had been set in place when the hotel was being built, back before all the walls were even put up. The thing was so big that it would have to be torn apart to get it out of the room. Without even closing her eyes, Sophia could imagine her grandmother sitting there as straight as a lightning rod with her reading glasses perched on the end of her nose.

That morning Clara sat down in the chair, turned on the desktop computer, and then looked up with a smile. "Take a deep breath."

Sophia inhaled and then nodded. "Youth Dew."

"What's that?" Hunter asked.

"That would be the faint scent of Mama Lizzy's perfume still lingering in this room," Clara answered.

"Well, she does spend a lot of time in here," Hunter said, "doesn't she?"

Sophia kissed him on the cheek. "Yes, darlin', she does, and if we take over the hotel, that chair will be Clara's brand-new throne."

"If I put a pillow in the chair, it'll be comfortable enough," Clara said as she poked a button and the printer sitting on a smaller file cabinet behind her began to churn out papers. "Mama Lizzy must've known that we would come looking. She's got a projected statement including the profit margin for next year and salaries for each of us, ready for us to view."

Three copies came out already collated and ready for them to look over. Clara handed them out and powered down the computer. "Looks like she's invested in a new, modern printer, even if we do still have old, black desk phones in the rooms."

Hunter hiked a leg on the edge of the desk and flipped through the pages. "Holy smoke! Sophia, darlin', are you seeing these numbers? How does a small place like this have such an income? And these salaries are at least thirty percent more than we were making at the oil company. We would be crazy not to take this job."

"Plus, she has worked in insurance and a retirement fund that matches what we put into it up to eight percent," Clara said without even looking up, "but it's not just about the money."

"I know, I know," Sophia whispered, "it's also about hanging on to what our ancestors started. This seems like a silver lining to a really dark cloud and almost too good to be true. Am I dreaming? If so, don't wake me. But still, I vote that we sleep on it for two nights before we really make up our minds."

"Look at you," Clara said. "The twin who was always so impulsive now becomes the careful one."

Sophia couldn't argue with that, but this decision involved more than making a choice on a whim. It had to do with the rest of her—and Hunter's—lives. Would their marriage survive if they lived in a hotel and worked together at a job where their paths would cross more than a couple of times a day? She loved him enough that she would rather be a greeter at a big box store or flip burgers in a greasy spoon diner than accept a position that would jeopardize their marriage.

"Sophia is right," Hunter defended her. "Let's give this some more thought before we jump right in and say yes."

Clara powered down the computer. "On that note, I'll be going out to the ranch for a couple of nights. I'll be back Thursday." The chair squeaked when she stood and pushed it away. "By then we should have all the pros and cons worked out."

"Do you think that . . ." Sophia said and paused.

"That we can work together and not argue about every single decision?" Clara asked.

"Looks like you two have more in common than you think," Hunter said with a chuckle. "Your sister just finished your sentence."

Sophia carried her set of papers across the room. "Well, it is something to think about."

Clara followed her and switched off the light at the door. "It's something to add to the con list you know we'll both start making up in the next few hours."

"Minutes, not hours," Sophia said.

"I'm already writing things down mentally," Clara said as she started up the stairs. "You've got the hotel to yourselves. Be sure to lock the lobby doors if you don't want to stand watch behind the check-in desk all night."

"That sounded just like Mama Lizzy," Sophia said, "but thanks for the reminder. I bet this place has never been locked up before in all the years it's been here."

Clara waved from the top of the steps. "Except

for the past few days, when even the night clerk has been given a paid vacation."

Sophia turned and wrapped her arms around Hunter's neck. "Darlin', we've got the next couple of days alone. As of right now, I'm going to pretend this is a fancy hotel, that we're already married, and you've rented the whole hotel so that we won't be disturbed. Neither of us will even have to get dressed."

"I love you so much." Hunter tipped up her chin with his fist and kissed her—long, lingering, and passionately.

"Hey, you two," Clara teased as she carried a small tote bag and her purse down to the lobby, "get a room."

"We've got one," Hunter said. "Would you please lock the door on your way out?"

"Of course," Clara said.

When she was gone, Hunter scooped Sophia up like a bride and carried her up the stairs and into their room.

"You don't even have to close the door," she whispered.

"What if Clara comes back?" he asked as he laid her on the bed.

"There's only one key and it's behind the desk. This is our honeymoon hotel and no one can come inside unless we let them," she whispered and pulled him down beside her.

Chapter Seven

Clara had no doubt that Trevor would tell her he would support any choice she made where her career was concerned, but it would be nice to talk the whole decision over with him. Trevor loved Mama Lizzy, and he always liked going to the hotel for dinner when they could carve out a few hours every month or two. The two of them would go over all the pros and cons—after they spent some time in bed together, she thought and smiled. The faint scent of Youth Dew perfume lingered with her, like an omen, as she drove from the hotel out to the ranch. She inhaled deeply and thought about how she could personalize that little office. Maybe put up some old pictures of her great-grandparents, who'd built the place, then add some of Mama Lizzy's folks, and even her favorite one of Sophia that her grandmother had taken last year at Christmas. The legacy would be on the walls to remind her that she was carrying on by doing her part.

So, you've basically made your decision? the voice in her head asked.

"I guess I have," she whispered with a smile as she turned into the lane that led up to the small trailer where Trevor would live until their wedding night. Cowboys were hurrying from one place to another, but she didn't see Trevor among them. He was probably out plowing a field or doing something with cattle that she could never quite understand.

She parked in front of the trailer, got out of her vehicle, and went inside. Trevor's dress boots were sitting beside his recliner and his breakfast dishes were in the kitchen sink. She carried her tote bag to the bedroom and dropped it beside the unmade bed. Clara had always been a neat freak, but then, she'd been raised that way. She could hear Mama Lizzy's voice in her head. *Make your bed when you get out of it. Do the dishes as you dirty them. Keep your bathroom spotless.* And that was when she was barely four years old.

She straightened the bed, moved on to the bathroom, picked up towels from the floor and took them to the kitchen, tossed them in the washing machine—after moving a load over to the dryer. Then she went to the kitchen and washed up the dishes. When she finished that she sat down in the living area and picked up a ranching magazine from the end table. Not one thing in it interested her, so she turned on the television and surfed through channels until she found one of her favorite old movies just starting, *Steel Magnolias*. The women in the movie were strong, and even if they were married, they made their own decisions and held on to their independence—just as her grandmother Lizzy had done.

Tears were streaming down her face at the end of the movie. When Trevor poked his head in the door she was sobbing. He hurried to her side, dropped down on his knees, and wrapped her up in a hug. "What's the matter? Is it your grandmother?"

She pointed at the television. "No, I always cry at the ..." she hiccupped, "the ..." she stammered as she tried to get control, "the end of that movie."

Trevor stood up and handed her a tissue from the box on the end table.

"Can't help it." Another hiccup as she wiped her eyes.

"Let's go up to the ranch house and have some lunch. My mother has made plenty, and good food and company will take your mind off the movie," Trevor said.

"Let's make a sandwich here and talk—just the two of us," she said.

"All of us boys have lunch at the ranch house every day," he reminded her. "The daughters-in-law join us when they can, but we brothers have always gone home for the noon meal. Then we all have supper in our own houses, except for me." Trevor extended a hand and pulled her up from the chair. "I still eat with Mama and Daddy at the end of the workday. I'm looking forward to changing that."

"What's going on after lunch?" she asked.

"Work, and then supper with the folks," he answered as he led her toward the door. "But pretty soon we'll be in our own house, and . . ." he tipped up her chin and kissed her, "I found out what the surprise is. I overheard two of my brothers talking about it, but you have to act surprised." He took a step toward the door.

"I'm not going with you to lunch," she said. "I want to hear about the surprise, but I'm going to burst if I don't tell you what's happened."

"Oh, yes, you are." Trevor tugged on her hand. "Mama will think something is wrong if I don't show up. This is the way things are done here on the ranch. I've told you before that I always eat with my folks."

Clara pulled her hand free and took her phone from the hip pocket of her jeans, scrolled down, and called her future mother-in-law.

"Hello, Clara," Donna said. "Trevor isn't here yet, but I'm expecting him any minute. What can I help you with?"

"I'm at the trailer, and we're having a sandwich here," Clara said.

Trevor took the phone from her and said, "She's jokin', Mama. We'll be down there in a few minutes. Don't wait for me, though. My brothers will string me up if that happens." He handed the phone back to her. "I do not appreciate that."

Clara had never seen Trevor angry and she didn't like it. She put aside her own feelings and said, "We are going to talk right now," and she went on to tell him about Sophia and Hunter losing their jobs, and about Mama Lizzy's offer. "We're going to think about it for a couple of days, but I'm leaning toward saying yes so we can keep the hotel legacy going."

Trevor let go of her hand and raked his fingers through his hair. "No."

"No? What do you mean by such a cryptic answer?" Clara asked. "I didn't ask you for permission. I just wanted us to talk about the pros and cons of me switching jobs. I'm pretty sure I'm going to do it if Sophia agrees."

Trevor's expression was set in stone and his mouth barely moved when he said, "Women on this ranch do not work outside. My sisters-in-law all take care of their homes, raise their children, and have things they do to help out here."

"You've known from our first date that I'm not a ranching woman like your sisters-in-law. They all came from that kind of background, but I didn't, and you know it. I want to be your wife, not a slave to this place." Her tone sounded chilly in her own ears.

"They consider themselves lucky, not slaves," he snapped. "Besides, you can't get along with your sister. Never have been able to, and you'd be miserable working in that hotel with her every day."

"My job would be five days a week and I would be working the same hours I'm working now, so what difference does it . . ." She clamped a hand over her mouth for a moment. "You are expecting me to quit my job when we have children, aren't you? Well, honey, I was raised in that hotel and I turned out well enough for you to fall in love with me, so I expect that I can take our kids to work with me until they're old enough to go to school."

"No," he said again. "The surprise is that my

folks will up my salary, just like they did all my brothers' wages, so that you don't have to work at all. You'll learn on Sunday that you can give your notice at the bank, and after the wedding you won't be going to a job anywhere but on the ranch. Mama said she could use some help with the books for a couple of hours every day."

Clara was stunned. Evidently, she had only thought she knew Trevor. "I have no intention of not working outside. I appreciate your folks' generous offer, but you and I are partners in this marriage and . . ."

Trevor opened the door. "I thought we were, and that you would be excited. You know my family and how we do things. I haven't kept anything a secret from you. We want four kids and we want them to be raised on this ranch, not bottled up every day in a hotel."

Clara propped her hands on her hips and walked outside ahead of him. "Then when they are old enough to walk and get around, you can take care of them while I work. I'm too angry right now to talk about this anymore. My mind is made up about the hotel and I'm not changing it. You go on up to the ranch house and have lunch with your family. I'm going home. Maybe we should have talked all this through before we planned a wedding."

He followed her out and slammed the screen door. "I thought we had. Are you really going to break up with me over something this small?"

"This is not small, Trevor." She opened the door to her car and slid in behind the wheel. "It's huge. You are making decisions for me and trying to control me. I need some breathing space away from you right now."

"Then, by all means, go get whatever you need," he snapped, then stormed off the porch, got into his truck, and slung gravel all over the front of the trailer when he spun out.

Chapter Eight

Tears flowed down Clara's cheeks and she pounded on the steering wheel a few times before she started the engine. She'd never seen anger in Trevor's eyes, and even if he hadn't physically abused her, she wasn't going to live in his world and potentially lose herself. She looked down at her engagement ring and wondered if he would ever place the little band that matched it on her finger. Was this the end of their relationship? When they had both cooled down would he give her an ultimatum—his way or the highway?

She started the engine and drove back to the hotel. By the time she parked, the front of her T-shirt was spotted with teardrops, and they were still coming down like hard rain. She tried to will them to stop, but that didn't work, so she got out of her car and made her way to the front door, only to find it locked.

Sophia's car and Hunter's truck were both parked in the hotel lot, but they wouldn't hear the doorbell if they were in the courtyard. She wiped her eyes and then turned around and walked around the hotel to the alley in the back. The gate was locked, but she could look through the scroll-work and there was nobody to be seen anywhere.

There seemed to be nothing to do but climb over the fence, so she hooked the toe of her athletic shoe in a space and slowly made her way up. When she flipped over the ornamental top her T-shirt caught on a spike, and she hung there like a rag doll until the T-shirt finally ripped down the front and she fell flat on her back. With the wind knocked out of her, she lay there for several moments, gasping for air. Dust from the concrete flew up around her and then filtered back down to settle on her wet face.

Finally, she was able to sit up and then stand. She pulled up a side of her torn shirt and wiped her eyes, then headed for the dogwood tree that stood right under the balcony to her room. Years ago, when they were teenagers, Sophia had shown her how to climb up the limbs to the balcony, and she figured with the anger that was still boiling inside her, she could do it again. She reached up, grabbed the first limb and, using it like the rung in a jungle gym, swung her body up onto it. Her stomach grumbled, but she assured it that there was food inside the hotel.

The third limb she stepped up on gave way and she had to scramble to get a hold on the next one up. Then it was a matter of hanging there like a monkey at the zoo for several seconds before she could continue the climb.

"Good God!" she heard her sister's voice above her. "What are you doing?"

"Trying to get inside," Clara answered between pants. "Help me."

"Go back down and I'll open the kitchen door," Sophia said. "What happened to you?"

"I'm not sure I can," Clara said.

"Then hang on," Sophia told her. "I'm coming right down. I'll help you."

Clara's hands had started to sweat. She glanced down and determined that the distance to the ground wasn't any farther than when she'd fallen off the gate. The main difference would be that she had kind of rolled off the fence; letting go of the limb would mean that she would most likely land on her feet. Which could mean she would break or sprain an ankle.

She tightened her grip until the bark on the tree bit into her palms. "I don't want to wear a cast or a boot to my wedding."

What wedding? the voice in her head asked.

That was all it took for her to decide to take her chances with a free fall, but then she heard a scraping sound and saw that Sophia was pushing one of the tables under the low limbs of the dogwood tree. "I'll climb up and grab you around the waist. Don't let go until I have a good hold or we'll both fall."

"Where's Hunter?" Clara asked.

"Taking a shower," Sophia said as she managed to get onto the table and reach up to Clara. "Why didn't you just call me? I would have unlocked the door for you."

"Crap!" Clara groaned and felt her sister's arms lock around her waist.

"Literally? Or just a Sunday school swear word?" Sophia asked. "Let go and we'll both ease down onto the tabletop until you can catch your breath."

"Sunday cuss word." Clara felt as if she was back at the Leadership Program she had taken the first year she worked at the bank. She had never quite mastered the art of trusting someone to catch her when she fell from a platform. "I can't," she said above a whisper. "What if we both fall off the table and break our necks?"

"Then I guess Mama Lizzy will push us up the aisle in wheelchairs. We had a double stroller when we were babies. Do you think they make double wheelchairs?" Sophia gave a tug.

Clara's sweaty hands couldn't hang on another second no matter how hard she gripped. One second she was swinging; the next, her feet were on the table. Sophia let go of her and she sank down into a sitting position and started to sob. Her sister eased down to sit right beside her and wrapped her arms around Clara's shoulders.

"You are crying mud, girl," she scolded. "Hush up and talk to me."

"Trevor and I . . . we . . ." Clara stammered and mentally relived the argument. "We . . . I might not be . . . he can't."

"What's going on down there?" Hunter asked from the balcony.

"I'm not sure, but I know Clara needs me," Sophia called back up to him.

"Need my help?" Hunter asked.

Clara shook her head.

Hunter covered a yawn with his hand. "Then I'll take a nap. Call me if you need anything."

"Thanks anyway, darlin'." Sophia smiled at him, but the grin faded when she looked at Clara. "Now, tell me what's happened. Were you in a car accident? You look like you've taken a dirt bath."

"I climbed over the fence and tore my shirt; then I fell and got the breath knocked out of my body. Someone has got to power wash this courtyard before the wedding. Trevor and I . . ." she wasn't sure how to begin, "we had a fight."

Sophia's hands knotted into fists. "Did he hit you and tear your shirt?"

"No! We just argued," Clara answered. "I told him about Mama Lizzy's offer and he said I couldn't do it. I'm supposed to stay on the ranch, not work outside, and raise kids. I love Trevor, but I'm not that kind of woman. I'm afraid we've broken up."

"If he can't compromise, you should break up with him, but honey, that man loves you enough that when he thinks about it, he'll be coming back and wanting to work through the problem," Sophia told her.

Clara shook her head. "I don't know about that. He's pretty upset with me. That surprise I was telling you about is that his folks want to raise his salary to the equivalent of what I make so I can stay home."

"What on earth would you do all day?" Sophia asked.

A picture popped into her head—making the bed, doing dishes, picking up wet towels. "I guess

I'd be waiting on Trevor and then doing some book work for the ranch two or three hours a day."

"And you said, 'No, thank you,' right?" Sophia asked.

"I don't think I added the thank you," Clara whispered, and her stomach growled.

"I heard that, and I'm hungry, too," Sophia said. "Let's go inside. I'll make some sandwiches while you take a shower and get cleaned up. Then we can talk some more. But I'm still puzzled about why you didn't call me."

"I was so mad, I didn't even think about it, and my phone was in my hip pocket when I fell on my back, so it might be smashed all to pieces," Clara replied as she eased off the table and started toward the kitchen door.

Sophia hopped down, beat her to the door, and opened it. "If your phone is ruined, it could be a sign that you don't need to talk to Trevor for a while."

Clara pulled the phone from her hip pocket to find the screen was cracked, but it appeared to be working just fine. There was a text from Mama Lizzy saying they'd stopped for lunch on the road and she would send another message when they reached the hotel.

"Nothing from Trevor," she muttered.

"He'll come around, but you should stand your ground," Sophia said and gave her a gentle push toward the lobby. "If you let him talk you into doing something you don't want to do, your marriage will fall apart anyway because you'll end up resenting him. Are you definite about taking over the hotel business?"

"I wasn't, but I am now," Clara declared as she headed out of the kitchen. She could already tell that by morning she was going to be sore in places she didn't even know she had. Thank goodness, she had time to heal before the wedding—if there even was one in the cards for her.

Chapter Nine

Clara had felt so smug when she was giving advice to Sophia about Hunter, but that attitude disappeared with a snap when it was her turn to be in the hot seat. Sophia had sat with her in the lobby until suppertime, and then Clara had insisted that she go spend time with Hunter. They'd gone into Palestine for ice cream, and the hotel seemed as empty as Clara's heart. If this was what it felt like after an argument with your husband, she wasn't sure she even wanted to be married.

She wandered through the lobby, into the kitchen, and then out to the courtyard. The shape of her body still lingered in the dust accumulated through the winter months, when few people came out to the courtyard. She made a mental note to ask Luther, who usually cleaned that part of the place.

She sat down on one of the chairs and watched

the sun paint a bright array of colors in the sky as it sank behind the gate at the end of the courtyard. She'd talked with Sophia about the argument, and now it continued to play in a never-ending loop through her mind—word by word, emotion by emotion. Could she have handled it a different way? Maybe just put the hotel idea out there a bit at a time without hitting Trevor with it all at once?

Millions of stars popped out to dance around the moon, and she stared at them without blinking, still trying to rewrite the whole day—but it didn't work. The argument had happened and she would have to deal with the fallout at some time. Her phone pinged, and she figured it was her sister, so she pulled it out of the pocket of her pajama pants. The message was from Trevor: **I'm sorry. Can we talk?**

She sent him the link to a song by The Chicks titled "Not Ready to Make Nice." The lyrics talked about not being ready to make nice or back down. Someone was still mad as hell. The words seemed to be fitting when they said she wasn't ready to do whatever it was he thought she should.

When she hit Send, she sat back and listened to the song all the way through at least half a dozen times before her phone pinged again: **When will you be ready to talk?**

"I don't know," she whispered as she typed the same words.

She listened to a soliloquy of crickets and tree frogs for an hour, but she didn't get an answer. Evidently, Trevor didn't like *what* she'd said, or what the lyrics to the song said, but she was standing her ground. She would not start out a lifetime commitment with the possibility of regrets, not even if she had to suffer a broken heart.

Finally, she went back into the hotel, waved at Hunter and Sophia, who seemed to be in deep conversation at the kitchen table, and went on upstairs to her room. She sat down in a rocking chair facing the double doors that opened to the balcony and got so lost in her thoughts that the knock on her door startled her.

"Come in," she said.

Sophia poked her head in the door. "I just wanted to let you know that Hunter and I have made the decision to keep the hotel, but only if you're in it with us. We could hire someone to do the books and help us, but we wouldn't trust them like we do you."

"I'm staying," Clara said. "I'll send my resignation or take it to the bank tomorrow."

Sophia came into the room and bent to give her sister a hug. "We won't always agree, and we'll argue."

Clara hugged her back and smiled. "We can't change who we are and we don't really want to, do we?"

Sophia took a couple of steps back and sat down on the edge of the bed. "Have you heard from Trevor?"

"He's sorry, and he wants to talk," Clara answered. "I'm not ready."

"You've always been the peacemaker and you hate confrontation," Sophia said. "What's changed?"

Clara shrugged. "I grew up. You've only got a couple of nights before we get bombarded with folks, and then the wedding is the next day. You need to spend this quiet time with Hunter, not sitting here trying to make me feel better."

"You *are* my sister," Sophia reminded her. "Hunter and I will have a lifetime of nights, but right now you need me."

"Thank you, but I'm fine," Clara assured her and pointed at the door. "I'm going to bed and . . ."

Someone knocked on the balcony doors and Sophia hopped up. She slung the door open to find Trevor standing there with his hat in his hand. She turned around and smiled brightly at Clara. "I guess you aren't the only one who jumps over fences and climbs up dogwood trees. Your knight in dusty armor has arrived, but he doesn't have a rose between his teeth."

"Trevor, I told you that I'm not ready to talk," Clara said.

Trevor took a step back and sat down in a white rocking chair. "Then I'll wait right here on this balcony until you are."

Sophia closed the balcony doors and locked them. "I'm going to my room now. If you need me, just call."

"I won't, but thank you," Clara said. "You and Hunter have a good night."

"Oh, honey, we will." Sophia winked and disappeared out into the hallway.

The Clara who had always hated confrontation of any kind wanted to go out on the balcony and have it out—again—with Trevor. The Clara who wasn't ready to forgive and forget stretched out on the bed and stared up at the ceiling. Sheer mental exhaustion took over, and she fell asleep a few minutes later and didn't wake up until sunlight flowed in the window and warmed her face the next morning.

She got out of bed, cracked the door enough to see that Trevor had kept his word about not leaving the balcony until she talked to him and was slumped down in the rocking chair with his hat over his eyes. She tiptoed down the stairs, made a pot of coffee, and carried two full mugs back up to her room.

She set them on the side table by the bed and eased the balcony doors open. Then she picked up the coffee and took it outside, sat down in the second rocking chair, and put the coffee on a small round table between the chairs. She picked up the mug with sunflowers on it, took a sip, and held the warm mug in her hands. It felt good in the brisk morning breeze.

The smell of the coffee must have awakened Trevor because he sat up, adjusted his hat, and rolled his neck around to get the kinks out. "Are we ready to talk?"

"Depends," she answered and pointed to the extra mug. "That's for you."

He picked it up and took the first sip. "Am I forgiven?"

"Not until we come to an understanding," Clara answered. "I'm going to work here at the hotel five days a week. If there's a full house, I might have to come in for half a day on Saturday, but Sundays should always be fairly free. Can you live with that?"

"My mother and my sisters-in-law have raked me over the hot coals," Trevor said. "They reminded me that living on the ranch and working there was their decision, and that I was a total jackass for expecting you to bend to what I wanted. I was angry with them at first, but then I realized that if you regretted doing what I wanted, you would be miserable, and I love you too much to be the one who hurts you in any way."

"I didn't ask you if you'd gotten in trouble," Clara said. "I asked if you could live with my decision."

"Yes, I can," Trevor answered without hesitation.

"Then you are forgiven," Clara told him.

Trevor set his coffee aside. "What if you and Sophia hate working together?"

"Then we'll work it out between us," she answered.

"What about our children?" Trevor asked.

"We'll cross that bridge when we have kids," Clara replied. "Like the old song says, 'One Day at a Time.' Let's plan for tomorrow, but let's enjoy today."

"So, you aren't mad at me anymore?" Trevor asked.

"Are you still upset with me?" she shot back at him. "In five years are you going to wish you'd married a woman like your sisters-in-law? That you had a wife who loved ranching as much as you do? I'm willing to compromise in this relationship. What do you want?"

He removed his hat and looked her right in the eye. "I want you, Clara." Then he stood up, moved to drop down on one knee in front of her, and took her hand in his. "Clara Delaney, you are the love of my life. Just thinking about my life without you in it is unbearable. Will you marry me?"

"You've already proposed," she whispered.

"Yes, but I'm doing it again, just so you know how much I love you," he said.

"Yes, Trevor Richmond, I will marry you." She wrapped her arms around his neck and then leaned back and kissed him. "I've heard that makeup sex is the best. Shall we see if the hype is all it's made out to be or do you need to get back to the ranch to work?"

He scooped her up in his arms and carried her through the double doors into her bedroom. "My family told me not to come home without settling this with you, so darlin', I've got all day to see if the hype is true. And honey, I realize now that the ranch comes second to you and always will." He kicked the doors shut with the heel of his cowboy boot.

Chapter Ten

"Hello the hotel!" Mama Lizzy yelled as she came through the lobby and into the kitchen on Friday morning. "I expected to see a parking lot full of vehicles out front!"

"Not yet." Clara met her in the middle of the room and hugged her. "We missed you so much."

Sophia dried her hands and then made it a three-way hug. "No one has arrived, but we're expecting a few to be here by suppertime. Luther will be here any minute and then we'll be run out of his kitchen."

"I'm surprised he's let us in here while he's been out on vacation this last week," Lizzy said.

Clara led her grandmother to the table. "Come sit down and have a snack with us. We've got doughnuts from that shop you like and coffee is made. How was your trip?"

Lizzy sat down and picked up a glazed doughnut from the box. "The trip was so good that I'm not sticking around until the end of summer. Marlene is looking into an Alaskan cruise for the two of us in June."

Sophia set a tray with three mugs and the full pot of coffee on the table and then took a seat across from Clara. She wasn't sure if she should make the announcement right then about the three of them making the decision to run the hotel or if she should wait for Hunter.

"Trevor and I had a big argument," Clara blurted out.

That's not the way I expected to start this conversation, Sophia thought.

"I helped her through it," Sophia said. "I found her hanging from a dogwood tree, trying to get up to the balcony. The front doors were locked because she was supposed to be at the ranch. I don't know why she thought she could get through the balcony doors any better."

"I thought they were unlocked." Clara shot a dirty look her way.

"Did you break any limbs off the trees?" Lizzy asked and then giggled.

"No, she didn't," Sophia replied, "but I do wish I'd taken a picture for you."

"Me too," Lizzy said and then turned to face Clara. "Start at the beginning and tell me what's happened since I've been gone. I know about Sophia and Hunter losing their jobs, but I need to hear from you, Clara."

"They fought because he was being a pompous pig from hell," Sophia said.

Clara cut her eyes around at her sister. "But he

apologized and changed his pig attitude into a sweet one, so he's got a chance of getting into heaven."

"What did you fight about?" Lizzy asked. "I thought you two were the perfect couple who would be able to say that they'd never had an argument on their fiftieth anniversary."

"Guess we'll have to give that trophy back," Clara said. "Maybe Sophia and Hunter will get it."

Sophia picked up a doughnut with chocolate icing. "That ship has already sailed."

"Do you have a trophy for no arguments, Mama Lizzy?" Clara asked.

"Lord, no!" Lizzy gasped. "Your grandfather and I had a doozy of a blowup the day before our wedding. I was ready to call the whole thing off. He thought that I should sell the hotel and be one of those little wives who stays home and raises babies."

"History really does repeat itself," Clara said with half a giggle, and then went on to tell the whole story from start to finish. "I guess men are the same today as they were back then."

Lizzy reached over and laid a hand on her granddaughter's arm. "Honey, human nature hasn't changed since the days of Adam and Eve. But women have fought for the right to make their own decisions since the beginning of time, and I'm proud of you for doing so. Does this mean y'all are going to take over the hotel, then?"

"Yes, ma'am," Sophia and Clara chorused together.

To Sophia, who admittedly liked fanfare, the answer seemed a lot less dramatic than she expected. "Because Hunter and I won't have a honeymoon, we'll be ready to learn the ropes starting on Monday. I noticed that the rooms are full that night."

Lizzy beamed and tears dammed up behind her eyelids. "You don't know how happy you've made me. The family legacy moves on to the next generation. Your ancestors would be so proud."

"We'll do our best to keep the place vintage," Sophia promised.

"Don't cry, Mama Lizzy," Clara begged. "We won't even change out those old landline phones."

Lizzy wiped her eyes with a paper napkin. "The wedding will be your celebration, but it will also be mine. Can I announce the news when I give the toast?"

"Of course you can," Sophia told her.

"I don't have time to arrange a honeymoon for either of you now, but next year I will come back and run the place for you for one week so you can have one for your first anniversary. Maybe you'll even choose to go on a cruise."

Sophia raised both her dark brows. "Separately?"

"Not on your life," Lizzy declared. "One week, and you have to compromise about where you'll go and go together. I'll pay for everything as your anniversary gift, but I'm only going to be tied down to the hotel for one week total."

"Well," Sophia said with a long sigh. "We've got a year to argue about it."

Clara reached across the table and laid a hand on her sister's. "Just think what fun we'll have fighting about it for a whole year. I hear folks coming in the front doors. Are we ready to check them in on our first day on the job?"

Lizzy took her last sip of coffee and pushed back

her chair. "Oh, no! Today and tomorrow, this place still belongs to me, but y'all can come on out and introduce me to your new families and friends. On Monday you can take over operations."

Sophia led the way out of the kitchen. "That's April Fools' Day."

"That, darlin' sister, will be our lucky day from now on," Clara said.

Chapter Eleven

Clara thought the alarm on her phone was telling her it was time to wake up on Saturday morning. Without even opening her eyes, she rolled over and reached to get it from the nightstand, but when she picked it up and hit what she thought was the Snooze button, Trevor's voice filled the room.

"Happy wedding day, darlin'!" Excitement was in his tone.

She opened one eye to see that she was FaceTiming with him. "Good mornin' and happy wedding day to you. We aren't supposed to see each other until the wedding. Mama Lizzy says it's bad luck."

"We're not really seeing each other, only blurry pictures on the phone. I just wanted to be the first voice you heard this morning and to wish you a wonderful day. I can't wait until this evening when

I can carry you over the threshold into our new home," Trevor said. "Remember, I love you."

"I love you too," Clara said as she threw back the covers and crawled out of bed. She could hear folks already up and around out in the hallway, and the blended aromas of bacon and coffee wafted through the air-conditioning vents.

She had brushed her teeth, pulled up her blond hair into a messy bun, and was on the way out the door when she stopped in her tracks. Today, this very day, she was getting married, and suddenly her slippers were filled with concrete and her feet were glued to the hardwood floor.

Sophia came out of her room a few doors down and met her. "Cold feet?"

"How did you know?" Clara whispered.

"Because an hour ago mine were freezing," Sophia answered in a low voice. "But then I remembered all the reasons why I love Hunter, and I thought about this new adventure we're starting on, not only in marriage but in our career."

"Did they warm up?" Clara asked.

Sophia looped her arm with her sister's. "Yes, they did. Did you reach across the bed this morning and feel a little fear that something was wrong because Trevor wasn't there?"

"Nope," Clara answered, "but only because he woke me up with a FaceTime phone call."

Sophia took a step toward the wide staircase. "I wish now that I'd only had one bridesmaid. The six I chose kept me up half the night, and after all these years away from my college sorority, I hardly know them anymore."

Clara couldn't keep the smile off her face. "I visited with Granny for a little while at supper, but then she said she needed her beauty sleep for the wedding. I got a wonderful night's rest. You should have snuck out and come over to my room like you used to do when you had a nightmare."

"You were the calm one, and I always thought that monsters wouldn't faze you," Sophia said as she started down the stairs. "We should have had the wedding in the lobby. That way we could float down these stairs in our wedding dresses."

"That could have worked if it had rained, but the weatherman is calling for a beautiful day and the dogwoods are putting on their show out there. Let's sneak out through the office door and see if the people are already here setting up chairs," Clara suggested.

Sophia took a detour before any of the early bird risers could stop them to chat, and in a few seconds she and Clara were standing in the courtyard, watching the cleaning staff power wash the concrete to a beautiful shine.

"This makes it so real," Clara whispered. She pinched herself to be sure she wasn't dreaming. It smarted, so she was pretty sure that she and Trevor had survived their first major argument and were really getting married. In just a little while folks would be bustling about, setting up chairs and the archway down at the end of the courtyard. The dogwood trees were in full bloom and the cleaning crew had already washed the ornate back fence. Everything was coming together—just as Mama Lizzy had told them it would.

"It will be even more real once we see everything all set up," Sophia declared. "I've been thinking that we should offer our hotel as a wedding venue to other couples. How do you feel about that?"

"That's a great idea," Clara agreed.

"We'll talk more about it later." Sophia tugged on her arm and steered her back into the hotel. "Right now we should go on in and have some breakfast with everyone. Then we've got hairdressers, makeup folks, and a manicurist all arriving throughout the day."

"I'm glad Mama Lizzy has the conference room set up for us or we'd be tumbling all over each other," Clara said as she and her sister headed back into the hotel office side by side.

Lizzy looked up from behind her desk and grinned. "Well, well, well! Look at you two getting along with each other and not fighting."

"It's a miracle, but remember what you said when we were kids?" Clara asked.

"I said a lot, trying to get you two raised up," Lizzy replied.

"'Miracles only happen in a moment,'" Clara reminded her.

"'And then they're gone,'" Sophia finished the sentence for her sister.

Lizzy stood up and rounded the desk. "Then I guess I'd better bask in the glory of the moment."

"Mama Lizzy, I want . . . to . . . say . . ." Clara stammered.

"Don't you dare cry or you'll make me start, and you know it takes hours to get the red out of my eyes once I begin sobbing," Sophia warned. "I swear, I'll trip you as we walk down the aisle if you don't suck it up."

"Thank you, Mama Lizzy, for everything," Clara managed to get out past the lump in her throat. "For raising us when you didn't have to, for being both mother and father to us, and for . . ." she swiped at the tears streaming down her cheeks, "for loving us when we weren't so lovable."

"Well, crap." Sophia grabbed the box of tissues from the desk and jerked out a fistful. "And for giving us the hotel when we don't deserve it, and for settling all our arguments in the past, and for the times you'll probably take care of us in the future. We could go on and on for the rest of this day and not even scratch the surface."

Clara swallowed several times, but the rock in her throat was still there. "But we want you to know that we love and appreciate everything, and we're sorry for ever taking you for granted."

Lizzy took the box from Sophia, pulled out a few tissues for herself, and then passed it over to Clara. "I'm proud of both of you, and even with your bickering I wouldn't trade a minute of the past for the promise of another hundred years of the future. You've made me a proud mother and I love both of you beyond words." She gave them each a hug. "And I'm glad we've had this little emotional jag before the wedding. We *all* would have had red eyes if we'd waited until then to talk about this."

Clara wiped her cheeks and pasted on a smile. "We're some lucky women to have one another."

"Amen to that," Lizzy agreed.

"Both past and future," Sophia said with a nod.

The words—past and future—stuck in Clara's mind. The past had molded all of them into what they were today, and she was grateful for every minute and every experience as she looked forward to the future right here at Dogwood Inn.

Trevor's granny was the first one in the crowd gathering in the hotel lobby to meet the three of them when they walked out of the office. "This is such a treat to get to stay here in the Dogwood Inn for a couple of nights. When I got married Wilbur and I spent our honeymoon right here and I felt like I was floating on air. We even got the same room we had back then. I don't know if Clara did that on purpose or if it was just by chance, but thank you. I'm so glad that Clara and Sophia are going to manage the hotel and keep it just like it is. I told Wilbur last night that we're going to start coming back here every single year on our anniversary to celebrate."

Several members of Trevor's family gathered around, and Clara scanned the bunch of them for her intended. Then she remembered that he, his brothers, and his father were at the ranch, along with his nephews. Only his mother, sisters-in-law, and nieces had spent the night in the hotel.

"Missing Trevor, aren't you?" his mother asked.

"Yes, I am," Clara admitted and wished she had asked all the sisters-in-law to be bridesmaids so the wedding pictures would be more balanced.

Her grandmother's eyes twinkled and she nudged Clara on the shoulder. "You could ask them right now. Sophia's bridesmaids are carrying a single red rose and your matron of honor is carrying two daisies. There's still time for the florist to whip up four more like that."

"But . . ." Clara started. She wondered if Mama Lizzy could read her mind.

"I'll do it," Lizzy said.

"What if they're offended because I waited until the last minute?" Clara asked.

"What color dresses have your sisters-in-law chosen to wear today?" Lizzy asked.

"Granny picked out a yellow one when we were thinking the wedding would be in a barn with lots of sunflowers and daisies," Molly, the oldest son's wife, answered. "So we all chose that color to make a pretty family picture."

"That's great!" Lizzy said. "I know it's last minute and we already had the rehearsal and all, but would y'all please serve as bridesmaids? I got this brilliant idea that each of you could walk down the aisle with one of Sophia's ladies. A yellow and a red to tie in the colors for the whole wedding, and the pictures will be gorgeous."

"We would be honored." Daisy, another sister-in-law, beamed.

"Thank you," Clara said. "I should have thought of that before now."

"No worries," Tiffany said.

"We'd do anything for Clara. She's our hero for putting up with Trevor," Penelope added with a giggle. "Does that mean we get our hair and makeup done too?"

"You bet it does," Sophia answered.

For the first time Clara felt like today was her special day as well as her sister's.

* * *

Sophia eased the kitchen door out onto the patio open just enough to see Granny and Delia, her maid of honor, making their way slowly down the aisle toward the archway in front of the gates. Only a few of the chairs were empty. One side was decorated with bright yellow bows and the other with red. Later Lizzy told them the tables that had been pushed to the back would be scattered around the courtyard with the same chairs placed around them.

"It's perfect," Sophia whispered. "Even the dogwoods have hung onto their blossoms just for us."

"Can you see Trevor? Does he look nervous?" Clara asked.

Sophia held her bouquet with one hand and put the other one on her sister's arm. "He looks a little nervous, but he's smiling. Hunter looks like he's the only rooster at a coyote convention," Sophia said. "His whole family loves this hotel, which shocked him to no end. He thought they'd think it was hickish."

"'Vintage' is the word," Lizzy informed her in a serious tone. "I like his folks and hope they come back to visit y'all real often. Clara, you need to remember that anytime you and Trevor need a night away from the ranch, your room is always available. Sounds like our music is starting."

"Mama He's Crazy" by the Judds started playing.

Sophia frowned. "That's not the traditional wedding song."

"No, darlin' girls, it's not, but it sure seemed appropriate to me," Lizzy said with a wide grin. "Sling those doors open and let's get this show on the road."

"Is the rest of the music the same as we practiced last night?" Sophia whispered as the three of them took their places at the end of the aisle.

"Yep, but I've chosen some special ones for the reception," Lizzy answered. "Now put on your best smiles. This is a very special and wonderful day."

A soft spring breeze made the dogwood blossoms dance as she, Clara, and Mama Lizzy took the first step down the aisle. Hunter's black suit fit him just right, and he'd chosen a red tie to go with her colors. The expression on his face, so full of love, put a smile on her own face that wasn't forced or fake. Right at that moment the rest of the world disappeared except for them.

Clara scanned the crowd of family and friends for a second or two as she slowly made her way toward the archway with the setting sun behind it. Everything was beyond what she ever could have imagined. She felt like Cinderella at the royal ball, and there was her prince waiting for her in his shined black boots and his cowboy hat set just right on his head. She had it better than the fairy-tale princess, though, because she and her cowboy would ride off together later that night.

When they reached the right spot the preacher asked, "Who gives these women to be married to these men?"

"No one," Lizzy said. "I will never give my girls away to anyone, but I will share Sophia with Hunter, and Clara with Trevor. Be good to them, but don't always let them have their way. Love them above and beyond just saying the words.

Prove your love to them in all the little ways every single day."

"Yes, ma'am," Trevor and Hunter said at the same time.

Lizzy kissed each of her granddaughters on the cheek and then said, "And the same goes for you two."

A few snickers were heard in the crowd, but most of the folks were nodding in agreement as she stepped back and took her seat in the first row of chairs.

"I feel like Lizzy should be doing this service," the preacher said, and then went on with a purely traditional ceremony.

Clara looked into Trevor's eyes as the preacher talked, and she heard the words he said, not with her ears as much as with her heart. When she promised to love him and respect him until death parted them and said her own personal vows, she meant them with all her soul.

After Sophia and Hunter exchanged vows the preacher pronounced them husbands and wives, "And now you grooms may kiss your beautiful brides."

"When I Found You," by Jasmine Rae played as the two newly wedded couples walked down the aisle. Clara and Trevor first, with Sophia and Hunter following behind. When they reached the office door Trevor took Clara in his arms and began a slow country waltz right there. "This song says it all, Mrs. Richmond."

"For the first time in my life I don't have to share my last name with Sophia," she whispered.

"I heard that and, sister, I'm just as happy about that as you are," Sophia said as she wrapped her arms around Hunter's neck and pulled his mouth to hers for another kiss.

"I agree with my new brother-in-law—this song does say it all," Hunter said as he began to dance with Sophia and sing along with the lyrics.

"Amen," Sophia and Clara said at the same time.

COWBOY TRUE

Stacy Finz

Chapter One

Jace Dalton's job as Mill County sheriff didn't ordinarily entail chasing hundreds of goats off the
road. But here he was, running across a two-lane
highway, waving his hat in the air, herding livestock as traffic came to a standstill.

Rush hour in Dry Creek.

It would've been funny if he wasn't in a hurry.
He was already ten minutes late for a state-of-the-
ranch meeting with his two cousins and his cousin-
in-law at the coffee shop for breakfast.

A pickup truck pulled past the line of stopped
vehicles. Jace feared the driver was about to speed
through the bottleneck. Goats be damned. But
then the pickup veered over to the shoulder and a
kid of about nineteen bounded out of the truck.

"Sorry, Sheriff," he called as he joined Jace in
chasing the goats off the road. "They must've gotten loose."

Ya think?

"We had them over at the Lloyd place, clearing brush. They probably got through an opening in the fence."

The Lloyds' fencing was sketchy at best.

"I hope you've got someone over there fixing it. Otherwise, they'll just get out again." The kid didn't seem like the sharpest tool in the shed.

"My dad's there now. And my brothers are on the way."

Just then, another pickup with a livestock trailer slid in next to the kid's and two beefy-looking fellows lumbered out with a pair of Australian shepherds. Between the four of them and the dogs, they got the goats safely back to the Lloyds' property, which was less than a quarter mile away.

"Thanks, Sheriff." One of the beefy guys shook Jace's hand. "It won't happen again, sir."

Jace hoofed it back to his truck, saw that traffic was flowing smoothly again, and headed into town. By the time he got to the coffee shop, Cash, Sawyer, and Tuff were mopping up the last of their eggs with Jimmy Ray's homemade biscuits.

"Where you been?" Cash pulled out the chair next to him.

Jace plopped down. "It's a long story. Hand me the coffee, would you?"

Sawyer reached over to the coffee station, snagged the pot off the warmer, and poured Jace a cup. They'd been coming to the coffee shop their whole lives and made themselves at home here. Laney was busy waiting on another table anyway. She and Jimmy Ray owned the restaurant and were as good as family.

"I presume you started the meeting without me." Jace took a sip from his mug. He had a feeling he was going to need the whole pot before the morning was over. Besides the goat fiasco, Grady had missed the bus this morning and Jace had to drive him to school. That was after his eldest, Travis, who was home from college, had woken up covered in poison oak. At least Charlie, Jace's wife, was handling that situation.

"We're solid," Sawyer said. "Cash went over the books, and it looks like this year Dry Creek Village is on the road to profitability."

"No kidding." The first good news of Jace's day.

When Jace and his cousins inherited Dry Creek Ranch from their late grandfather, it had been a flailing 500-acre, cow-calf operation with back taxes the size of California. To save the ranch from foreclosure, the four of them had taken a portion of the land and turned it into an agricultural-themed shopping center, including a florist, Tuff's saddlery, a specialty food market, a farmhouse furniture store called Refind, and a steak house run by Sawyer's wife, celebrity chef Gina DeRose.

They hoped that if they built it, they'd come. Except for a while it seemed as if they'd miscalculated because the village wasn't taking off the way they'd hoped. But with perseverance and the Gina DeRose name, business picked up and it had been going gangbusters ever since.

"According to my estimation, we'll be able to pay off the last of the back taxes, each get a decent draw, and put some money in the bank for lean times," Cash said.

"What about the cattle part of the equation?" Tuff asked, and three pairs of eyes turned to Jace.

"We're a little ahead. Beef prices are up this year. But don't go buying any big-ticket items just yet. Let's see how we do at market first."

Jace waved Laney over from across the room. "What does a guy have to do to get some breakfast around here?" He winked, then gave her a hug.

"It's about time you made an appearance. These boys have been waiting on you. You want your regular?"

"Yes, ma'am. But add a side of grits. I'm starved."

"You got it." She kissed Jace on the cheek and went off to put in the order.

Done with business, the four of them turned to other conversation, including Cash's cases as investigator for the Bureau of Livestock Identification. Unfortunately, cattle rustling was still alive and well in California's Sierra Foothills. Sawyer's next article for whatever fancy magazine he was writing for these days. And Tuff's latest leather project. Angie's husband was regarded as one of the top saddle makers in the country.

"How's Charlie doing?" Cash asked, addressing the elephant in the room. Everyone, Jace most of all, was on edge about her pregnancy. She was high risk, having had two previous miscarriages. The first one, a late-stage miscarriage, was at the hands of an abusive boyfriend, who Jace had put behind bars.

"So far so good. We're just taking it one day at a time."

"We're all pulling for her." Cash pushed away from the table. "As much as I'd like to sit around shooting the breeze, I've got cow cop duties. See you all Sunday night." It was spring, which meant they took turns hosting a weekly barbecue. Because they all lived on the ranch, no one had to travel far.

Tuff, who had to open his saddlery shop, followed Cash out, leaving just Jace and Sawyer.

"I'll sit with you while you eat."

Laney brought Jace's breakfast to the table. "Here you go, Sheriff Hot Stuff."

Sawyer let out a bark of laughter. "Hot stuff?"

Jace pinned Sawyer with a scowl. "I wouldn't talk if I were you. You look like hell these days."

Sawyer smirked. "You'll feel my pain soon enough."

"What are you talking about? I'm still feeling your pain. You think teenage boys are any easier than a baby girl? If you do, you're crazy."

"It's been a while since you had to deal with the terrible twos."

"Mia's only eighteen months. Jeez, don't you know your own kid's age?" Jace jabbed Sawyer in the arm.

"The thing is my daughter is so advanced that she may as well be two."

Jace rolled his eyes and washed down a bite of chicken fried steak with another slug of coffee.

"I need a bigger place, man. Some alone time with my wife," Sawyer said.

"Did you talk to that architect Aubrey knows about expanding your place?"

"Not yet. But soon because one bedroom isn't going to cut it much longer."

Jace laughed and shoveled another forkful of

grits into his mouth. "There's always the Skank for a quick romantic getaway." It was actually named the Swank, a roadside motel next to a biker bar out on the highway. Locals called it the Skank for obvious reasons.

Sawyer shook his head. "Are you almost done gorging yourself because I've got a deadline to meet."

"Get out of here. I'll see you Sunday night."

Jace finished his breakfast, spent a little time talking sports with Jimmy Ray in the kitchen, and headed to his office.

The sheriff's department was in the Civic Center. Unlike most of the historical buildings in Dry Creek—some dating back to the gold rush—the sheriff's department was a nondescript, twentieth-century building. Jace's office was even blander. White walls, a sofa and chair, a small conference table, a few certificates on the wall, and a collection of framed pictures of Travis, Grady, and Charlie on his desk.

The truth was he'd rather be out in the field than sitting in a stuffy office anyway. But as Mill County's top cop, the bureaucracy and paperwork kept him inside most days.

He closed his door, hoping for a few hours of peace to go through reports. Annabeth, his assistant, had already left a stack of messages on his desk. While waiting for his computer to boot up, he called Charlie.

"How'd it go with Travis?"

"The doc gave him prednisone. His first week home for summer break and he gets poison oak. Poor baby."

Jace was no stranger to poison oak. Every Dalton on the ranch had had an intimate relationship with it a time or two. "He'll be feeling better in a few hours. How about you?"

"I'm feeling great. As soon as I get Travis settled in, I'll probably head over to Refind and get some work done."

"Don't push yourself too much, okay?"

"I won't. Travis is calling me, so I better go."

"Charlie? I love you."

"Love you too."

As soon as he signed off, line one on his office phone lit up. Annabeth.

"What's up?"

"Grady's school called. Principal Martinez asked that you call her ASAP. Don't ask, I have no idea."

"Terrific," he said under his breath. "Thanks, Annabeth."

Jace didn't even have to look it up; he had Marta Martinez's phone number on speed dial.

"Hi, Jace." She answered on the second ring. Usually, she was too harried to take a coffee break, let alone answer her phone. Dry Creek High School was understaffed, and on any given day Marta was juggling four different roles at the same time. She'd taken the job two years ago and the district was lucky to have her.

"What did he do this time?" Grady was a good kid, kind and polite. But his energy levels were through the roof and he liked to play the class clown.

"Nothing. He's fine. But there was a woman here maybe twenty minutes ago. She came to the office and asked to take Grady out of class. I'd never seen her before and when Doreen asked her who she was, she said she was Grady's mother. When Doreen told her she knew Grady's mother, she walked off in a huff."

A sense of unease lodged itself in the pit of Jace's gut. "Did she give you a name?"

"We didn't get that far. I called you as soon as she left."

"I'm on my way over. Make sure she isn't on campus and that Grady is in class." Jace was already moving.

"Do you know who she is?"

"Just don't let that woman anywhere near my kid."

Chapter Two

"Jace! Jace, stop!"

But Jace continued to race down the corridor to Grady's classroom.

"Jace, for God's sake, Doreen saw her get in a car and drive away and Grady's teacher has been notified." Marta was right behind him. "Slow down, please. He's fine. Grady is fine. And if you barge into his classroom, you'll scare him and the other kids."

She was right, of course. But Jace needed to see Grady for himself. It was visceral, not because he was a cop but because he was a parent.

It was after eleven. Freshman Spanish. Jace knew where it was because he himself had taken Spanish in this very high school when he was fourteen.

He got to Grady's classroom, slid to a stop, and peered inside the door's glass window. There was

Grady, sitting in the fourth row with his head bowed, taking a quiz. He'd studied hard for it, practicing vocabulary words with Jace and Charlie the previous evening.

He ducked away before his son saw him and let out a long breath.

"You know we would never release a student to the care of anyone who isn't authorized, right?" Marta had her hands on her hips and was chastising him like he was one of her students.

"I know the protocol, Marta." Hell, he'd helped write it.

"What's going on, Jace? Do you know who this woman is?"

"What did she look like?"

"Gosh, it happened so fast. The only reason I saw her at all is because I happened to come in off the quad while she was talking to Doreen."

"Let's talk to Doreen, then."

The moment they walked into the office together, Doreen rose from her chair behind the counter and held out her arms to Jace for a hug. "What's going on, Jace? Who do you think she is?"

"I need a full description, Doreen. Anything you can remember, any little detail, is important."

"Now you're scaring me."

From the moment he'd talked to Marta, he had his suspicions. It was like an instant premonition; he could even feel his ex-wife's presence. But for Mary Ann to show up after more than six years of radio silence . . . well, it didn't make sense. Of course, he couldn't rule out that it was someone else. Although Mill County was relatively small and peaceful, being sheriff came with a fair number of enemies. And although Charlie's ex was safely locked up, Corbin could have friends on the outside willing to exact revenge for him.

"Let's start with the car and work backward," Jace said. "Marta said you saw her drive away. Any chance you got a license plate number?"

Doreen covered her mouth and shook her head. "Oh, dear, I should've taken a picture. It just happened so fast."

"Don't worry about it. Most people miss it." He gave her arm a reassuring squeeze. "How about a description of the car?"

"It was white and compact. Other than that, I didn't think to look at the make or the model. Nothing like this has ever happened before. It's Dry Creek, for heaven's sake."

"I know. White and compact is good." He tried to be encouraging, but it sure would've been helpful if she'd gotten a license plate number. "What did she look like?"

"Uh, pretty. Blond, blue eyes. About my height. Thin build. About your age, maybe a little younger. It's hard to tell."

Mary Ann.

"Did she give you a name?"

"No, only that Grady Dalton was her son and she wanted to speak to him."

"What happened after she asked to talk to Grady?" Jace asked.

"I said Charlie was Grady's mother and I think I said something about calling the police. But I can't remember for sure. All I know is that she left and something told me to follow her outside. That's when I saw her get in the white car and drive away." Doreen looked ready to collapse. "I'm sorry, Jace. I should've done more. She just caught me off guard."

"You did great, Doreen. Really, you've been extremely helpful."

It had to be Mary Ann. The matching description and the fact that she'd said she was Grady's mother. Too many coincidences. And Jace didn't believe in coincidences.

He turned to Marta. "It sounds like it was my ex-wife, Mary Ann. I don't know if she still goes by Dalton or uses her maiden name, Culbertson. She's Grady's biological mother. But she's been absent from both my sons' lives for a long time. I have full custody. And for now, under no circumstances is she allowed to have any contact with Grady. If she comes around here again, I'd appreciate you calling me. I'm sorry for the inconvenience."

He started to leave, needing space to wrap his head around the fact that Mary Ann was here in Dry Creek after leaving him, Travis, and Grady without so much as a glance in her review mirror. In the beginning she sent the boys an occasional birthday card or a small trinket from wherever she happened to be. Mexico, Costa Rica, Portugal, Spain. Last he'd heard, she was living with some dude in the French countryside. But who really knew with her?

"Jace, is she dangerous?" Marta asked as he made it to the door.

"No. Just flaky." And a crappy mother, but Jace kept that to himself. "Still, I don't want her ambushing Grady. He should hear about her from me first." Both his boys should hear it from him before Mary Ann decided to crash into their lives on one of her misguided whims.

He drove back to the sheriff's department, sat in his truck, and decided he needed a couple of mental health hours or whatever the hell they were calling it these days. On his way home, he called Annabeth and told her he was off the clock but available by phone.

It wasn't until he drove through the Dry Creek Ranch gate that he could breathe again. This place had always been his refuge. Even as a kid, when has parents and baby brother had been killed by a drunken driver, it was the ranch and his grandparents who had salved his grief and made him whole again.

Grandpa Dalton had loved the ranch as if it was his fourth son and built it into a profitable cattle enterprise. But when California suffered drought after drought he'd had to cull the herd. Without the revenue stream, the ranch had fallen into decay. By the time Grandpa Dalton died, the ranch, all except for the beautiful home he'd built for Jace's now late grandmother, was on its last legs.

That was where Jace, Cash, Sawyer, and Angie came in. Instead of selling to a hungry developer, who would've turned the Daltons' five hundred acres into a planned community of minimansions, swimming pools, and golf courses, the four of them had turned things around. And although his cousins had grown up elsewhere, they all called Dry Creek Ranch their homes now.

He pulled up to the sprawling ranch house, the

place he'd called home since his parents' deaths, and cut the engine. The dogs, Sherpa and Benson, greeted him with their usual slobbery exuberance. Scout, his favorite hound, had gotten cancer last year and they'd had to put him down. He was buried by the big oak tree down by the horse barn.

The TV was on in the house and Jace followed the sound to the family room, where he found Travis lying on the couch.

"How you doing, kiddo?"

Travis shrugged but looked miserable just the same. "How come you're home?"

"Wanted to check in with you and Charlie. Where is she?"

"Down at the barn." That's what they called Refind because Charlie and Cash's wife, Aubrey, had commandeered one of the old ranch barns to use for their furniture store and design business.

"You eat?"

"Mom made me a sandwich." There was a half-eaten PB and J on a plate on the coffee table next to a glass of milk.

"You going to eat that?" Jace grabbed the un-eaten half and took a bite.

"Guess not," Travis said.

"You okay here while I drive down to the barn?"

"Go for it. But bring me back one of those big cookies from the Dalton Market."

"I see you're milking this poison oak thing for all it's worth."

"Don't forget," Travis called as Jace headed out the door.

He'd get Travis his cookie and one for Grady too. He'd also be waiting for his younger son when

Grady got out of school today. Jace wasn't leaving anything to chance.

He found Charlie behind the barn, painting an old china hutch, making it look new again. She'd made a lucrative business out of upcycling old furniture pieces she bought at garage sales, antique markets, craigslist, even stuff she rescued from the landfill. She and Aubrey had made quite a name for themselves in the Sierra Foothills and had furnished and decorated homes from Lake Tahoe, an hour up the road, to three hours away in San Francisco. They even had clients as far away as Vail and Park City who wanted to hire them to dude up their vacation homes.

"Should you be painting?" He came up behind her and wrapped his arms around her swollen belly.

"Hey, what are you doing home?" She turned in his arms and kissed him.

"It's been a day." He huffed out a breath. "I'll tell you about it. But first more of this." He draped her arms over his shoulders and finished what she had started with a much deeper kiss. Man, he loved the taste of her and the sweet way she hummed her pleasure as his mouth devoured hers.

The kiss was over too soon, but if he kept going like this, he'd never make it back to work.

"Can we go inside for a few minutes?" He wanted privacy, but he also wanted his wife off her feet and away from paint fumes.

They took the back door that bypassed the store and followed the hallway to Charlie's office. It was a closet-size room with a desk, a laptop, two chairs, and walls that were covered in magazine pages, paint chips, and fabric swatches. Charlie called them her inspiration walls.

"Where's Aubrey?" He loved his cousin's wife, who also happened to be one of his best friends, but she had a big mouth. It was only a matter of time before the whole family found out about Mary Ann and how she'd surfaced at Grady's school. But for now he wanted to keep it under wraps until he figured out his next move.

"She's in Sacramento, doing a bid for a couple who want to redo their pool house."

"Who's minding the store?" Sometimes his cousin Angie helped out. She was better at keeping confidences than Aubrey, but in this instance it was best to keep her out of the loop too.

"That nice girl who sometimes works at the floral shop. Kelly. She and her boyfriend are saving for a wedding and she can use the hours."

Jace had no clue who Kelly was, but as long as she wasn't one of his busybody family members, he didn't care. "So Marta Martinez called me today."

"Uh-oh, what did Grady do?"

"Nothing. There was a woman at the school today claiming to be Grady's mom and wanted Doreen to get him out of class so she could talk to him."

"What?" Charlie's eyes grew large. "Who was she, Jace?"

Jace let the silence stretch between them, giving her time to figure it out.

"Oh, no, you don't think it was Mary Ann?"

"Doreen's description matches. And who else could it be?"

"I don't know, some psycho. It's not like you

don't hear or read every day about some awful person going into a school and—"

He cocked his brows. "You trying to protect my delicate sensibilities?"

"I can't bear to say it. My point is how do we know it's Mary Ann?"

"We don't for sure. But if it walks like a duck . . ."

"Why would she show up after all these years without calling or somehow notifying you? It doesn't make sense."

"Nothing about her ever made sense." Who leaves their children? He could forgive her for leaving him, but Travis and Grady? Never.

"What are we going to do?"

It meant a lot to Jace that Charlie always used "we" when they were talking about the boys. Ever since she'd come into their lives, she'd fixed a part of them that Jace hadn't even realized was broken. And the boys had welcomed her into the family with open hearts. They loved her as much as Jace did.

"I don't know. A part of me hopes this is a one off, that she was in the area and showed up to the school on impulse. She's got family in Roseville, so it wouldn't be out of the realm of possibility. And maybe she'll just go away. Also not out of the realm of possibility because leaving is her MO."

Charlie looked skeptical. "I'd say that's wishful thinking. Extremely wishful."

"Probably. But before I go off half-cocked and tell the boys, I'd like to check it out first. Do some nosing around."

"Okay. But what if she shows up again? Grady's got all kinds of activities outside school. What if she comes to one of his Little League games or a 4-H event? It seems like we should give both Travis and Grady a little warning."

She was right of course. But he wasn't ready to shake up their worlds for a woman who was as unreliable as his grandfather's old John Deere tractor.

"Just a day or two," he said. "I'm not going to let Mary Ann wreck them again."

"Wrecked" was an understatement. After Mary Ann left the boys were complete shells of their former selves. For years they worried themselves sick that Jace wouldn't come home, that he would up and leave them like their mother did. Grady slept with a sock puppet Mary Ann made him until he was nearly ten years old. And poor Travis believed he had to assume the role of second parent until Charlie came along. If it hadn't been for Jace's aunts, uncles, and cousins, who loved his sons like they were their own, the boys wouldn't have the sense of security they had now.

And Jace would be damned before he let Mary Ann blow it up again.

"But don't wait too long, Jace. I would hate for either Grady or Travis to be broadsided by Mary Ann."

"I won't. I just want to get a bead on the situation, a little background."

"You think she's moved back to the States?"

"I have no idea. I lost track of her years ago. But that's what I'm hoping to find out."

"I still don't understand why she wouldn't have called you first."

He held her gaze. "It's pretty obvious to me. What's that saying? 'It's better to ask for forgiveness than it is to ask for permission.' Because she wasn't getting any permission from me."

He pulled Charlie up from her chair. "Come here and kiss me before I go back to work."

She leaned in and touched her lips to his, teasing. She never failed to drive him crazy.

"Please don't work too hard." He rested his hand on her stomach. "And leave the painting for someone else."

"It's perfectly safe, Jace. But I will take it easy, I promise. Same goes for you." She poked him in the arm. "I know it's difficult, but please don't work yourself up about Mary Ann. Whatever happens, we'll work through it as a family."

He nodded but wasn't so sure it was that easy. Mary Ann had the power to rock the hard-won balance he'd managed to maintain these last few years. And his gut told him she was about to shake the ground out from under him.

Chapter Three

Charlie finished up the last of her painting and left the hutch out to dry. The temperature was in the high seventies and the sun was showing off today, not always the case in spring in the Foothills. May and June could be gloomy. They'd had a cold and wet winter, so the warm weather was a welcome change.

She cleaned up in the bathroom and peed for the dozenth time that day, one of the not-so-fringe benefits of pregnancy. But she was counting her blessings that she'd made it to her third trimester. The first two times she hadn't been that lucky.

That was why she was cutting herself plenty of slack these days, including not pushing herself too hard at Refind, even though she and Aubrey were on the precipice of real success. And she was letting herself give in to her constant cravings for sweets.

Today she had a yen for ice cream and headed over to the Dalton Market. Angie had just signed on to carry a local creamery's gelato, and it was to die for. She rationalized that she'd burn off the calories by walking, even though the store was only on the other side of Dry Creek Village, not more than six minutes away.

When she first came here three years ago the village was nothing more than an open cattle field and a kernel of an idea to save the ranch. Now, with the hard work of four Dalton families, it was a burgeoning agritourism destination/shopping center. And it was as pretty as it was utilitarian. A mixture of old, converted barns and new buildings made to look original. Meandering trails. Picnic tables along Dry Creek. And adorable, old-timey kiosks, selling everything from Jimmy Ray and Laney's popular sarsaparilla to a local woodworker's signs.

The truth was that the village was keeping the ranch afloat as much as the men liked to believe it was their beef business. In good years the cattle certainly helped supplement their income. Still, it was too inconsistent to rely on.

But after a long, hard push, the village was bursting with business. She liked to think that she, Aubrey, Angie, and Gina were key in its success.

And now, with everything going so well, there was this . . . Mary Ann. Charlie hoped Jace was right and Mary Ann would move on. But her intuition told her it was unlikely. As a soon-to-be mother, she couldn't imagine anyone not wanting to reclaim a relationship with their children. Then again, she couldn't imagine leaving them in the first place.

The Dalton Market was crowded, even for a weekday. It was a popular stopover for folks traveling between the Bay Area and Lake Tahoe. Dry Creek Village had a slew of electric charging stations. So, while motorists waited for their cars to charge, they shopped. Or ate.

Thanks to Angie's marketing genius, Dalton Market included a deli counter with sandwiches and salads and premade picnic baskets to eat creek side here on the property. For the full-fledged Dalton beef experience—also the pricier one—they could eat at Gina's steak house.

"Hey there," Angie called from the top of a rolling library ladder. She was stocking one of the top shelves with boxes of Gina's organic cake mixes. They flew out of the store faster than a bullet train. Gina's popularity as a FoodFlicks Network star came in handy.

"Jace was just here buying cookies for the boys."

"Did he tell you?"

Angie scrambled down and joined Charlie by the ice cream counter. "Did he tell me what?"

It was clear he hadn't mentioned Mary Ann to Angie, which signaled to Charlie that he wasn't ready for his family to know about her yet. Not before the boys. "Oh, about Travis's poison oak."

"He said the doctor prescribed steroids."

"Yep. Poor guy. His first week home from school, can you believe it?"

"It's all over the place. Tuff washes Buddy with that anti-itch stuff every time the dog goes out to do his business. You want some?" She pointed to the gelato.

"You read my mind. It's sooo good."

"Right?" Angie slipped behind the counter. "Cone or cup?"

"Cup, please."

Angie filled a cup with two generous scoops and Charlie didn't even try to stop her.

"Let's eat outside." Angie served herself a cup and led the way to the only vacant picnic table.

"Wow, it's bustling today. Anything going on?"

"A beautiful spring Thursday. I suspect people are cutting out of work early to take advantage of it and head up to Tahoe or the American River. Things busy at Refind?"

"Not like this." Charlie nudged her head at a group of six going inside the market. "But business is good. Really good." She smiled.

Angie leaned in closer to Charlie. "Did you hear about Mitch?" Mitch was Aubrey's ex-fiancé, Jace's ex-best friend, and, according to everything Charlie had heard, a world-class jerk.

"He's getting married," Angie continued. "He actually had the nerve to come into Tuff's shop and order three leather engraved flasks for his groomsmen."

"You're kidding." Charlie laughed because it did take gall given that the Daltons had shunned him. "I have so many questions. First, who's he marrying? The poor, deluded woman. Second, does Aubrey know? And third, did Tuff take the order?"

"Some girl from Sacramento. Tuff said she

came into the shop with Mitch and seemed nice enough. Someone should probably warn her to run. No, Aubrey doesn't know because this just happened yesterday and you're the first person I'm seeing except for Jace. And he wouldn't find the humor in it the way we would. And hell no, Tuff didn't take the order."

"What did he say?"

"He said he didn't have time, which, honestly, he doesn't."

"I wonder where they're having the wedding and whether Jill Tucker knows." Jill was the woman Mitch was cheating with when Aubrey left him.

"Don't know about Jill," Angie said. "And Mitch said something to Tuff about having the wedding at his house."

"Seriously? What else did Tuff find out?"

"We're talking about Tuff here. Gossip gives him hives."

Charlie laughed because it was true. Tuff was good as gold, but he sucked at gossip. "Well, I guess Mitch will be able to show off the minimansion. He'll probably invite the whole town."

"Everyone but us." Angie snorted. "Maybe he'll ask Gina to cater it."

"As if Gina would lower herself. But it would be great if we could talk her into it just so we could hear all about it."

"I've got that covered."

Charlie gave Angie a quizzical look.

"Tiffany. You can be sure the grand dame of Dry Creek will get an invitation. And let me tell you, that girl can dish."

"Oh boy, can she." Charlie finished the rest of

her gelato, scraping the bottom of the cup for the last drop. "I need to get home to check on Travis." It took her two tries to get to her feet, she was so top heavy now. "Thanks for the ice cream and the gossip. Can I tell Aubrey about Mitch?"

"Please do. See you on Sunday."

"Or maybe tomorrow." It was their inside joke because all of them lived a stone's throw away from one another and, with the exception of Jace, Cash, and Sawyer, worked in the village.

Charlie walked home. It was only fifteen minutes away on the south side of the ranch and too beautiful a day to waste.

She followed the creek to the house, taking a tree-lined path. Sunshine filtered through the canopy of branches, dappling the trail in the most magnificent light. The wild irises had bloomed, painting the shoreline in vivid stripes of yellow and purple. Soon, the snow from the mountains would melt and the crystal-clear water would cascade off the rock formation at their favorite swimming hole. In the summers they'd cool off from the hot sun by standing under the icy waterfall for as long as they could take the cold, then swim until their skin wrinkled.

Dry Creek Ranch was the most beautiful place she'd ever lived and she counted every day here as a blessing.

Sherpa and Benson met her on the last leg of her hike, their tails wagging madly, then escorted her to the front porch, where they plopped down in the shade for a rest.

She found Travis in the kitchen, eating leftover lasagna from the night before. The kid was a bottomless pit. She put the milk carton away in the refrigerator and started in on a small pile of dirty dishes in the sink.

Charlie loved this kitchen, with its enormous picture windows and sweeping views. The marble countertops, industrial-sized appliances, and large center island was a dream for their big family dinners. But what made the room all the more breathtaking was the tall, open-beam ceilings and the enormous, handcrafted, deer-antler chandeliers that hung from the iron trusses.

It looked like something you'd see in Wyoming and nothing like the densely spaced rows of painted ladies in San Francisco, where she had lived before moving here.

"Feeling better?" she asked Travis, who, judging by his appetite, was better off than when she'd left him a few hours ago.

"A little bit. At least the itching has stopped."

"That's half the battle, right?"

"It still throbs."

Charlie suspected his rash hurt plenty bad for him to complain. The Dalton men were cowboys through and through and subscribed to the notion of what doesn't kill you makes you stronger.

She kissed him on the forehead. "I know. But as soon as you take a couple more doses of the medication, you'll feel a lot better."

"I was thinking of meeting up with a few friends tonight. But I look like a freak."

If Travis was worried about how he looked, "friends" was code for a girl. He'd had a girlfriend before leaving for Cal Poly, but they'd broken up, deciding they should both focus on school. Which she and Jace had fully supported.

"You don't look like a freak." She ruffled his hair, which needed a good trimming. "You look like you have poison oak. Why don't you invite them here?"

"How's that going to make me look better?"

He had a point.

"Better lighting."

"Ha ha, very funny."

"You can hang out on the porch or in the backyard. That way, God forbid, you won't have to be near us. And if you start to feel uncomfortable, you can turn in for the night. And remember what the doctor said. Don't mix alcohol with your medication."

"I won't," he said. "Maybe we'll hang out at the creek."

"That's a wonderful idea. You can take some of the folding chairs from the garage and I could pack you some snacks."

He laughed.

"What?"

"Maybe some Lunchables in my old Star Wars lunchbox." He hugged her. "I'm good, no worries."

"You may be a big, bad college student now, but you'll always be my little brat."

The phone rang, startling both of them. It was the landline, an old cordless that hung on the wall that no one used anymore. The only reason it was still connected was because Jace wanted it in case a cell tower went down in an earthquake or a wildfire. Charlie couldn't remember the last time she'd heard it ring, if ever.

She got to the phone before Travis did. "Hello."

There was someone on the other end. She could hear him or her breathing. Not heavy breathing like an obscene phone call, just soft intakes of air.

"Hello. Can I help you?"

No response, but the person was still there. Charlie heard background noise. Maybe traffic, but it was hard to tell.

"I'm going to hang up unless you say something," she said.

Still nothing, so she clicked off.

"What was that about?" Travis had retaken his spot at the center island and was looking at her expectantly.

"Either a wrong number or a prank call," she said, but she was sure it was neither.

Chapter Four

Jace got to work early Friday morning to make up for the time he'd lost the previous day. He wasn't in the office ten minutes when he got called out on a disturbing the peace. Ordinarily, he'd send one of his deputies. But he knew both parties involved. One of them used to be his best friend and the other one still was.

"Be nice," Annabeth warned him on his way out.

"I always am."

She let out a snort.

"I heard that."

It took him less than five minutes to get to Brett's workshop, a double-sized metal garage a few miles out of town. In the driveway sat Mitch's tricked-out, jacked-up pickup truck, the kind that made a man look like he was trying to compensate for his shortcomings.

Jace took a few seconds to collect himself. He wanted to be professional, but Mitch brought the mean out in him. Four years ago his former best friend did something unforgivable to Brett and spread a nasty rumor about Jace to cover it up. It had nearly cost Jace's reelection bid for sheriff, but the toll on Brett was worse. Much worse.

The moment Jace hopped out of his duty vehicle he could hear shouting coming from Brett's workshop. No wonder someone had called the cops. He crossed the gravel driveway and pulled open the door to find Brett pinning Mitch against the wall with his wheelchair. They were so busy going at it, neither of them noticed Jace.

He let out a shrill whistle, startling both men into silence. "We've gotten three calls complaining about you two. What the hell is wrong with you!? You're grown men, for God's sake."

Mitch at least had the decency to look contrite. Brett not so much.

"Back up, Brett."

Brett put his chair in reverse but continued to stare daggers at Mitch.

"What's going on here?" Jace looked from Brett to Mitch. "Brett?"

"Why don't you ask him?"

Jace turned his gaze on Mitch. "Start talking."

"I came here to ask him"—Mitch bobbed his head at Brett—"to be the best man at my wedding and the sumbitch threw a goddamn cabinet door at me."

Jace didn't know what surprised him more, that Mitch had asked Brett to be his best man or that Brett, a usually peaceful guy, had thrown a cabinet door at Mitch. That's when he noticed Mitch's arm was bleeding.

"You," he pointed at Brett, "stay over there. And you, over there. If I come back and find you at it again, I'll arrest you both." He went to his vehicle to get a first-aid kit.

When he returned both men were in their respective corners, glaring at each other. Jace threw Mitch the kit. He'd be damned before he doctored Mitch's arm. Let him do it himself.

"Now let me get this straight. Brett threw a cabinet door at you because you asked him to be your best man." Jace had heard through the grapevine that Mitch was getting married, but he was pretty sure there was more to this story. Like, for example, Brett hated Mitch's guts, so why the hell would Mitch ask him to be his best man?

"That's right," Mitch said. "The damn thing is made out of MDF, weighs a ton. He could've killed me."

"You look alive and well to me." Jace turned to Brett. "Is what he's saying true?"

"Nope, my cabinets doors are made from one-hundred percent walnut."

Jace rolled his eyes. "Brett, did you or did you not throw a cabinet door at Mitch?"

"I did."

"Was it in self-defense?" He was trying to throw Brett a lifeline here.

"It was not. Let's stop pussyfooting around here. We all know why I threw a cabinet door at Mitch. I should've done it four years ago when he was sleeping with my wife. But I'd say now is as good a time as any. What kind of home-wrecking douchebag comes waltzing in here and asks me to stand up for him at his marriage when he destroyed mine?"

Jace thought it was a legitimate question. Unfortunately, as the law, he couldn't take sides.

"Mitch, do you want to press charges?" He didn't want to have to haul Brett in, but he would if he had to.

Mitch was thinking about it. Jace knew that because Mitch rarely thought about anything. And when he did he had a tell. His left eye would twitch, like it was doing now.

"No," Mitch finally said. "I want him to be my best man."

Brett spun around in his chair. "Can you believe this guy? Get him out of here, Jace. Get him out of here before I throw more than a cabinet door at him."

"Let's go, Mitch." Jace walked him to his truck. "What the hell were you thinking, man?"

"I was thinking this has gone on long enough. Look, I made some mistakes, some really bad mistakes, but Cheryl has made me a better person. A better man."

Jace presumed Cheryl was the bride-to-be. Whoever she was, she ought to run as fast as her legs would carry her as far away from Mitch as she could go.

"Brett made it crystal clear that he's not ready to forgive and forget, so it would be best if you didn't show up here anymore."

"You too, Jace."

"Come again?" Brett didn't have a problem with

Jace. He could come here as often and as much as he liked.

"This has gone on too long. The three of us used to be thick as thieves. And now look at us."

"Mitch, have you lost your ever-loving mind?" Jace shook his head, wondering if Mitch had indeed suffered brain damage. "Your best friend in there went to war, got blown up by an IED, and you welcomed him back by screwing his wife while you were engaged to Aubrey. Then what did you do? When Aubrey found out and dumped you, you exacted your revenge by telling everyone that she and I were the ones having an affair. And if that wasn't bad enough, you plotted to steal Brett's wife's family's cattle ranch, so you could develop it. Can you now understand why Brett might not want to be your best man?" Jace slapped the side of his own head because he couldn't believe he even had to spell it out.

"And I've been paying the price ever since. I want my friends back. You know how many times I picked up the phone to call you, how many times I thought about coming over to your house and begging your forgiveness? You know how badly I want you to stand up for me too? The most important day of my life and neither of my best friends will be there."

"And whose fault is that? Go home, Mitch!" Jace turned on his heel.

"Mary Ann's in town," Mitch called to Jace's back. "She's renting the Stoddard cottage on Miners Road."

Jace stopped in his tracks, frozen. "What about it?"

"I thought you should know."

He waited for Mitch to drive off and went back inside. "He's gone," he told Brett.

"The guy's got a set of balls on him, I'll say that for him."

"He always did." Jace hopped up on one of Brett's work counters and took in the workshop. Brett kept his tools neat as a pin. "What do you have over there?" In the corner of the room was an entire kitchen minus the sink, appliances, and countertops.

"It's for a house in Nevada City. A couple from the Bay Area bought it and then promptly gutted it."

Jace got down to take a closer look. "Nice." Brett did beautiful work. A few years ago, after he came back from Afghanistan, he took a course through the VA to learn a trade and joined his uncle in the cabinetry business.

Jace let out a breath. "Mary Ann is in town. According to Mitch, she's renting the Stoddards' place out on Miners Road."

"Damn. When did that happen?"

"I don't know." Jace told him about the incident at Grady's school. "Until now I wasn't completely sure it was her. But Mitch confirmed it."

"I wouldn't believe anything that knucklehead says. If he told me it was raining outside, I'd go out and look."

"Except it's too much of a coincidence. She's here, Brett. She's here and she's going to make trouble for me, Charlie, and the boys."

"Why do you think she didn't call you first and at least give you a heads-up? It doesn't seem like Mary Ann."

Jace pinned Brett with a look. "It seems exactly like her. She's always done whatever the hell she wants with no regard for anyone but herself. If she cared, she wouldn't have walked out on her children and ignored them for six years."

"How are you planning to play this?"

"I've got full custody of Grady. Let her try to fight that because I'll crush her. As for Travis, he's an adult now. He'll have to make his own decisions, but it's killing me. It's freaking killing me."

"You're not gonna like what I have to say, but she is their mother, Jace. She may be a lousy mother, but she's their own flesh and blood."

"Are you telling me I should let her back into their lives only so she can walk out again? Because she'll do it at the first sign of a shiny dime that draws her attention elsewhere. Maybe it'll be cooking school in Paris or a job working as a safari guide in Africa. Who the hell knows with her?"

"I don't like it any more than you do, Jace. But maybe Grady should have some choice in this. He's fourteen, not the baby he was when she left."

Jace didn't want to talk about it any longer. The whole thing made him sick to his stomach.

"What's going on with you and Jill?" Jace leaned against the wall.

"She's seeing a guy in Roseville. A pool contractor she met online." Brett shook his head. "He seems decent enough. Has two kids of his own about the same age as ours."

"And you're okay with it?" Jace asked.

"It's not like I have a choice, but yeah. We're over, Jace. There's no coming back from her and Mitch. From me . . ." He trailed off, but Jace understood what wasn't being said. Jill hadn't supported Brett when he'd come home from war a different man from when he'd left.

"How about you?" Jace cocked a brow. He knew Brett had started dating.

"Nah. I'm in no rush."

"It'll happen when it happens. And when it does, ooh doggy, it'll knock you right between your eyes." He grinned, remembering how he fell for Charlie. "Who would've guessed about Mitch? He's a better man now my ass."

Brett threw his head back and laughed. "Between you and me, I kind of feel sorry for the guy. He doesn't have any friends anymore. He went from being town hero to pariah."

"Nah," Jace said. "You've always been our town hero, Brett, not Mitch. I've got to get back to the station. Do me a favor, stay out of trouble. No more throwing cabinets at people."

Brett followed Jace to the door. "Let me know how this Mary Ann thing shakes out. Take it easy, okay?"

"Yeah. Sure."

Jace decided to swing by the Stoddard cottage. He told himself it was on the way to his office, which it wasn't. But he was anxious to see if Mitch's information checked out. At some point he'd have to confront Mary Ann, but he wanted to consult with his attorney first. In the meantime he'd do some reconnaissance.

He took the exit to Miners Road, a residential area just outside of Dry Creek. The burbs, he and his cousins liked to joke. Despite a farm supply store and a new strip mall with a sandwich shop, a laundromat, and a dollar store, there wasn't a whole lot out here besides homes. It was a hodge-podge of new construction—lots of two-story mini-mansions with swimming pools—and older homes that were a little worse for wear.

But it was only a matter of time before Mitch and his development company bought up the eye-sores, tore them down, and built shiny new ones.

Dry Creek, like every small town in California, was experiencing a growth spurt. Folks from the cities were coming to retire because the real estate prices were better here than wine or ski country. And young people who could work from home enjoyed the bucolic charm, the good schools, and the relatively low cost of living that Dry Creek had to offer. Located only an hour away from Sacramento and three from the Bay Area, it was close enough to "civilization" that it wasn't too much of a compromise.

Not everyone in Mill County liked the influx—Grandpa Dalton would've hated it—and it sure didn't make Jace's job any easier. But it was what it was.

In the self-interest department, the changing demographics had certainly been a boon for Dry Creek Village. The new residents, accustomed to all the amenities of city life, loved eating at Gina's steak house, buying farm-fresh groceries, including the ranch's beef, at Dalton Market, and furnishing their new homes with pieces they bought at Refind.

Jace had no reason to complain.

He hung a right on East Creek Lane and a left on Miners. It was a nice-looking street. Two years ago some of the residents petitioned the city to turn the vacant lot behind one side of the street into a soccer field and a small park. The city went for it and, with the help of volunteers and private donations, they had their park a year later.

The Stoddards' property backed up to the park. After Dick Stoddard's wife died of cervical cancer a few years ago, he moved to Folsom to be closer to his daughter. But he couldn't bear to sell the cottage, where he and his wife had raised their two children. So, he rented it out. Last Jace heard, an elderly couple from Arizona was leasing it. But that must've changed if Mary Ann was living there now.

At the last minute he turned the corner and parked his marked vehicle near the soccer field on Juniper, then walked around the block to Miners. He stayed on the opposite side of the street from the cottage, passing the neatly trimmed front yards and well-kept houses.

He knew almost everyone who lived here, many of whom were the parents of kids he'd gone to school with or his former classmates, who'd inherited their family homes.

As he got closer to the Stoddards' place, he climbed up onto Christy Wheeler's front porch. Christy and her partner, Tammy, were both sheriff's deputies, so he knew they were at work. And even if they weren't, they wouldn't mind Jace making himself at home. He'd known Christy his whole life. Her grandfather had been one of Grandpa Dalton's best friends.

Christy and Tammy's wide deck was a perfect vantage point for spying. He could see the cottage perfectly from here, but it was just far enough away that someone across the street wouldn't be able to identify him. Just a guy with a cowboy hat, sitting in a rocking chair. Pretty par for the course around here.

Sure enough, there was a white compact car in the driveway. Jace zoomed in with his phone camera and snapped a picture, then sent it to his watch commander to run the plate. He suspected the car was a rental, which meant he'd have to do some fancy footwork to get the rental company to give up the driver. It wasn't like this was official police business.

Then again, he really didn't have to corroborate that it was Mary Ann because he knew it was. There was a time when he could sense her presence with his eyes closed.

He'd been no more than a kid himself when he'd fallen for her. And the more he loved her, the more she'd acted like a caged animal ready to bolt the minute the door opened. Then they got pregnant with Travis and she was stuck. Stuck with him is what she'd said. Stuck with Dry Creek Ranch and living in a nothing town.

Next came Grady and she was jumping out of her skin, so filled with wanderlust that she spent half her days glued to the Travel Channel.

Everything he did to try to make her happy only made it worse. Joining the Mill County Sheriff's Department so he could be closer to home instead of commuting to Roseville, where he'd been a police officer. Hiring Mitch to draw up plans for a house so she'd have her own domain instead of living with Grandpa Dalton.

Loving her until he thought he'd go crazy with it.

She'd called his love suffocating. A fortress built to keep her in. So she scaled the walls, ran as fast as she could go, and put an ocean between them.

And now she was back. For how long he couldn't say. But long enough to do some serious damage.

He sat there for a while. Why? He didn't know. He supposed the cop in him wouldn't be satisfied until he got indisputable proof that it was really her.

His phone rang, disrupting the silence.

"Hey, Annabeth, everything okay?"

"Everything is fine. I just wanted to make sure you're planning to be in the office this afternoon."

"Why?" Annabeth could be a pain in the ass sometimes, micromanaging him like she was his boss instead of it being the other way around. But his job was unpredictable. Because it was a small department he often went out on calls himself. This was all to say who knew where he'd be this afternoon?

"Uh, you have a deadline with the city council to get that proposal in for the new body cameras."

What the hell was she talking about? "That's not until next week."

"Uh . . . oh, for goodness' sake. Just be here." With that she clicked off.

He shook his head because there was never a dull moment around this place; then he got up to leave. Jace was halfway to his vehicle when a call came in on his radio. It was a burglary in progress at the Dry Creek Market. He looked at his watch. Lunchtime at the middle school, which meant another kid lifting a candy bar.

He put his light bar on his roof, turned on his siren, and took off.

Chapter Five

"Why are we doing this again?" Charlie got in Aubrey's car.

"Because it'll be fun."

Charlie was too tired to have fun. The fact was she was dead on her feet from working in the store all morning. Just buckling her seat belt was a chore and the bumpy ride out of the ranch was going to make her have to pee. Again.

And something about Aubrey's story about going to town to look at some old furniture the sheriff's department was giving away didn't make sense. Charlie could work wonders with upcycling most furniture. She'd even been known to filch an old chair or table from the side of the road waiting for garbage pickup and make it look like a million bucks. But she had her limits. She drew the line at metal desks and swivel chairs.

"What kind of furniture?" Because if it was anything worth salvaging, Jace would have told her about it.

"Annabeth said it was stuff they had left over from years ago, back when they used good, hard woods."

Charlie was dubious, but Aubrey seemed so excited, she didn't want to burst her balloon. At least she could pop in on Jace. He'd been so tense when he left for work that she'd thought about him all morning.

"I still can't believe Mitch is having a big wedding at his house," Aubrey said. "After the debacle with Jill and then her family's ranch, I would've figured he'd want to lay low. Or have his wedding in another county, where everyone didn't hate him."

"Maybe they don't have anywhere else to have it."

"Or he just wants to show off that ridiculous house of his. The one he built for me"—she put air quotes around "me"—"was bad enough. But at least it wasn't any showier than Tiffany's house, or any of the new builds in Dry Creek. But this new one . . . uh, can you say Medici Palace? What a tool."

Charlie laughed because the house, a fake-looking Italian villa, really was ostentatious. Like Tuscany threw up. He'd even planted a small vineyard to give it that wine country feel.

Mitch, a successful developer, had sold the old house—the one he and Aubrey shared before the breakup, before she'd married Cash—at a hefty profit to a tech guy from Silicon Valley who could telecommute and wanted his kids to grow up in the country. And he'd built the Italian one. Charlie suspected it was Mitch's way of waving his middle finger at the good citizens of Dry Creek, who'd disowned him.

"It's actually kind of sad," she said.

"Nah, not sad. Douchey." Aubrey turned off on Main Street, heading for the Civic Center "I hope the bride has a large family, otherwise it's going to be a tiny reception. Just his assistant, Mercedes, and Mitch's mom."

Aubrey pulled into City Hall lot and found a parking spot close to the sheriff's headquarters, which Charlie was eternally grateful for. There was only so far her aching feet would take her.

Aubrey flipped down the passenger seat's visor and pointed to the mirror. "You want to put on some lipstick?"

"Why?" It wasn't as if they were going nightclubbing. For the next hour they'd be rooting through a bunch of dusty furniture in the bowels of the sheriff's department. "Are you trying to tell me that I look awful?"

"No, of course not." Aubrey pinched Charlie's cheeks. "You're just a little pale. Put on some lipstick, Charlotte. You'll thank me for it later."

Charlie was starting to get the sense they weren't really here for furniture.

That suspicion was confirmed eight minutes later when two dozen deputies, support staff members, and county workers yelled, "Surprise!" at the top of their lungs as she and Jace simultaneously entered the conference room. The usually drab space had been decorated in pink streamers, yellow balloons, a baby shower banner, and a sheet cake topped with a fondant pair of tiny pink cowboy boots.

A smile spread across Jace's face that took Charlie's breath away. He loved his staff and this community so much that it warmed her heart to see how much it loved him back. Even Tiffany was here. Although she didn't work for the sheriff's department, she was Jace's campaign manager and had her hands in every Dry Creek cause, charity, and ad hoc committee.

"Did you know about this?" Charlie asked him when they had a moment alone.

"Not a clue. You?"

"Not until a few minutes before we walked in, when Aubrey made me put on lipstick. This is so sweet. I can't believe they went to all this trouble."

"You two. Pose by the cake. I want to take a picture." Tiffany herded them to the cake table, where she proceeded to snap photos of them with her phone.

Charlie cornered Annabeth, who she presumed was the architect of the party. "This was enormously kind of you to organize. It's just so . . ." Charlie choked up, waving her hands over her teary eyes. "Don't mind me and my pregnancy hormones."

Annabeth gave her a hug. "It was a group effort. Everyone wanted in on it. Now go open your presents and then we'll have cake."

A folding table was piled high with gifts wrapped in lots of pink paper and frilly bows. She and Jace were having a girl, which was public knowledge. They had chosen the name Keely but weren't broadcasting it because Charlie was superstitious and didn't want to jinx anything. The name, though, had been Grady's idea. He had a classmate named Keely, and Charlie and Jace adored the girl as much as they did her name.

It took a good hour to tear through the packages of adorable onesies, receiving blankets, toys, books, and even a high-tech high chair, a group gift from Jace's top command. But Charlie's favorite present was a handmade quilt made of vintage Western fabrics that Annabeth had no doubt spent weeks sewing.

If Charlie felt weepy before, she was only seconds away from a monsoon of tears. There was no way to describe the gratitude and joy she was feeling. She'd come to this beautiful town almost four years ago, running from a monster. The people of Dry Creek had not only taken her in and given her their protection but they'd also helped her heal. And now these very same people would be there for her child.

Keely would not only have a big, loving family, she'd have the adoration of a whole community that would watch her grow.

Jace and Cash loaded the gifts into the back of Aubrey's car.

"I'll be home in a few hours." Jace brushed a stray hair away from Charlie's face. "How about I bring home dinner from the coffee shop—fried chicken and Jimmy Ray's smashed sweet potatoes?"

"That sounds heavenly."

"I don't want to ruin the day, but I've got news."

Charlie braced herself. "She's here, isn't she?"

"Yeah. She's renting the Stoddard cottage."

"Oh boy, here we go. How'd you find out?"

"From of all people, Mitch."

"What? When did you talk to Mitch?"

"That's a whole other story that's too long to get into right now." Aubrey was waiting patiently in the driver's seat. But she needed to get home before Ellie got out of school. And little Carson was probably throwing a fit by now. Cash and Aubrey's toddler had a bad case of separation anxiety.

"Can't wait to hear it. To hear everything. Sounds like you had quite an interesting day."

"Yep. But this was nice." He was talking about the shower.

"The party was beautiful. Tell Tiffany to send me her pictures. And come home soon." She started for the passenger door when Jace called her back.

"Are you forgetting something?" His lips curved up and then he kissed her.

On the ride home Charlie couldn't hold back any longer and told Aubrey about Mary Ann.

"All I want to do is bask in the afterglow of that wonderful shower, yet all I can do is think about her and how she's going to come in here and screw everything up. And then I feel guilty about it because as much as I want it to be otherwise, Travis and Grady are hers."

"Travis and Grady love you, Charlie. Those boys worship the ground you walk on. And Mary Ann is awful. I've only seen Jace cry twice. The day Brett Tucker came home from Afghanistan a paraplegic and the day Mary Ann failed to show up for

Grady's sixth birthday party. She's that awful. But the one thing you can count on with her is she can't commit, not even to her own children. So whatever the hell she's doing here, she'll take off again as soon as something better comes along. And this time the boys won't be brokenhearted because they'll have you."

Charlie doubted it would be that easy. No matter how much Travis and Grady loved her, being abandoned by their birth mother not once but twice would leave lasting scars. She didn't have to be a child psychologist to know that.

"Jace doesn't want to tell them. But I think that's a mistake. If she's rented a house here, it tells me she's intent on seeing them. And no child custody order is going to stop her."

"Jace needs to tell them," Aubrey agreed. "Should I talk to Cash? He'll talk some sense into him. Maybe at the barbecue."

"No, don't say anything yet. When Jace gets home tonight we'll discuss it. Now that he found out she's staying here, he might be more inclined to talk to the kids. Before, he thought, or hoped, that she was just passing through and if we ignored it long enough, she'd go away. But it's clear now that's not happening."

When they got to the ranch house Travis was waiting on the front porch.

"Oh good, he can help us unload the gifts," Charlie said. She barely had enough energy left to make it from the car to the house, let alone carry in all the packages from the shower, including left-over cake.

Travis met them in the driveway, scowling. Charlie could tell instantly that something was wrong.

"When's Dad getting home?"

"A couple of hours. Why? What's going on?"

"My mother called. She's here in Dry Creek and she wants to see us."

Well, that hadn't taken long.

Chapter Six

"**I**'m not meeting with her. She can go to hell for all I care." Travis threw himself into a dining chair for breakfast

"I'm doing whatever Travis does," Grady said, but to Jace he seemed less adamant and more conflicted than his older brother.

"It's entirely up to you guys. I'll support you in whatever decision you make," Jace said.

Mary Ann was moving fast. Jace hadn't even heard back from his lawyer yet.

He had no idea what kind of resources she had or how far she would push the issue, but he was willing to guess not a lot on both questions. A tiger doesn't change its stripes. And Mary Ann had never been the focused type. Besides, how do you force a kid you abandoned to take you back as if nothing happened?

"I don't want her living here either." Travis rested his arms on the breakfast table, his fists clenched.

"It's a free country, Trav. She can live wherever she wants," Jace said. "But if it makes you uncomfortable, you should tell her that."

"Except I don't want to talk to her." Travis scratched a patch of poison oak on his neck.

"Don't scratch, sweetie." Charlie fetched a bottle of anti-itch cream from the mudroom and applied a handful to Travis's neck.

"Then send her a text or an email," Jace said. "You have a voice in this." He'd always taught his sons to speak up for themselves as long as they did it respectfully. "I don't know that she'll listen, but I do know that she loves you boys. That she wouldn't want to make you uncomfortable." Jace spoke the truth. Mary Ann did love her sons, just not more than she loved herself.

"Yeah, she loved us so much that she took off and never came back. That's some love all right."

"What if she comes to my school again?" Grady wanted to know.

"She's not authorized to have contact with you at school. Mrs. Martinez knows the situation and will bar her from campus. But if she does approach you, you call me. Okay, Grady?"

He nodded.

"Look, I'll talk to her if you want me to. I'll explain to her that you guys aren't cool with this. But only if you want me to."

"I do," Grady said, but he seemed torn and that was tearing Jace apart.

"You got it, buddy. Travis?"

He shrugged. "Whatever. But if she comes around me, I'm not going to be nice about it. Not like you'll probably be. I'll tell her to go straight to hell. She's nothing to me. As far as I'm concerned, Charlie's my only mother."

"I'll talk to her," Jace said. "Why don't you guys finish the rest of your chores, then enjoy your Saturday? I don't want you to worry about this anymore. Okay?"

Grady got up from the table first. He'd never been good at sitting for too long. "Ellie's got a horse show today in Auburn. Uncle Cash said I can go with them if it's all right with you."

"Sure. Just make sure the dogs and horses have water before you go." Jace made a mental note to give Cash a heads-up about the Mary Ann situation before Grady spilled the beans.

"What are you up to today?" he asked Travis.

"I'm meeting a couple of friends down at SB."

SB was what they called the Mill County State Park's swimming hole. It was a public beach where tourists and local kids liked to hang out and swim or tube in Dry Creek. On almost any given night you could find groups of high schoolers there, holding bonfires. It was a rite of passage for teenagers here. Jace and Aubrey had spent many a weekend at SB. When Cash, Sawyer, and Angie were visiting for holidays or summers, they came too.

"It's still a little cool for swimming," Charlie said.

Travis shrugged his shoulders. "We'll probably just hang out."

"No drinking and driving," Jace warned.

"I know. We won't."

"I've got to get to the store." Charlie started clearing the breakfast dishes.

"I'll do the cleanup." Jace said. "You want a ride?" Refind was only fifteen minutes away by foot, and in good weather, Charlie liked to walk it. But he wanted to talk with her.

"Sure." She pressed her hand into the small of her back.

"Meet me at the truck. I've got to get my keys."

She was already in the passenger seat when Jace got behind the wheel. "How'd you think it went with them?"

Charlie looked away and gazed out the window. "It broke my heart. I just hope we're doing the right thing."

"I left it up to them, Charlie. I can't force Travis to see her and Grady . . . what's the point? She's only going to leave again."

"I know. But maybe we should've encouraged them to at least hear what she has to say. Maybe it would be healthier."

"Healthier?" He let out a bitter laugh. "She deserted them when they needed her the most. She doesn't get to march in here six years later and decide she's ready to be a mother now."

"I didn't say it was about her. But I understand your concerns. It's just . . ." she trailed off.

"It's just what?"

"Never mind. My hormones are all over the place and I guess I feel sorry for her."

"Well, don't. You're such a good person, Charlie. It's one of the many reasons I love you so much. But she doesn't deserve your sympathy." He started the engine and nosed down the driveway.

"Are you really planning to talk to her?"

"Hell yeah. I want to know what her intentions are. Why she's here."

For some reason Jace got the impression that didn't sit right with Charlie. But he'd promised Grady he would talk to Mary Ann and there was no reason for him not to.

"I've got to call Cash and tell him what's going on. I don't want him hearing it from Grady first. Then I'll get around to Sawyer and Gina and Angie and Tuff."

"Uh, I may have already said something to Aubrey on the way home from the shower."

Jace chuckled. "Then Cash and half of Dry Creek already knows."

He cut the engine in front of Refind. The old livestock barn had been falling down when Charlie had started using it to refurbish her found and rusted treasures. She, Aubrey, and a crew of construction workers had given it a second life.

In the beginning Jace had been dubious that the barn would ever serve as a legitimate store and design center, or that the money it took to rebuild it could ever be recouped. He was proud to say he was wrong on both fronts.

"When's Aubrey coming to relieve you?" He didn't want Charlie working too hard.

"After Ellie's horse show."

Jace snorted. "That'll be all day, babe."

"She's driving her own car and coming back right after Ellie's event. And Kelly should be here in a couple of hours." She leaned over and brushed his lips with hers. "I'll be fine. Spring is a good time for us. Something about the warm weather puts people in a buying mood. Fingers crossed that the only energy I expel today is working the cash register."

"Fingers crossed." He crossed his. "Just no heavy lifting. If you need some muscle, call me."

"I will, I promise." She hopped down from the truck and shooed him away. "Now go mow the lawn."

He would, but first he texted Cash to meet him at the horse barn.

Cash came down the dirt trail from his and Aubrey's house and joined Jace on top of the fence. "What's up?"

They'd been holding impromptu meetings here for so long Jace couldn't recall when they'd first started doing it. Probably as far back as childhood.

"Mary Ann's in town." Jace figured there was no sense beating around the bush. With Cash it was best just to lay it out there. Before his cousin became a livestock investigator, he was an FBI agent and liked his facts unvarnished. "She's rented the Stoddard place. So I assume she's sticking around for more than a few days. She wants to see the kids."

Cash scrubbed his hand under his cowboy hat.

"This is kind of sudden. Did she contact you ahead of time?"

"Nope. Just showed up. Marta Martinez called me a couple of days ago. Mary Ann came to the school and asked Doreen to get Grady out of class. They didn't do it, of course. Then she called Travis on our landline. Told him she wanted to see him and Grady."

"Jeez. What did Travis tell her?"

"That he's not interested. Grady isn't either," though Jace wasn't so sure about that. He told Cash that he was in the process of consulting with his lawyer.

"What the hell do you think brought this on? I mean, the woman all but vanishes off the face of the earth for six years and suddenly she wants to be mom of the year."

Jace hitched his shoulders. "Don't know, but I plan to find out."

"How?"

"I'm going to ask her."

Cash let that settle in. "I'd be careful of that if I were you. Did you tell the lawyer you were planning to confront her?"

"Confront her? You make it sound like I'm planning to arrest her."

Cash pursed his lips. "I know you, and let's just say when you're angry you're not subtle about it. And there's a lot of water under the bridge where you and Mary Ann are concerned. A lot of pent-up resentment. You don't want to give her any ammunition to put your job in jeopardy or, for that matter, custody. In my opinion, you let the lawyers handle it."

Jace would take Cash's advice under submission. His cousin was the most rational person he knew, except for maybe Angie, who was generous and kindhearted to a fault. But it wasn't as if Jace was a hothead. In fact, he prided himself on keeping his cool in the most trying of situations. It was a requirement of his job.

"Have you talked to Sawyer yet?" Cash asked.

Whereas Cash was rational, Sawyer was practical. Jace respected Sawyer's opinion on just about everything. "You're the first person in the family I've told. Sawyer's next."

"I would definitely get his take on this." Cash became pensive. "Look, you're not going to like this but no matter how absent she's been, she has a right to see her kids, Jace. And maybe it would be good for Travis and Grady. They're not babies any more and don't need you as a buffer. I'm no therapist, but I suspect they have things they want to say to her, things they want to get off their chest. Things Mary Ann should hear from them, not you. All I'm saying is if the boys are amenable, maybe there should be a meeting. Something with your blessing; otherwise even if they want to talk to her, they'll say no out of loyalty to you."

"If they want to talk to her, they can. But I'm not giving my blessing to anything having to do with her."

Cash looked away, realizing he wasn't going to win this battle. "How's Charlie holding up under all this?"

"Like a trooper."

"You've got a lot of emotion where Mary Ann's concerned. It's coming off you in waves. I get it. I do. It's impossible to watch the mother of your children break their hearts. I hope for your sake Charlie doesn't misconstrue that emotion." He caught Jace's gaze and held it. "Remember, there's a thin line between love and hate."

Jace had no worries where Charlie was concerned. She would back him 100 percent. As far as love for Mary Ann, that ship had sailed the minute she headed for the high seas.

Cash jumped off the fence and slapped Jace on the back. "I've got a horse show to get to." He started for the trail back to his house and called over his shoulder, "Don't do anything rash."

Jace gave a slight nod and went in the opposite direction.

There were at least three baby gates in Sawyer's upscale apartment, which made Jace chuckle at the humor of it. When Sawyer hired a fancy San Francisco architect to convert one of the ranch's old barns into a contemporary one-bedroom loft, he'd been a confirmed bachelor. Now the only sign of Sawyer's bachelor days was a basket of dirty laundry on the sofa.

"Hey," Sawyer grunted. Jace could tell by the pillow imprint on the side of Sawyer's face that he had just woken up.

"You want coffee?"

"Sure. Where's Mia?" Gina was probably at the restaurant, which left Sawyer on kiddo duty.

"Angie took her for the day so I can get some

work done. I can't ask for any more extensions on my book deadline without getting blacklisted by the publishing world. We need a nanny." Sawyer glanced around the open floor plan, cluttered with toys. "But first we need a bigger place."

"You working on that?"

"Yeah, Aubrey's architect came through. He thinks we can expand this place, but we might have to move in with you during the work." His lips curved up in a wicked grin to let Jace know he was joking. "But seriously, he's drawing up plans. Between drawings and pulling permits, it's going to take a while, though."

"What about Tuff's old cabin?" They had two cabins on the property. One that Angie and Tuff lived in and a second one that had been used at one time or another by almost every Dalton on the ranch but was now vacant.

Sawyer turned up his nose. "Or I could just move onto the set of *Deliverance*."

Granted, the cabin was a little rustic for Sawyer's taste, but "At least it has two bedrooms," Jace said.

"Yeah, it's a hard no."

Sawyer poured them each a cup of coffee and motioned for them to sit at the kitchen island. Jace wiped the counter with his hand, clearing a path of Mia's leftover Cheerios.

"Sorry about that." Swayer got a dishrag and gave the counter a good cleaning. "We also need a housekeeper."

"I came by to let you know that Mary Ann's here. She's living in town at the Stoddard place and wants to see Travis and Grady."

"Whoa. When did this happen?"

Jace told him the whole story, starting with Mary Ann showing up at the high school and Mitch tipping him off about her renting the cottage.

"Mitch? Since when do you talk to Mitch?"

"He and Brett got into it at Brett's workshop. I got called in on official sheriff's business."

"Okay. We'll circle around to that story in a minute. First tell me about Mary Ann."

"I told you everything I know. I was planning to have a chat with her, find out what on God's green earth she's doing here. But Cash thinks I should leave all communication with her to my lawyer."

"When did you talk to Cash?" Sawyer asked.

"Right before I came here to talk to you."

"Yeah, I'm in agreement with Cash." Sawyer shook his head. "I guess it was bound to happen eventually."

"What was?"

"Her showing up. Her wanting to see the kids. How do you want this to go?"

"How do I want it to go?" Jace thought it was obvious, but Sawyer the journalist had a habit of asking a million and one questions. "I want her to get in her car, turn around, and drive back to wherever she came from."

"What about Travis and Grady?"

"Travis is adamant that he doesn't want to see her and Grady . . ."

"And Grady what?"

"He says he doesn't want to see her, but I'm not so sure of that," Jace said.

Sawyer sighed. "She's his mother, Jace."

"I know." Jace pinched the bridge of his nose. Why did this have to be so damned complicated? "Remember Grady's birthday party? I think it was his sixth or seventh. Mary Ann and I had just separated and she was living in some crappy apartment in Roseville. She promised Grady she would come for the party, promised him that afterward she, Grady, and Travis could do something special, just the three of them, to celebrate. And then she never showed up. The entire party, Grady stood by the window, watching for her, waiting for her. Later, after I finally managed to reach her, her excuse was she'd caught a cold and didn't want to get everyone sick." He cursed under his breath. "I don't want that happening again. I don't want her setting the kids up for disappointment. Because the one thing I know definitively about Mary Ann is she's not a mother any child can depend on."

"I remember." Sawyer nodded, but he looked contemplative. "I'm pretty new at this fatherhood thing. But experience tells me that you can't always protect your children from disappointment, Jace, as much as you want to. It's a cold, hard fact of life that there will always be someone out there who does a number on you. Look at Tuff. His late mother makes Mary Ann look like a saint by comparison."

Tuff's mother was a drunk and had turned on her son in the worst way imaginable. And he had no one to look after him. That wasn't the case with Travis and Grady. As long as Jace had breath left in him, he'd protect his sons with his life.

"So the bottom line is that you're with Cash on

this," Jace said. "I should leave it to my lawyer to deal with."

"Yes. If your objective is to keep her from seeing Grady, I think you should do this by the book. But before you do anything, you should find out what the kids want. What they really want. It's bigger than what you want, Jace. Try to remember that."

"Yep," was his only response because deep down inside he knew Sawyer was right.

But that didn't stop him from getting in his truck and driving straight for Miners Road.

Chapter Seven

Charlie recognized him the minute he came into the store with a blonde on his arm. Though Mitch and Jace had fallen out before Charlie moved to Dry Creek Ranch, she'd seen Mitch around town and at various functions. It was a small community.

Given the way things had ended with Mitch and Aubrey, Charlie found it strange that he would show up at Refind. Then again, he seemed to be making the rounds with his enemies these days. Luckily, Aubrey wasn't here or she'd probably throw more than a cabinet door at him.

"Can I help you?" She flashed a tight smile, trying to decide how to play this. She could either ask him to leave or find out what he wanted.

She decided on the latter, mostly because she had a store full of customers and didn't want to make a scene.

"We're interested in the arbor you have out-side," the blonde said.

Charlie thought the woman looked a little like Jill Tucker. Silky blond hair, big brown eyes, great figure. Apparently, Mitch had a type, though Aubrey was a brunette with green eyes.

Mitch, on the other hand, was a little worse for wear. His hair was thinning and since the last time Charlie had seen him, his beer paunch had become more pronounced.

Charlie came out from behind the counter and followed them outside to the shop's French-style garden. She and Aubrey had finished it last summer so they could display patio furniture, back-yard fountains, and outdoor bric-a-brac. The small investment had proven to be a success, drawing people in from the rest of the center.

Flagstone lined with antique wooden posts and handmade birdhouses made a pathway through sections of Dave Austin rosebushes, French laven-der, and purple lupine. There were benches and wrought-iron bistro tables and chairs arranged on a moss-covered patio with gurgling fountains. But the pièce de résistance was the raised vegetable beds, each section defined by an arbor that Char-lie had constructed from something else. Doors, old fencing, farm tables, anything she could reimag-ine.

"It's for our wedding," the woman volunteered. "I just love it." She wrapped her arms around the arbor, which Charlie had made from three chippy, white antique French doors, and hugged it.

"How much is it?" Mitch asked.

"I'll let it go for four hundred dollars." It had been such a great conversation piece that Charlie had decided to hang on to it. But why walk away from an easy sale? she told herself.

"We'll take it," the woman said before Mitch could respond, then jumped up and down, clapping her hands. "My fiancé brought his truck." She pointed to a black pickup that looked like it was on steroids.

"Would you like help loading it?" Charlie prayed the answer was no; otherwise she'd have to call Jace. And that would be too weird for words.

As if sensing her hesitance, Mitch shook his head. "I've got it."

"Ooh, I want to look around," the blonde said, gazing around the garden. "Everything is sooo pretty here."

Mitch rolled his eyes but couldn't stop grinning at the woman. It was clear to Charlie that he was besotted. Charlie would be offended on Aubrey's behalf if it wasn't for the fact that her best friend and business partner was madly in love with Cash. They had two beautiful children and were living the dream.

The woman had moved on to an old farm table that Charlie had put outside because she'd run out of space in the store. "We could use it as a gift table or . . . something."

Mitch snuck a peek at the price tag. "Whatever you want, Cheryl."

Cheryl beamed, then turned to Charlie. "You make all this stuff yourself?"

"Well, it's already made. I just spiff it up or repurpose it. And I work with a partner." Charlie couldn't help but look at Mitch for that last part. He had the good grace to look away.

"You are sooo talented." Cheryl obviously wasn't aware of the weird undercurrent here.

"Thank you."

"OMG, I've got the best idea." She started clapping her hands again. "I can hire you to decorate our wedding. Would you do it? Don't you just love it, Mitch? Just like this." She turned in a circle, indicating the garden. "This is exactly my dream."

Mitch looked as uncomfortable as Charlie felt. "Babe, I'm sure Charlotte is too busy for something like that."

Cheryl turned to Charlie. "I saw on your website that you do all kinds of design work. I loved the pictures of Picnic in the Park." It was an annual fundraiser for the local Boys & Girls Club that Charlie and Aubrey had decorated last year.

"Thank you," she said. "But I'm afraid I'm going to be out of commission pretty soon." She stared down at her belly, hoping that would put an end to any of Cheryl's ideas.

"That soon, huh? You look amazing." Out of the blue, Cheryl hugged her, which was sweet but also awkward.

Mitch's fiancée was so charming, Charlie was finding it difficult not to like her. And why shouldn't she? Cheryl had nothing to do with Mitch's past.

"You know what? I can show you some pictures that might give you some good ideas," Charlie said. "I take it it's an outdoor affair, right?"

"It's in Mitch's backyard." She blushed, then her whole face lit up. "I guess it's our backyard now. Anyway, it's in the vineyard, so I kind of wanted to go for a real old-timey, country theme."

Charlie nodded. "Come in and I'll show you something Aubrey and I did in Napa a year ago. It was for this darling couple renewing their vows after forty years of marriage. They'd purchased a number of pieces here for their home that Aubrey worked with them on and they wanted us to work with their event planner on the décor for the party."

Charlie grabbed her portfolio from the office and motioned for Mitch and Cheryl to take a seat at one of the tables in the showroom to look through the photographs of the event, while she helped other customers.

Kelly was ringing someone up at the cash register. Luckily, Aubrey wasn't due in for another hour. By then Charlie would make sure Cheryl and Mitch were gone. In the meantime it didn't hurt to show Cheryl a few ideas.

"You see anything you like?" She pulled up a chair.

"This." Cheryl pointed to a picture of the dining setup Charlie and Aubrey had devised. It was a row of farm tables that spanned the size of a football field covered in white butcher paper, so the guests could write salutations for the couple to read later. For seating they'd used bales of straw as benches and lit each table with a crystal chandelier hung from a ten-foot-tall post. Glamour meets rustic. The result was breathtaking. "I would love this. Wouldn't you, Mitch?"

Mitch shrugged. "I don't know where we'd get all this stuff."

"This was all rented," Charlie said. "It's a place in San Francisco. They'll deliver it, set it up, and tear it down. But it's pricey, I'm not going to lie. If you're interested, I'll give you their contact information and I'll make you a copy of the picture. Just tell them I sent you and that you want exactly what's here."

"I can't believe you're willing to give us your design. This is like copyrighted stuff," Cheryl said. "Please let us pay you."

"Don't be ridiculous. This picture has been everywhere, including a couple of magazines. Anyone could replicate it. It's just the nature of the business."

It was in that moment that Aubrey chose to walk through the door and announce, "Ellie came in first place!" She did a little victory dance, then abruptly stopped short when she spotted Mitch.

Mitch got up so fast he nearly knocked his chair over. Cheryl, who was clearly in the dark about Mitch and Aubrey's history, just sat there smiling. Charlie started to mouth, *I'll explain later*, but Aubrey beat her to the punch.

She marched up to Mitch and did the last thing Charlie expected.

She plastered on a warm smile, took his hand, and said, "Hi, Mitch. You still owe me two thousand bucks."

Chapter Eight

This time Jace wasn't concerned about being incognito. He parked his personal truck on the street in front of Mary Ann's house, walked up to the door, and rang the bell.

She didn't seem at all surprised to see him. In fact, it appeared to Jace that she had been expecting him, judging by the way she simply waved her hand over the entryway of the cottage for him to come inside.

Mary Ann looked good, he'd give her that. She'd always been beautiful, but there was a maturity about her now that she wore well. She was in jeans, a T-shirt, and a pair of sandals. Her blond hair was tied back in a ponytail and her face was bare. No makeup. When they'd been together she wouldn't leave the house without taking at least an hour to do her face and hair. It used to drive Jace nuts. They lived on a cattle ranch, for goodness' sake.

He could tell she was taking him in the same way he was her. Jace watched her gaze fall to his left hand, where he wore his wedding ring. It hadn't occurred to him until now that she may be married too. But when he snuck a glance he saw that her ring finger was bare. Still, it didn't mean she wasn't in a committed relationship. For all he knew she was still with the French dude.

He took a quick look around the cottage. It was sparsely furnished. Just a sofa, matching chair, coffee table, and medium-sized flat-screen TV, which he suspected came with the place. Through the dining room he could see a table and four chairs. There wasn't anything on the walls or any of the usual personal items you'd find scattered throughout a room, like books or photographs or even a stray pair of shoes. It gave him hope that Mary Ann wasn't planning to stay, and that the cottage was just temporary lodging while she was passing through.

"Would you like something to drink?" Mary Ann broke the strained silence.

"No, thanks. Why don't I just cut to the chase?"

She gave a solemn nod, as if she was resigned to a confrontation. "At least take a seat. I'd rather not do this while you're towering over me, being intimidating."

It was a cheap shot. He was standing a good five feet away and had never once in their entire marriage done anything that could be construed as intimidating. But Jace took the chair and waited for her to settle in on the sofa.

"What are you doing here, Mary Ann?"

"I think that's obvious. I'm here to see my sons."

"Why? For six years you couldn't be bothered with them. So why now?"

Her gaze dropped to her feet and there was a long stretch of silence before she said, "Because I miss them."

"You miss them." He let out a bitter laugh. "That's pretty rich, don't you think?"

When she didn't respond he continued, "But you didn't miss them a year ago, or a year before that. You didn't miss them when Travis graduated from high school or when Grady hit his first home run in Little League or any of the other milestones mothers celebrate with their children. You didn't miss them when they cried themselves to sleep at night because you promised to call and never did.

"But now you miss them."

She was sobbing. He hadn't been prepared for that and he resented it. It was manipulative, and he wouldn't let himself be moved by her tears. Travis and Grady had shed too many for him to feel sorry for her.

"You don't think I regret missing all those things, missing a huge part of their lives? I regret it every day. All I want to do is make up for it." She wiped her face with her hand, then got up and came back from the bathroom with a wad of tissues.

"You can't make up for it," he said. "Leave them alone, Mary Ann."

She shook her head. "No. They're my children. I love them and I want to make this right."

"How? By leaving them again? If you love them, you'll leave them alone."

"You're wrong. I have every right, Jace. They're every bit my flesh and blood as they are yours."

"Then why the hell didn't you help raise them?"

"I made a terrible mistake." She choked on a sob. "It was selfish and it was wrong, but I was a different person back then. I was a child, for God's sake. A lot has happened, Jace. I've had time to reevaluate my past . . . my future . . . I'm ready to be their mother."

He laughed that bitter laugh again. What a piece of work. "That's not how parenthood works, Mary Ann. Look, I'm asking you to back off. The boys are good, they're happy, they're loved, they're growing up to be fine young men. Travis and Grady have asked me to explain to you that they're not interested in a meetup. If they change their minds, they'll let you know." He handed her his phone. "Go ahead and put your contact information in there. In the meantime, please don't go to Grady's school again. It's disruptive. Not only to Grady but to the other students and school staff. And please don't call the house again." He took his phone back and got to his feet. "What are your plans as far as Dry Creek?"

She seemed confused by the question.

"Staying here," he said. "How long are you planning to stay here?"

She rose too and wiped her eyes. "That's really not any of your business."

"Nope, it's not." He made his way to the door. "For once try to think about the boys and not yourself."

"Is that what you're doing, Jace? Thinking about the boys."

"That's what I've always done, Mary Ann. While you were out seeing the world, doing God knows what, I was thinking about the boys. Our boys, who you left."

He walked out before things got really heated.

"There you are." Charlie was on the couch when Jace got home, her feet elevated on a mound of pillows. "I tried to call you twice, hoping you'd bring home dinner."

"Sorry. I went to talk to Mary Ann and didn't hear the phone ring."

"You went to talk to Mary Ann? Why didn't you tell me?"

He threw up his hands in the air. "I did it on the spur of the moment." He bent over her and kissed her on the lips. "Long day?"

"You don't know the half of it. Mitch came into the store with his fiancée, but I want to hear about Mary Ann first."

"Where are the boys?" Jace would talk to them later, but he wanted his conversation with Charlie to be private.

"Travis went out and Grady is still with Cash, Ellie, and Carson. Ellie got a first place, but I think she has one more event. Tell me what happened." She pulled him down onto the sofa and moved her legs to make room for him, then put her head on his shoulder.

"It was weird seeing her again."

"What do you mean? What was weird about it?" Charlie pulled away and sat up.

He looked at her. "Not like that. Come on, Charlie. It was weird how she was remorseful and thought that was enough. It was like, 'Yeah, I really screwed up and now I want to make amends, and everyone should just let me.' It was cavalier and it pissed me off."

"Was it really cavalier or does she simply recognize that what she did hurt Travis and Grady immeasurably and she wants a second chance to make it right?"

"What's the difference?" He was getting annoyed. First Cash, then Sawyer, and now his own damn wife. "Why are you taking Mary Ann's side in this?"

"I'm not taking her side. I'm just trying to understand where she's coming from. At the end of the day it's about the boys."

"You heard them this morning. They made it perfectly clear how they feel about her being here."

"What I heard was anger and defensiveness."

"Yeah, imagine that. They're angry that their mother ditched them six years ago." He got to his feet, angry. "I'll go scrounge up something for dinner."

"Talk about defensive," she called after him. "Can't we just have a conversation about this?"

"Apparently not."

"Well, who's fault is that?"

He went in the kitchen, rummaged through the fridge, and didn't find a damned thing to make, even though there was plenty of food. He plopped down on one of the stools, rested his face in his hands, and let out a long sigh. He took a moment, then went back to the living room.

"Let's go to Gina's," he said.

"What about the kids?"

"They can fend for themselves. You up for it?"

"I'm up for anything that doesn't involve me cooking—or fighting." She gave him a hard look.

"I'm sorry," he said and tugged her up off the sofa into his arms. "I'm wound up."

"Why are you letting her do that to you? Why are you giving her that kind of power?" She locked eyes with him.

He thought it was obvious why and was about to tell her that when he thought better of it. It would only trigger another argument.

"Let's have a nice dinner out and not talk about this tonight. Tell me about Mitch." He wanted to talk about Mitch like he wanted a hole in his head, but it was better than dwelling on Mary Ann.

Charlie found her purse and on the way to Jace's truck said, "I liked her."

"You liked who?"

"Mitch's fiancée, Cheryl. She's so open and sweet. And just a bundle of enthusiasm."

"Well, Mitch will fix that."

Charlie stopped in her tracks and Jace could feel her instantly tense. "Is he really that awful?"

"No. He's not like that." Physically abusive. He didn't have to spell it out for Charlie. She'd lived it with her ex. "At least not that I know of. He's a pompous son of a gun, but I grew up with the guy and he's never laid a hand on a woman in front of me. Ask Aubrey."

"Aubrey just thinks he's a joke." Charlie started laughing.

"What's so funny?"

"When she saw him today at the store Aubrey told him that he owed her two thousand dollars for her out-of-pocket wedding expenses. You should've seen the look on his face."

Jace laughed too. It was the best thing he'd heard all day. "How did old Mitch take that?"

"You wouldn't believe it, but he wrote her a check on the spot. I don't think he ever told Cheryl about Aubrey, or Jill, and was mortified."

"As he should be. Aubrey better hurry up and cash that check before Mitch puts a stop payment on it."

"He wouldn't, would he?"

"Nah. He's probably afraid Aubrey will kick his ass."

"I hope he's good to Cheryl because she's truly lovely. He did seem dazzled by her, I will say that."

Jace parked in front of the restaurant so Charlie wouldn't have too far to walk.

"He told Brett and me that she'd made him a better man." Jace threw back his head and laughed. "The guy is so full of crap."

Charlie poked him in the arm. "When did you become so cynical? Maybe it's true."

"Maybe you just want to see the best in people."

"Maybe," she said. "Maybe because I've seen the very worst it makes me want to believe."

He squeezed her arm. "You're a good person, Charlotte Dalton. Best thing that ever happened to me, that's for damn sure."

Chapter Nine

When Charlie got to Refind the next morning to open the shop there was a woman there. She was waiting at the locked door. Charlie knew instantly who the woman was and her heart sank. Not because Mary Ann was even more beautiful than she was in pictures, which admittedly made Charlie feel insecure. But because Charlie knew intuitively why she was here.

Mary Ann's gaze dropped to Charlie's belly and something flickered in her eyes. Sadness maybe. But Charlie couldn't say for sure.

"Can I help you?" Charlie's voice was tight.

"I'm Mary Ann Dalton, Jace's ex-wife."

Dalton.

Charlie flinched. Dalton was now her name. And yet another woman had come before her. It was Mary Ann's not-so-subtle way of reminding Charlie of that.

"I know who you are. And you shouldn't have come here." Charlie unlocked the door and flicked on the lights.

Mary Ann followed her into the store. "I hoped we could talk."

"You should talk to Jace, not me."

"I already did that and it didn't go too well." Mary Ann let her eyes drop to Charlie's belly again. "I thought we could talk mother to mother."

The phone rang and Charlie went behind the counter to take it, hoping it would give her time to compose herself. Or even encourage Mary Ann to leave. Her surprise visit had ruffled Charlie. The right thing to do—for Jace and for the boys—was to tell Mary Ann to go, that her ambush—because what else would you call it?—was inappropriate. But her curiosity outweighed good sense.

The call was from a client who was redoing her den and wanted to know what kind of coffee table she should use for her crescent-shaped sofa. While Charlie ticked off a couple of ideas and dimensions, Mary Ann browsed around the store. She wasn't leaving, that was clear.

"You have a lot of beautiful things here," Mary Ann said after Charlie got off the phone. "The Village is interesting." She nudged her head to indicate the shopping center. "It doesn't strike me as something Jace would've gotten behind. He was always about preserving the ranch. About the cattle."

While Mary Ann was just voicing an honest observation, Charlie resented it. Perhaps it was petty, but it felt as if Mary Ann was trying to show that she knew Jace better than Charlie did.

"Dry Creek Village was Jace's idea. It was the best way to preserve it for the next generation of Daltons." Charlie said it with an edge in her voice. But Mary Ann didn't appear to notice because she just nodded.

"It's impressive. So is your store." Mary Ann toyed with the stack of business cards on the counter. "So Aubrey's your partner, huh?"

Charlie had it on good authority that Mary Ann and Aubrey couldn't stand each other.

"Yes, she is." Charlie locked eyes with Mary Ann and, to borrow a phrase from Jace, said, "Why don't you just cut to the chase?"

"Okay. I'll be direct, then. I came here to ask you to lobby Jace on my behalf. I realize that you don't know me, that you've heard what a lousy mother I've been, and that you probably dislike me. But if you have any feelings for my sons, which I assume you do, you understand how important it is that I make peace with them. Not for me but for them."

"May I be direct too? Because what I'm going to say next will be hurtful to you."

Mary Ann gave an imperceptible nod, but Charlie could see that she was girding herself for a verbal assault.

"I'm sorry," Charlie said softly. "But I must abide by Travis and Grady's wishes. And they've asked not to have contact with you."

Pain washed over Mary Ann's face. It was so pronounced that Charlie could feel it deep down in her own chest.

"I would hate me too," Mary Ann said in a whisper of a voice and swatted at her eyes.

Charlie went into the back room and returned with a box of tissues.

"Do you have any pictures of them?"

Charlie was torn. To continue engaging with her felt like a betrayal of Jace, Travis, and Grady. But she couldn't help but feel for the woman. And what would it hurt to show her a few pictures?

Charlie fished her phone out of her purse and cued up the most recent pictures she had of the boys from her photo gallery. Travis in his dorm room at Cal Poly. A picture of him with Grady at a restaurant in San Luis Obispo the weekend they'd moved Travis to college. And one of Charlie's all-time favorites, a photo of Grady wearing a Santa hat at Christmastime sprawled out on the floor with the two dogs under the tree. There was also a picture of both brothers sitting on top of the fence at the horse barn, the brims of their cowboy hats pulled low over their foreheads.

"They're so grown up." Mary Ann's hands shook as she held the phone. "Oh God, I've missed so much."

"Why?" It was something Charlie couldn't fathom. "Why did you leave them?"

Mary Ann looked up from Charlie's phone, her eyes brimming with tears. "If you're looking for a good sob story, I don't have one. I'd always wanted to travel, see the world. Then I met Jace, got pregnant, and before I knew it I had two toddlers at my knee. It wasn't the plan. It was never the plan, but it just happened."

She wandered over to the window and stared outside. "I got depressed. I don't know if you would call it clinical or anything, but I felt like a shell of myself. Like there was nothing left in me. And then one day I couldn't take it anymore and I left, figuring the boys would be better off with Jace than they were with me. I didn't go far at first. But just being away . . . from them . . . made me feel free, like a bird that had been allowed to fly after its wings had been clipped. I used to come and visit. But even that got hard. The boys—and Jace— would cry and beg me to stay and I couldn't. I just couldn't. It was crippling being here. Like the minute I drove onto the ranch, my arms and legs felt shackled, literally chained. Sometimes I'd sit in my car just trying to catch my breath, just trying not to die. Have you ever felt that way?"

Charlie had. Right after Corbin would hit her or kick her or berate her until she felt like nothing. Like zero.

But with Mary Ann it was different. Jace and the boys loved her. She'd been cared for here. She'd been safe.

"Do you think it might've been a form of post-partum depression?" Charlie was by no means an expert, but that's what it sounded like to her. "Did you seek help?"

Mary Ann let out a wry laugh. "Yes. My help was a ticket on the first outbound plane to anywhere. I visited every place I'd ever wanted to go, every place I'd ever dreamed of. Africa, Central America, South Asia, Eastern Europe, you name it. I wound up in France at a small artists' commune in Antibes, where I fell in love."

Charlie suspected there was more to the story, but Mary Ann was far away now. Somewhere painful, judging by her glassy expression.

"What happened?" she finally asked.

"Denis, a man I met in France, came into my life. And everything changed. My whole world opened up. He was a painter, an artist of some renown, and we fell desperately in love. We were expecting our first child together." She paused and that faraway expression returned. "A car broadsided us on our way to Paris for Denis's gallery show." She stopped again and tried to compose herself, then in a shaky voice said, "They said Denis died instantly. It took me two days to lose the baby. And two years to mourn."

Charlie knew what it was like to lose a child and her heart folded in half. "I'm so terribly sorry, Mary Ann."

"Even now I wonder if it was my punishment for what I did. For me abandoning Jace and my boys." She turned to Charlie. "You must think I'm a horrible person."

"I think you've made mistakes, yes. Horrible? All I know is that you've hurt the people I love most."

"I know I can't take back what I did, but I want my boys to know that I never stopped loving them, that I never stopped feeling them right in here." She placed her hand on top of her heart. "When I lost Amélie—that's what we had named her, a baby girl—all I could do was think about Travis and Grady. About what I'd done to them. About how I missed them."

She dried her eyes with the tissues Charlie had given her. "Please help me make it right with them again."

* * *

Charlie had never seen Jace this angry. He was trying desperately to keep his cool, but she could tell he was fuming.

"What was I supposed to do? Tell her 'I'm sorry about your tragedy, now get out of my store'?" Charlie said.

"You shouldn't have let her worm her way in in the first place. I thought we were united on this."

"We are. But is this really the right thing to do for Travis and Grady? Shouldn't they at least hear what she has to say?"

"You're going to lecture me on what the right thing for my sons are? I'm their father; I'll decide what's right for my kids."

He may as well have slapped her across the face or kicked her in the stomach.

I'll decide what's right for my kids. My kids.

It was the first time he'd ever drawn a line in the sand, the first time he'd ever told her that he considered her an outsider when it came to Travis and Grady. That in essence she wasn't an integral part of their family. His first family.

He immediately realized his mistake and went toward her. "I didn't mean it the way it sounded."

She pulled away. "How else could've you meant it, Jace?"

"Not like that." He rubbed his hand down his face. "Not like how you think I did. Ah, jeez, Charlie. I'm upset. That's all."

"I have to wonder why you're upset. Is it for the boys? Or for you?"

"What the hell is that supposed to mean?"

"You tell me. Ever since she came roaring into town you've been angry. Are you angry for Travis and Grady? Or are you angry for you? Because she left you. You!"

She turned on her heels, went to the bedroom, and slammed the door. That was when a cramp sliced across her stomach, making her double over. She made it to the bed and lay on her side the way her obstetrician told her to do.

It's nothing, she told herself, just normal third trimester cramping or Braxton-Hicks. She'd be fine as long as she rested.

Jace came charging through the door, took one look at her, and his expression turned from fury to fear. "What's wrong?"

"I had a cramp. That's all. It's probably all the stress this is causing. It's gone now. I just need a few minutes."

He lay down next to her on the bed and rubbed her back. "You sure? Should we call the doctor? Maybe you're going into labor."

"No, it's too soon. Dr. Orville said occasional cramping is normal. I'm doing exactly what she told me to do. Do you have your boots on the bed?"

He laughed, and the sound of it was so reassuring that it filled her with love, even though she was still angry with him.

Jace swung his legs over the bed and she heard each boot drop to the floor, then he was spooning her again, his warm body encasing hers like a weighted blanket. He left a string of kisses across the back of her neck. "Better?"

"Much better."

"Just rest, okay?" He pressed against her.

"You too. But we're not done talking about this."

The barbecue was at Cash and Aubrey's. Besides Charlie and Jace, they had the biggest house, with an outdoor kitchen and a large smoker. Cash liked getting his grill on as much as Jace did. All the Dalton men considered themselves pit masters, although Gina and Tuff were no slouches either. You couldn't live on a cattle ranch without mastering the art of the grill.

Everyone brought sides and Gina always made the dessert, which tonight was strawberry shortcake. The strawberries were from the restaurant's garden and Charlie couldn't wait to taste a slice. They set everything out buffet style on a long picnic table. There were at least three salads, heaping bowls of chips, a Crock-Pot full of beans, and garlic bread. The host always provided a big jug of Jimmy Ray and Laney's sarsaparilla and they all brought beer and wine. It was enough food to feed two counties, yet they rarely had leftovers. The Daltons had big appetites.

Charlie's nap with Jace had only temporarily quelled her uneasiness about the Mary Ann situation. The more she thought about it, the more she realized that Jace wasn't as done with his ex-wife as he let on. After six years his hostility toward her should've mellowed. She could understand a fresh resurgence of resentment toward Mary Ann for showing up here and demanding to see the boys, but not a burning fury that consumed him. It was too much emotion for a man who was supposedly over his ex-wife.

Charlie didn't doubt Jace's love for her, but what if he still loved Mary Ann? What if he loved his first wife more?

She excused herself from the party to use the powder room in Cash and Aubrey's sprawling hacienda-style ranch house. Aubrey had worked side by side with the architect to design it and it was marvelous Saltillo tile floors, thick white walls, vintage Mexican rugs, and chunky wood-beam ceilings.

Charlie loved hers and Jace's home, but she envied Aubrey for getting to put her own personal touch on this place. Charlie's home had been designed by Jace's grandfather and except for a few knickknacks, pieces of furniture, and artwork that she had added, it was exactly the same as Grandpa Dalton had left it.

The powder room was one of Charlie's favorite rooms in Aubrey's house. It was small, but Aubrey had gone all out with handmade Mexican tiles, a vessel sink stand made of wrought iron with matching towel and tissue holders, and forged-iron light fixtures.

She took a quick look in the mirror; even that was a work of art, framed in carved wood from an old Mexican barn. Her face was pale and slightly puffy and she had dark circles under her eyes.

The memory of Mary Ann's flawless skin flashed in her head and she quickly swatted it away. She was being ridiculous. She was pregnant, not ugly. Despite all the BS about pregnant women glowing,

Charlie had never looked worse. Her petite frame was carrying an extra twenty pounds, her feet were swollen, her hair was limp, her skin was sallow, and she looked perpetually exhausted.

Even though it was only a temporary state, she couldn't help but compare herself to Mary Ann, who had the figure of a goddess and probably turned every head in a room. Charlie was sure Mary Ann was turning Jace's head. Ever since he'd found out she was in town, Charlie sensed a difference in him. He was behaving like the hero in one of Charlie's enemies-to-lovers romance novels. And she knew how those ended.

By the time she got around to using the facility she was so worked up she was ready to leave the barbecue and walk home. It was the three specks of blood on her underwear that stopped her. She reminded herself that it could be normal, that one out of ten women spotted in their third trimester, according to all the literature she'd read. But just to be safe, she would call Dr. Orville in the morning.

"Hey, you okay in there?" Jace knocked on the door.

"I'll be out in a minute." Charlie pulled herself together and came out of the bathroom to find Jace leaning against the wall.

"Everything all right?"

"Jeez, can't a woman go to the bathroom in peace?"

His lips curved up in his signature cocky smile. The one she'd fallen completely, hopelessly in love with. "I thought you might've fallen in and needed rescuing."

She shook her head and headed back to the party, calling over her shoulder, "You're an idiot."

Later that evening Aubrey took her aside. "I heard Mary Ann showed up at the store."

Charlie did a double take. "Jace told you?"

"Yeah, what's the big deal?" Aubrey waved her hand in the air dismissively. "What's important is that the woman had a lot of nerve putting you in the middle like that."

"In the middle? That makes it sound like I'm a third party to all this. Is that how you see me? As a third party? As someone who isn't an essential part of this family?" Charlie clutched her stomach as another cramp seized her.

"What's wrong?" Aubrey grabbed Charlie's arm and pulled her over to one of the patio chairs. "Are you cramping?"

"Just a little one. It's probably Braxton-Hicks. Nothing to worry about."

"Does Jace know? I'll get him." He was over at the grill with Cash, Sawyer, and Tuff.

"Don't! Aubrey, please, don't."

Aubrey, not one to be cowed or mince words, pinned Charlie with a look. "What's going on with you? First you bite my head off and then you don't want me to get Jace. You're right, the cramping is probably nothing, but Jace should know about it in case you're going into early labor."

"I'm sorry. I think it's a combination of raging hormones and stress. That's all." Charlie couldn't bring herself to tell Aubrey about her suspicions of Jace's feelings for Mary Ann. It was too raw and too personal, even though Aubrey had seen Charlie through her worst times with Corbin. Plus,

Aubrey would only tell her that she was being ludicrous. And while Charlie wanted to hear those words she didn't believe it was the truth.

"Are you sure? Because it seems like there is more going on here." Aubrey took the chair next to Charlie. "Stress over Mary Ann?"

"Over Mary Ann, over the boys, over the baby. What's there not to be stressed about?" She smiled to show Aubrey that it was nothing, just normal baby jitters.

"Are you still cramping?" Aubrey dropped her gaze to where Charlie's hand still rested on her stomach.

"No, I'm good now." It had only been one sharp pain and then nothing. It was all fine, Charlie told herself. She was getting closer to her due date and her body was reacting, that was all.

"Let me get you a drink." Aubrey went over to the bar and returned with a glass of sarsaparilla.

Charlie took a few sips even though she wasn't thirsty.

"I want to make something very clear," Aubrey said. "I have never, ever thought of you as a second party. I . . . all of us . . . think of you as Travis and Grady's mother. Not stepmother, do you hear me? You have done more for those boys than their biological mother ever did. All I meant is that Mary Ann is putting you in the middle because she's relying on the fact that as a mother"—she emphasized the word "mother"—"you'll side with her. That you'll persuade Jace to convince the boys to see her. She's sneaky that way. And conniving."

Charlie had not gotten the impression that Mary Ann was sneaky or conniving. Her only take away from her was that she was sad and sorry for the things she'd done. For the things she'd lost.

"Do you think there's a chance that Jace still loves her?" Charlie blurted out, then immediately wished she could take it back.

"Oh my God, you're seriously hormonal. My mood swings were so intense during my third trimester that Cash is lucky I didn't kill him. Listen to me carefully: You are the love of Jace's life. Mary Ann is the bane of his existence. How do I know this? Because I was there. I was there through the whole sordid thing. No, let me correct that. I was there long before Mary Ann came along. I mean, Jace and I go back to splashing each other in a baby pool while his parents were still alive. This is all to say that I know the man as well as I know my own brother. Mary Ann is nothing to him. Nothing."

It was exactly what Charlie expected Aubrey to say. But it didn't mean it was true. Because while Aubrey was one of Jace's oldest friends, there were some things that only a wife knew.

Chapter Ten

It was one in the morning and Jace was sitting in an exam room holding Charlie's hand. Soon after they'd gotten home from the barbecue Charlie started experiencing extreme cramping. They didn't know if she'd gone into false labor or was losing the baby.

Charlie wanted to wait for Dr. Orville, but Jace wasn't taking any chances. He'd loaded her in the truck and rocketed to the emergency room. And here they were, waiting for the results of tests to see what was going on.

"It'll be okay," Jace said, even though he wasn't at all sure whether he was giving her—or him—false hope. She'd told him about the blood, which in his mind wasn't a good sign. The fact was he was terrified.

"I can't do this again." She turned on her side and stared at the wall.

"Don't say that. Whatever happens we'll get through it."

Dr. Orville came in the room, surprising Jace. Earlier it had been an ER doc. Charlie turned at the sound of the door and it was the first time Jace had seen her smile all night. The relief at seeing their regular obstetrician was short-lived, though. The fact that they'd called in the big guns told him it probably wasn't good news.

He didn't think that realization had caught up to Charlie yet and squeezed her hand tighter.

"Did they get you out of bed for us?" she asked the doc.

"Not quite. I was at a graduation party at my in-laws'." She pretended to stick a finger down her throat. "So thank you for getting me out of there."

"What's going on, Doc?" Jace wasn't in the mood for small talk.

"It appears you've gone into early labor."

"Oh, no," Charlie said, her face going sheet white. "It's too soon."

Dr. Orville nodded. "We would prefer that you were at least thirty-seven weeks. So we're not too far off, but far enough that I'd like to slow this baby down, give her lungs time to mature a little more. I'm going to give you nifedipine. It's a to-colytic medication that suppresses labor. And hopefully that'll give us a few more days."

"A few more days?" Jace said. "Don't we need more than that?" Charlie was only thirty-four weeks along.

"Ideally yes. But this baby wants to come. So, let's see how much time the nifedipine buys us.

I'm also going to put you on bed rest, Charlie. No more working, okay?"

"Do I have to stay in the hospital?"

"No, but given your history I want you to call me and be ready to come to the hospital at the first sign of labor."

Jace knew the doctor was substituting the word "labor" for "trouble." As calm as Orville was, Jace understood they were on shaky ground. And he could see by the haunted look in Charlie's eyes that she understood it too. The stress of knowing that she could lose the baby at any time only added to the risk factor. Jace realized that too.

A nurse came in and gave Charlie the nifedipine and a little paper cup of water and they waited to see if the cramps subsided.

By sunlight they were on their way home to the ranch. For now the emergency was averted. Charlie slept in the truck, but even in sleep Jace could see tension. Her hands were fisted in her lap and her mouth was pulled taut.

The boys were waiting for them on the front porch when they pulled into the driveway. Jace planned to carry Charlie inside, but she jarred awake as soon as he cut the engine.

"We're home, baby. Let's get you to bed." He came around to her side of the cab, but she'd already gotten out of the truck.

Grady trotted down the steps and gave Charlie a giant bear hug.

"Jeez, Grady, let her breathe." Travis was more ginger with her, but he too hugged her.

As the boys fussed over her, Jace saw the last

seven hours of anguish melt away from her face. She looked like the old Charlie again.

"Are you hungry?" Grady asked. "We can make you eggs."

"That sounds perfect," Charlie said.

Travis and Grady ran up the stairs to get breakfast started. They wanted to feel useful and Charlie understood that. Jace beamed. His wife was one in a million.

"You want to get in bed and I can have the boys bring you breakfast on a tray."

"I can eat in the kitchen. There will be plenty of time for bed later."

They sat at the breakfast table where the boys continued to dote on Charlie.

"Hey, Grady, you need to get ready for school, buddy."

"I figured I'd stay home today with Mom."

Both he and Charlie laughed.

"Yeah, I don't think so. But good try." Jace playfully patted his head. "Get a move on before the bus comes."

"I'll do his chores for him," Travis said.

Both boys started to leave when Charlie called them back. She got up and wrapped her arms around both of them and pulled them into a huddle. "Do you know how much I love you guys? To the moon and back, that's how much."

Jace watched his two tough hombres get a little teary-eyed.

He got up and cleared the dishes while Charlie lingered over the herbal tea she liked.

"I'll take a personal day and we can hang out in bed." He waggled his brows.

"I don't want you to do that. Save your personal days for when the baby comes." There was an edge to her voice. But Jace chalked it up to stress and exhaustion.

"You sure?" He wanted to stay. "I like the idea of spending the day with you."

"I plan to spend it sleeping, so what's the point?" She brought her mug to the sink and cupped his face in her hands. "Maybe tomorrow, okay?"

"Whatever you want. I'm at your service. In the meantime I'll come home at lunch to check on you."

She gave him an imperceptible nod, like she was somewhere else entirely.

Jace wasn't in his office fifteen minutes when Travis called. "Everything okay?"

"Yeah, it's not Charlie. Don't worry. Mom called again. I thought you told her to leave me alone."

"On the landline?" Damn it, he didn't want the phone disturbing Charlie.

"No, she somehow got my cell phone number. I hung up on her."

"Ah, jeez." Jace scrubbed his hand through his hair. Why couldn't the woman go away? "I'll take care of it, Travis. Okay?"

"Okay. But maybe I should just talk to her." There was a hesitancy in his voice and Jace couldn't tell whether Travis was trying to be helpful or if a part of him really wanted to talk to his mother.

"If you don't want to talk to her, I'll take care of it, Travis. But it's up to you."

"Maybe we should just ignore her."

"We could try that, sure."

"Yeah, let's do that."

But as soon as Jace got off the phone, he grabbed his hat and headed to the parking lot. "I'm on cell if anyone needs me, Annabeth."

He got as far as his truck when Mitch of all people waylaid him. "Unless you're here to report a crime, I don't have time for you now."

"I heard about Charlotte," Mitch said.

Jace wasn't surprised that word had traveled about their midnight run to the emergency room. That was how it was in a small town.

"I wanted to see if there was anything Cheryl or I could do. If it's all right with you, Cheryl was planning to run over later with a casserole. Between you and me, she's not the greatest cook, but she's crazy about your wife and would like to help anyway we can."

"I've got no beef with Cheryl. According to Charlie, she's great, which makes me wonder what she sees in you." Jace popped the lock on his truck. "And Mitch, don't steal any of my cattle while you're over there." It was a long story, but a few years back Mitch had been popped for cattle rustling. To this day he hadn't been charged, which still stuck in Jace's craw.

As he drove away, Mitch gave him a middle finger salute, which had Jace smiling all the way to Mary Ann's house.

Like the last time, Mary Ann seemed to be expecting him and invited him inside.

"This won't take long," he said and didn't even

bother to take off his hat or sit down. "Leave my wife and kids alone!"

"They happen to be my kids too."

"Only if you count DNA. I'm serious, Mary Ann. Leave them alone."

"You can't stop me from talking to my children, Jace. Travis is an adult; it's up to him. And you may have custody of Grady, but that doesn't preclude me from having visitation rights. I'll go to court if I have to."

"Then go to court. Until then, back off."

"You're not being fair, Jace."

"That's the thing about life, Mary Ann. It ain't fair." He caught her gaze and held it, punctuating his point. Life certainly hadn't been fair to Travis and Grady.

"I'm going to keep trying with Travis until there's no breath left in me and there's nothing you can do to stop me. As far as Grady, we both know I have rights. And I plan to exercise them to the fullest."

Jace contained his anger. "Why? If you love them the way you say you do, why would you come here and disrupt their lives like this? Why?"

"Because they need their mother. Even a once-bad mother is better than no mother at all."

"That's the thing, Mary Ann. They already have a good mother." With that, he turned around and walked out.

Chapter Eleven

There were people in and out all day, so much so that Charlie couldn't get any rest. First Aubrey came with a pile of home magazines to keep Charlie busy. Then Gina came with enough food and fresh berries from the restaurant's garden to feed half of California. Soon after Angie arrived with a bag full of romance novels.

It was like Christmas in June.

Jace came home for lunch all smiles, but Charlie could tell something was wrong. When she tried to press him on it all he would say was that it was a work thing, which she could see through a mile away.

It was Mary Ann.

She could sense it like a deer in the woods sensed danger. By the time he left to go back to work, she was sure something had transpired between the two of them. Something that made her already queasy stomach sink.

Later that day she was surprised to find Cheryl at the door. Mitch waved from his truck, which was idling in the driveway.

"Does he want to come in?" Charlie asked.

"No, that's okay. He'll wait for me there. I just came to bring you this." In her arms was one of those insulated casserole dish holders. "It's my mother's recipe. Mitch loves it."

"Come in." Charlie opened the door wide. "This is so nice of you. Thank you."

"Oh gosh, it's the least I can do. After all you've done for us."

Charlie really hadn't done much. Just gave them a couple of pictures and a contact number for a vintage party rental company.

"How are you feeling?" Cheryl said.

"Much better now. The doctor gave me some drugs to stop the prelabor contractions and for now they seem to be working."

"That's good, right? I mean . . . is it too soon?"

"If I can make it another two weeks, that would be ideal. Well, not ideal, but safer for the baby," Charlie said.

"Is there anything I can do?" Cheryl peeked through the foyer into the great room. "Everything looks so nice, but I could tidy up if you'd like, or run errands, or just anything."

"That is so kind of you, Cheryl. But between Jace, the kids, and the rest of the Daltons, I'm set. Come into the kitchen so you can set that down. I'm being so rude." Charlie wasn't even dressed, unless you counted a pair of old sweats.

"No, you're not." She followed Charlie into the kitchen. "This is beautiful."

"Thank you. It was Jace's grandparents' house. Would you like a cup of coffee or tea? Juice or a soft drink?"

"I'm fine." Cheryl slipped the casserole out of its holder and tucked it in the refrigerator. "I should let you get some rest. But I'm going to leave my phone number just in case. Don't hesitate to call. I'm pretty much living at Mitch's full time now and can be over here in less than fifteen minutes."

"You're so sweet." Charlie gave her a hug. How bad could Mitch be if this delightful woman loved him? And she clearly did.

She walked Cheryl to the door and waved good-bye to Mitch, who was still patiently waiting behind the wheel.

"Who was that?" Travis came in the door after taking the dogs to the creek just as Mitch was backing out of the driveway.

"Mitch and his fiancée, Cheryl."

"Mitch? I thought Dad hated him."

"I don't think your father hates Mitch as much as everyone thinks. In fact I think he might even miss him." As soon as the words left her mouth, she wondered if she was talking about Mitch or Mary Ann.

Grady was upset when he came home from school. Charlie sensed it the moment he walked in the door with his shoulders slumped, frowning. He further confirmed her suspicions when he turned down some of Gina's homemade oatmeal cookies.

"Tell me what happened today."

He gave her a nonchalant shrug and said, "Nothing," then went in his room.

Jace was still at work, but as soon as he got home, Charlie would get him to pry it out of Grady.

Of everyone, Grady was the happy-go-lucky one of the Dalton bunch, always smiling and cracking jokes. But occasionally he'd become sullen at something that happened at school. A bully who was picking on one of the smaller kids or some other infraction. He was a sensitive boy and, not unlike his father, felt the need to protect people from the injustices of the world. Travis was like that too.

She'd just nodded off to sleep in front of the TV on the couch when Jace came through the door with a huge bouquet of flowers, awakening her. He leaned over the back of the sofa and kissed her on the cheek.

"How was your first day of bed rest?"

"Busy," she said. "I've had an endless stream of visitors, including Mitch's fiancée."

"Yeah, he told me they were coming by."

Charlie sat upright. "You two are talking now?"

"No. But he ambushed me in the sheriff's parking lot and told me Cheryl wanted to bring you a casserole."

Charlie laughed.

"What's so funny?"

"I'm picturing how that conversation went." She got to her feet and took Jace's flowers. "These are lovely. I'll put them in water and figure out dinner."

"Oh no," Jace said and took back the flowers that Charlie was sure he bought in the floral shop in Dry Creek Village. "I'll put them in water and make us dinner. You stay there." He pointed at the couch.

"Jace, I can do light duty, you know? And you need to talk to Grady. He's been locked in his room ever since he got home from school. Something upset him today and he won't talk about it. Go coax it out of him." She took the flowers out of his hand, shooed him toward Grady's room, and went into the kitchen.

After arranging the bouquet in a vase, she slid Gina's famous lasagna into the oven and had just started on a salad when a cramp gripped her. She grabbed onto the edge of the counter to hold herself up and waited for the pain to subside.

"Mom, what's wrong?" Travis came up behind her.

She hadn't heard him come in. "Nothing. Just a small cramp."

He helped her to a chair. "I'm getting Dad."

"No, don't. I just need to sit here for a few minutes. You finish the salad."

She could see Travis vacillating, but ultimately he relented and took over in the kitchen, first bringing her a glass of water, then putting Gina's garlic bread in the oven.

"This is much better," she said. The cramp hadn't been like the others, not like a contraction but more like a sharp pain. But it hadn't lasted long, and she vowed to stay off her feet.

Travis's cell phone rang. He fished it out of his pocket and took one look at the caller ID and grimaced, letting out a soft curse.

"What's that about?"

"Mary Ann. She won't stop calling me." In an act of defiance he'd started calling his mother "Mary Ann." Or maybe it was out of deference to Charlie.

"Have you thought of just taking the call and listening to what she has to say? Maybe it's something you need to hear."

"Damn it, Charlie!" Jace came into the kitchen, furious. "Travis doesn't want to talk to her. Leave it alone."

She could feel her face heat. Once again Jace had made it clear that she wasn't part of this. That her opinion didn't count.

She walked out, making a beeline for the bedroom. Jace came in behind her and shut the door.

"I shouldn't have done that." He held up his hand in the classic surrender gesture. "I'm sorry. I let my emotions get the best of me and flew off the handle. I'm sorry, Charlie, it was the wrong way to handle it."

He moved in to hold her, but she pulled away. "Corbin used to do that. Right after he hit me, right after I lay bleeding on the floor, he would start in with the apologies. '*Oh, Charlotte, I'm so sorry. I just love you so much. No one loves you like I do.*' "

Jace backed away as if she'd burned him with a blowtorch. Stunned. Hurt. "How can you compare me to him? I was angry and I said things I shouldn't have said, which I regret. But husbands and wives argue, Charlie. Sometimes they yell at each other. Sometimes they say things in the heat of the moment they can never take back. If you don't like what I say, tell me to go to hell, tell me I'm full of crap. I can take it. What I can't take is you comparing me to that piece of garbage. I'm not him, Charlie."

"You embarrassed me out there. You made me feel like I'm not part of this family, that my opinion doesn't count."

"Look, there's no excuse for what I did. It was wrong. I should've waited until you and I could have a private conversation. I screwed up. I let my emotions on the issue override the proper way to handle it. I'll do better. But that woman is pushing me over the brink. Today she threatened to go to court over Grady."

"You talked to Mary Ann today?" She'd sensed it all along. "When? And why didn't you tell me?"

He gently led her toward the bed and told her to sit. "Let's both take a deep breath."

"Don't you dare patronize me! When did you talk to Mary Ann?"

"I went over there today before lunch. Travis was upset that she was calling him on his cell. I told her to leave him alone. We had words and that's when she told me she would go to court over visitation with Grady. I told her until she had a judge's order to back off."

"When were you going to tell me this? Or were you?"

"Of course I was. I just got home. You told me to find out what was bugging Grady. When was there time, Charlie? It's not like I'm keeping stuff from you."

She wondered. "Why did you find the need to go over there? Travis is nineteen years old. He's perfectly capable of telling her that he doesn't want any contact with her. Why are you obsessed with her, Jace? Ever since she got here you've been consumed."

"You've got to be kidding me." He threw up his hands in the air. "Yeah, Charlie, I'm obsessed with my ex-wife. Give me a break. You know what I'm obsessed with? I'm obsessed with protecting my family. You ought to try it sometime."

He walked out, slamming the door behind him.

Chapter Twelve

A week went by in a silent truce, but Jace felt a shift in Charlie. He told himself it was stress over the baby. They were all tense, counting the days until the thirty-seven-week mark of Charlie's pregnancy when, for all intents and purposes, the baby would be out of the woods.

Mary Ann had gone radio silent, giving Jace hope that she'd skipped town. Once a quitter, always a quitter.

Or worse. Perhaps it was the calm before the storm.

Travis's poison oak was all but gone and Grady was preparing for summer break. Next week there were finals and then, according to Grady, it was lazy days hanging out at the creek or the Dry Creek public pool.

Whatever had been eating him seemed to disappear along with Mary Ann's relentless phone calls.

"Shake a leg." Jace banged on Grady's door. "Pancakes in five. If you miss the bus today, it's a long walk to school." Jace's way of saying he wasn't driving him.

He had a cattlemen's meeting in the opposite direction of the high school and his schedule was tight today. He was trying to clear the decks before the baby came so he could take time off.

Charlie wandered into the kitchen just as Jace was serving up Travis and Grady's pancakes.

"Morning, sunshine. You want pancakes?" She was hardly eating these days and it worried him.

"I'll have one or two."

"Coming right up." He made them extra thick and passed her the syrup.

"What's on your plate today?" he asked her and she rolled her eyes.

"Same old. *ER* reruns, followed up with sleep, and then more sleep."

He grinned. "It's almost over. And when it is, you'll pray for sleep."

"I suspect that's true." She smiled back.

It was the first one he'd gotten out of her in a while and it lit him up.

Travis excused himself to do chores and Grady took off to meet the bus, leaving Jace alone with Charlie.

"I'll try to get home early today," he said.

"Don't worry about it. Between the boys and the cousins, I'm waited on hand and foot."

"You ever think I might just want to spend time with you?"

She didn't say anything and he shook his head.

"You're still pissed that I went to Mary Ann's house? Jeez, Charlie, let it go already."

"When you let her go I'll stop being pissed. How's that?"

"What do you want from me? You want me to tell her she can see Grady whenever she wants or that she can keep on harassing Travis until he relents? Would that make you feel better?"

"All I'm saying is that the boys should be able to make their own decision. First, though, they should hear what she has to say. But as long as you go around bullying everyone, that's not going to happen."

"Bullying everyone?" He snorted. "I'm tired of talking about this. We haven't heard from her in a week. She's probably gone. She probably went back to France or whatever place she saw last on the Travel Channel. Can't we just give it a rest? I'm tired of talking about her."

"Are you, though?"

"Okay, I'm leaving to go to work now before this turns into a fight, which for the sake of our baby neither one of us needs." He swiped his hat off the hook in the mudroom on his way out and got as far as the ranch gate before he pulled over to the shoulder of the road and dialed Charlie on his phone. "I love you."

"I love you too."

This would pass, he told himself as he caught the highway to the Auburn Cattleman's Hall, then sat through a boring meeting on beef prices. Cash, Sawyer, and Tuff usually joined him for the biannual meetings, but today his cousins were MIA. He'd give them hell for it later.

When he got back to his office he found Brett waiting.

"Annabeth let me in. I have something for you in my truck."

"Yeah, what's that?"

"Come on out and see."

He followed Brett to the Civic Center parking lot. Brett's truck had been modified with all kinds of nifty hand controls so he could drive it, and even had a lift for his wheelchair. A veteran's group had paid for it and Jace made sure to donate to the nonprofit every year.

Inside the bed was a cradle made of pink ivory wood. Jace only recognized the wood because he'd seen it in Brett's shop and had commented on how beautiful it was.

"Take it out," Brett said.

Jace hoisted it out of the bed of the truck and ran his hands over the fine workmanship. It was as much a piece of art as it was furniture. "This is freaking amazing. I don't know what to say, man. This is just . . . you're an artist."

Brett's grin spread across his face. "It swings." He pushed the cradle to show Jace how it worked.

"Charlie's going to go nuts. Wow, I can't believe you did this for us. This is like an heirloom . . . something to cherish." Jace was too blown away to put into proper words how much the gift meant to him. Not just because it was a thing of beauty but because Brett had gone through so much and had come out the other side.

"Enjoy it, amigo. I've got to motor, but I'll see you around."

Jace stashed the cradle in his office for safe-keeping. As usual, his inbox was clogged with dozens of emails. Most of them junk. But there was one that stood out from the rest, making him curse under his breath.

Jace: Attached is the original court filing for custody. Note that I get visitation rights one day a week, every other weekend, and half of all calendar holidays. I would like to spend the day with Grady Friday, after he gets out of school. Then we'll take it from there. Please let me know if that works with everyone's schedule. If not, I'm willing to choose another day next week.
Thanks,
Mary Ann

He clicked on the attachment, even though he remembered exactly what it said. He was the one who'd initiated the custody arrangement, with no pushback from her. In the beginning, for the sake of the boys, he'd wanted joint custody. But she wasn't interested. Hell, most of the time she didn't even show up for her weekends, let alone the weekday visits. And then she left the country.

Jace forwarded the message, then called his lawyer and told him to check his inbox.

"Is the agreement still valid after all this time?" Jace asked. "Can she disappear for six years without exercising her visitations and then just like that demand them? Tell me this is BS, Jerry."

"Let's calm down and give me a second to read everything."

Jace hung on while Jerry read the court order.

"It looks pretty clear-cut as far as Grady, Jace. As I told you before, Travis is aged out. It's up to him whether he wants to see his mother."

"Even after all this time? Even after she disappeared on the boys? Isn't there something in the law that says if you don't use your visitations, you lose them?"

"Maybe, but that would require going back to court, making a case against her. I'm not going to lead you down the garden path, Jace. It's a difficult case to make unless there is evidence of abuse. The judge would likely want to hear from Grady. If you want to fight, we'll fight. But take some time to think about it."

Jace couldn't believe that a woman who had all but thrown her children away could actually have rights.

He caged his fury and asked, "What do I do in the meantime? Force my kid to spend the day with her?"

"If you don't want to be in contempt of court, you do. You could try stalling. Tell her Friday won't work and schedule something for the end of next week. Then if you want me to seek an emergency change in visitation, I could try. But the chance of getting one is slim to none given that this isn't considered an urgent situation. And Jace, it's only temporary. You'd still have to go through the regular hearing process, which could take more than a year."

Jace got it. Mary Ann was an absent mother, not a violent one. He'd seen the ravages of abuse in a home and he'd never compare that to his situation with Mary Ann.

"Okay, let me think about it," he told Jerry.

"Let me know what you decide. And I'm sorry, Jace."

After he hung up he considered paying Mary Ann another visit, but what was the point? It was now clear that his ex-wife was here to stay. And to fight for the children she should've cared for six years ago.

That evening he called a family meeting and explained to Grady about the original custody agreement and how Mary Ann got to see him once a week, every other weekend, and on alternate holidays.

"So, I couldn't be with you guys on Christmas, I'd have to be with her?"

"We're going to try to change that," Jace said. "I don't want you to worry. And as far as this Friday, I'll send her a message that you're not available. Sound good?"

"What about Travis?" Grady wanted to know.

"Travis is nineteen, so none of this applies to him," Jace said.

"But he can see her if he wants to, right?" Grady turned to his older brother.

"I'm not seeing her. She can go to hell for all I care."

"Travis, please don't talk like that," Charlie said.

"Sorry."

Jace reached over and squeezed Grady's arm. "Hey, buddy, I don't want you to worry about this. No one is going to force you to do anything you don't want to do, *comprendes?*"

Grady worried his bottom lip. "Yeah, I guess. Can I go do my homework now?"

Jace and Charlie exchanged glances. Grady asking to do homework was as common as Jace winning the lottery, which was to say never.

"Go for it, kiddo."

"If the meeting is adjourned, I'm going over to Ruben's to see his new car." Travis got to his feet. "I'll be home in a few hours."

"Be careful," Charlie said. "It's foggy at night."

"I always am." He kissed her on the top of her head and left through the back door.

"I thought he was on the outs with Ruben." Jace couldn't stand the kid. He was a spoiled brat and a bully, but he made it a policy to let his kids pick their own friends.

"My guess is he's more interested in the car than hanging out with Ruben," Charlie said. "What are you planning to do about Friday?"

"Tell her Grady already has plans, which isn't a lie. Last I looked his dance card was packed with end-of-the-school-year activities."

"And then what? You can only come up with so many excuses."

Jace leaned back his head. "Go back to court."

"I thought the lawyer said it was a long shot, that judges tend to favor the mother in situations like this?"

"I don't know, Charlie. What do you want me to do? You saw Grady. He wants no part of her."

"Or he thinks you want him to want no part of her."

They were back to this again. He'd had a long day and was exhausted.

"Could we table this for now?"

"Sure. But we're going to have to deal with it eventually," she said, her voice terse.

Chapter Thirteen

Charlie was alone when the pain started.

It began with pressure in her back and slowly moved down to her abdomen, the pain radiating from back to front. The nausea had come on so fast that she hadn't even realized it was happening until she had a heavy urge to vomit.

At first she tried to ignore the symptoms, telling herself it was probably more Braxton-Hicks contractions. But she could no longer deny the reality of the situation. She was experiencing preterm labor.

She should've called Jace, but lately it felt like there were three people in their marriage and the delivery room wasn't large enough for Mary Ann too. So instead she dialed Aubrey.

Fifteen minutes later Aubrey was at the house, packing Charlie a bag.

"I should've done that already, but I hoped I still had at least another five weeks," Charlie said.

"It'll be fine." It was the seventh time Aubrey had said that. Charlie got the sense that Aubrey thought if she said it enough times it would be true.

"I'd be lying if I didn't say I'm scared," Charlie said.

"It'll be—" Aubrey stopped herself. "Let's get you to the hospital. While I drive, you call your doc. Can you do that?"

Charlie nodded and immediately dialed Dr. Orville.

"Until today I had tons of energy. No pain, no nausea, no nothing," Charlie told Dr. Orville. "Could it be Braxton-Hicks?"

"Has your water broken?" she asked.

"Not yet."

"That's a good sign. We'll see what's going on when you get here."

"Should you call Jace?" Aubrey asked when Charlie signed off with Orville.

"Not yet. He'll freak out, and there's a good chance this is a false alarm. Why pull him away from work for nothing?"

"Gotcha." Aubrey pulled off at the hospital exit and drove to the turnout at the entrance doors. "Can you walk in while I park? Or should I go get a wheelchair?"

Charlie had paced the floor until Aubrey had gotten to the house and it had actually eased some of the pain. "No, I'm good to walk."

"I'll be right behind you. Promise."

As soon as Charlie got inside, she was escorted to a room where a nurse gave her a gown to change into.

"I'm here." Aubrey rushed in, out of breath. Charlie suspected she ran all the way from the parking lot.

Dr. Orville knocked, came in, and glanced around the room. "No Jace today?"

"He's at work," Charlie said. "I'm waiting to call him until we know more." She introduced the doctor to Aubrey.

Dr. Orville washed her hands, slipped on a pair of gloves, and pulled a stool up to the foot of the bed. "Okie doke. Let's take a look at your cervix. How often are the contractions?"

"I don't know. Maybe every five or six minutes. They feel more like cramps, like I'm having my period. So maybe this is a false alarm, right?"

"Could be. Let's have a look."

In the middle of the doctor's exam another cramp ripped through Charlie. She grabbed her abdomen and let out a groan.

Dr. Orville checked her watch and went back to business. "You're dilated and I see the mucus plug."

"What does that mean?"

"It means this baby is coming."

"But it's too soon," Charlie cried.

"I'm on my way." Jace raced out of his office so fast he nearly forgot his hat.

"Let Tobin know he's in charge while I'm gone," he called to Annabeth as he flew past her desk on the way to his truck.

"Don't drive like a madman."

"Yes, Mom."

If it wasn't a violation of policy, Jace would've put his light bar on the roof of his truck and turned the siren on. But Charlie said there was no rush. She was still in early labor and it could take hours, even days before the baby came. Still, he didn't want to miss a second of it.

He hung a right and merged onto the on-ramp for the highway when his phone rang. One glance at caller ID told him it was Marta Martinez from the high school. Either Grady was in trouble or she needed law enforcement assistance with a student.

I don't have time for this.

"Hey, Marta, what's up?" He got into the fast lane and punched the gas pedal.

"Grady didn't show up to his first-period class this morning. According to the driver and his cousin Ellie, he was on the bus. But no one has seen him since."

"Are you sure he's not on campus and just skipping class?"

"We've looked for him, but he's not in all the usual places."

Goddamn Mary Ann.

"Okay, I have an idea where he is. I'll let you know as soon as I find him. In the meantime can you call me if he shows up?"

"Absolutely. And Jace, it's the end of the year.

It's not unusual for a group of kids to ditch their classes and go to SB over at the state park."

"Are any of his friends missing?"

She let a long sigh. "So far they're all accounted for, but we're still checking."

As soon as he hung up with Marta, he hit automatic dial for Cash.

"Hey, Aubrey says Charlie's in labor," Cash said by way of a greeting.

"Yeah, I'm on my way to the hospital now. But I need a favor. Mary Ann nabbed Grady as he got off the school bus. She wanted a visitation with him today, but I told her it wasn't in the schedule. Apparently she took matters into her own hands. Can you go over to the Stoddard cottage to see if they're there? I can't believe she freaking did this. I'm going to nail her for it, but I don't have time right now."

"I'm on my way," Cash said. "And Jace, take it easy until we've got all the facts. Focus on Charlie and the baby. I'll take care of this and call you as soon as I find Grady."

Jace found parking at the hospital and followed the information desk volunteer's directions to Charlie's room. He found her in the maternity wing's hallway in a johnny gown, pacing the floor.

"You're here." She fell into his arms.

"Why aren't you in bed?"

"It feels good to walk."

He pulled away to take a closer look at her. "Are you in a great deal of pain?"

"Not too bad." Just as she said it she grabbed on to him and shuddered. "That was another one. They're getting closer."

"Let's get you inside your room." He took her arm and let her lead the way.

"Aubrey went to the cafeteria to get us drinks. Call her if you want something."

"I'm good," Jace said, but he was freaking out a little. Besides the baby being early, he couldn't stand seeing Charlie in pain.

"The doctor said this could take a while," Charlie said.

"That's good, right? The longer the better."

"I think at this point we're only talking hours. A day maybe. The baby will still be born premature."

"But we're still okay, right?"

"She'll be late preterm, which is better than early preterm but it's still not ideal."

He rubbed her back. "She'll be strong like her mother and stubborn like her father, so we're all good."

His phone vibrated in his pants pocket. "I've got to take this." He stepped out into the hallway. "Cash?"

"They're not here."

"Is there a white Toyota parked in the driveway?"

"Jace, believe me, I checked for her car. There's no one here. I peeked inside the windows and saw plenty of her stuff, so I don't think she took off with him. You have her phone number? I'll call her."

"Yeah. I'm sending it to you now. Call me as soon as you hear something."

He could've called Mary Ann himself, but he didn't want to lose it with her in the hospital with Charlie in the next room. Things between them had been tenuous these last few days where Mary Ann was concerned and Charlie didn't need the extra stress.

"What's going on?" she asked him when he got in the room. Aubrey was sitting in the corner with a cup of coffee. "Aubrey heard you talking to Cash."

Jace hadn't even seen Aubrey come in.

"It's nothing. Just something work-related."

Charlie cocked her brows and Jace could tell she wasn't buying it.

Aubrey, knowing when to beat a hasty retreat, got to her feet. "My work here is done. Call me if you need anything." She kissed Charlie on the cheek. "Break a leg. We're all rooting for you."

"Jace what's going on?" Charlie asked as soon as Aubrey closed the door behind her.

"Grady didn't show up at school today. Mary Ann's got him, even though I told her not today."

Charlie grimaced and wrapped her arms around herself. "Oh boy, the pressure is starting to bear down on me."

"Should we call Dr. Orville?"

"Not yet. She's close by when we need her, but my water hasn't even broken yet." She started to ask more about Grady when Jace's phone vibrated again.

It was Cash. This time he took the call in the room. "Did you get her?"

"She drove up right after I got off the phone with you. Grady's not with her, Jace. She's right here and swears she hasn't seen Grady all morning."

"Put her on the phone!"

"I don't know where he is." Mary Ann sounded as panicked as Jace was starting to feel. "I would never have gone against your wishes, Jace. I would never have taken him out of school."

He didn't have time for this. "Put Cash back on."

"Could you check the SB? Maybe talk to Ellie to see if she knows something. Hang on a second, I've got another call coming in. Hopefully it's Grady." He switched over. "Grady!"

"No, it's Mitch."

"I don't have time for you right now." Jace switched back to Cash. "It wasn't him."

"Take it easy. I'll find him. If he's not at the state beach, I'll call in for reinforcements. Between all of us, we'll find him. Just hang tight with Charlie." Cash signed off.

Charlie was shaking her head, "Go, Jace. Just go find him."

His phone vibrated again. "Jesus, Mitch is calling me again." He was just about to let it go to voice mail when he thought better of it. "What!"

"I've got Grady."

The world seemed to turn on its axis. Charlie had heard it too because she grabbed his hand and squeezed it.

"He's in the truck with me. I was on my way to a job site and saw him walking toward the park on Juniper. He said he was on his way to his mother's to, and I quote, 'see her and give her a piece of my mind.' Poor kid is a mini you. Hopefully there's help for that. Do you want to talk to him?"

Charlie pulled the phone out of Jace's hand.

"Mitch, it's Charlotte. Please take Grady to Mary Ann's and tell her to drop him off at the ranch when they're done having their day together, okay?"

"Yes, ma'am."

"And Mitch, Jace has something to tell you."

She handed the phone back to Jace, who held up his arms in the air and shrugged.

"Tell him 'thank you,' you idiot."

"Mitch, my wife says I should tell you 'thank you.' And that you're an idiot."

"Yep, don't mention it," Mitch said and Jace could hear the laughter in his voice.

He dashed off a text to Cash to call off the cavalry and left a message with Marta that Grady had been found safe.

"If you weren't so obsessed with your ex-wife, you would've seen what Grady wanted. What he needed." Charlie turned away from him and winced. It was another contraction.

"You're right," he said and sat in the bed next to her. "We're focusing on you now and our baby." He put his finger to his lips.

"So you admit that you're obsessed with your ex-wife?"

"The only woman I'm obsessed with is you, Charlie. From the day I met you, you were the one. The only one."

"But you realize that Mary Ann is also part of our family?"

He started to say she wasn't, that she would never be, when Charlie interrupted him. "She'll always be Grady and Travis's mother. And if she wants a place in their hearts, it's our job to accept it. Can you do that, Jace?"

"I don't know," he said truthfully.

"Why? Because she hurt you so badly?"

"Yes. But not in the way you think. When your children hurt, you hurt. And she hurt them, Charlie. She tore them apart."

"Do you still love her?"

He did a double take. "What? I stopped loving her a long time ago. And when I fell in love with you, I started to wonder if what I had with her was even love at all. I mean, I loved her. Of course I did. But it wasn't an enduring love, it wasn't the kind that sticks. I think she understood that right from the start. And when it was over between us the truth was I was relieved. Not that she left the boys but that she'd left me.

"Do you know how much I love you?" He cupped her chin in his hand. "If you don't, I'm doing something wrong because there's no one but you. You, this baby"—he touched his hand to her belly— "Travis and Grady are my everything. Nothing is ever going to change that."

She reached for him and he wrapped his arms around her. "You just seemed so . . . I don't know . . . consumed with her. It felt too passionate to me."

He remembered what Cash had said about the thin line between love and hate. He didn't even hate Mary Ann, let alone love her.

"Remember how *consumed* I was with your ex coming back to hurt you?" he said. "Do you think I had the hots for Corbin? No one is ever going to hurt my family. If you call that consumed or passionate, so be it." He held her gaze to see if she understood, to see if she comprehended how much he loved her.

She grimaced.

"Come on, Charlie. You don't believe me?"

"I believe you," she said. "And I love you so much. But my water just broke."

Epilogue

Keely Jo Dalton was born at 4:45 in the morning, weighing in at five-and-a-half pounds. After a week in the hospital she was coming home to Dry Creek Ranch.

Charlie wrapped her in a swaddling blanket, clipped her into her car seat, and rode next to her in the back of Jace's king cab.

"You two okay?" Jace watched them in his rearview mirror.

"We're great."

Twenty minutes later they pulled up to the ranch gate, which had been decorated with pink ribbons and balloons and a giant banner that read, "Welcome home, Keely!"

There was more of the same at the house, including fresh bouquets of pink gerbera daisies. The entire Dalton clan was waiting. Keely got passed around like a football, everyone wanting to hold her, most of all Travis and Grady. The two of them were so in love with their new baby sister that Charlie feared Keely would be spoiled rotten.

Everyone moved into the kitchen, where a feast had been spread out on the center island. Gina had outdone herself. Charlie's parents and sister had sent a giant basket of cookies and planned to come in person later that month to help with the baby.

Mitch had brought over a rocking horse almost identical to the one Jace had as a kid. Jace took one look at it and suppressed a snarky grin. Yes, Mitch was trying too hard. But Charlie suspected that eventually Jace would pardon his old friend. And that was good. Friendship was more important than old grudges.

While the Daltons were eating and Jace had Keely cradled in his arms, she managed to pull Travis aside.

"How did it go with your mom?"

"You're my mom." He was adamant. "But it went okay. I did what you said and told her how angry I am with what she did. She said she's sorry and I think I believe her. I think she wishes she'd done things differently."

"I'm proud of you." Charlie brushed away a stray hair that had fallen into his eye. The boy still needed a haircut. "And Travis, it is a blessed child who has two mothers instead of one, you know?"

"We'll see," he said, but Charlie could tell that Travis and Mary Ann were already making headway.

Grady would be easier. He was younger and more forgiving than his big brother. But Charlie

realized they all had a long way to go in the forgiveness department. They'd get there, though.
Charlie's heart was too full not to.

Jace joined her to the other side of the room.
"What were you and Travis talking about?"

"Mary Ann. He and his mother are trying.
Grady too. She's planning to stay in the Stoddard
place through Christmas, you know?" Charlie had
gathered that information from Mary Ann herself,
who'd brought a gift to the hospital for Keely
when Jace wasn't there.

"That's what I hear." Jace nodded. "I guess it's
good. Healthy." For the sake of all of them, Charlie knew Jace was putting his best spin on the situation.

"I told Travis that I'm proud of him. And I'm
proud of you too for accepting that Mary Ann may
very well be back to stay."

"I'm trying," he said and grinned. "It's difficult
to remain angry with her when I have everything I
ever wanted." He wrapped his arms around her
and held her tight. "Thank you for giving me
that."

"Giving you what?"

"Everything I ever wanted."

She reached up and pulled down the brim of
his Stetson. "Thank you for being my cowboy
true."

Please read on for an excerpt from *Proof*.

Page-turning suspense and adventure combine with masterful storytelling in the newest novel in the Lost and Found series from acclaimed #1 New York Times bestselling author Fern Michaels, as a cache of mementoes is the catalyst for a search into Luna's own past.

Sometimes, two very different pieces of furniture just pair perfectly together. Brother and sister Cullen and Luna Bodman work much the same way. While practical-minded Cullen Bodman focuses on their family's antiques restoration business, his sister Luna's next-door Namaste Café brings in new clientele. As a thank you to his sister, Cullen retrieves Luna's childhood dresser from storage and refinishes it. A delighted Luna rummages through the drawers and discovers a shoebox full of mementos of her friend Brendan, reviving memories of love and a broken heart. But a flurry of emails and texts leads to a very brief death notice: Born. Died. Nothing else.

Beyond Luna's sadness is her uncanny intuition that something about the announcement is off, a feeling that intensifies when she later glimpses a person who seems to be Brendan's doppelganger. His laugh, his walk—Luna remembers both so well. Is her old friend really alive? And if so, who faked his death, and why? It's not the first time an item of furniture has spurred Luna to solve a fascinating puzzle. But this time, the mystery is much more personal, and the stakes infinitely higher . . .

Prologue One

Stillwell Art Center was coming up on its third
anniversary. The forty-acre complex was home
to a two-story lavish building where dozens of
artists occupied glass-enclosed workspaces over-
looking a meticulously landscaped atrium in the
center. The rear of the building had large glass
sliding doors that opened to a stone patio with
café tables. Beyond the patio was an equally metic-
ulous park where visitors could bring their dogs
and let them run in a designated area, where they
were supervised by an attendant.

The genius behind the artisan village was Ellie
Stillwell, a seventy-something former art professor.
It was when her husband Richard passed away that
she discovered how much money her real estate,

bonds, and investments were worth, and that the farm and land she'd inherited from her family spanned hundreds of acres.

Ellie and Richard had never had children. The farm, Richard's law practice, her position at the college, and their dogs were all they needed. But Ellie wanted to leave a legacy, something for the community of artists, and for the community as a whole. It took almost two years and a lot of council meetings, surveys, revisions, building plans, and cajoling before they broke ground. Initially many of the council members were dubious about the viability of an art center outside Asheville, North Carolina. *Who would go watch people paint? Throw pottery?* Ellie had ready answers: It would be a place of interest. A destination. She explained that the atrium would be surrounded by gourmet shops, where people could purchase sandwiches, salads, pastries, cheese, wine, tea, and coffee between visits to the many artists' studios, where they could watch the artists at work—and hopefully purchase something. Strategically placed café tables in the atrium as well as on the outdoor patio would provide a place to eat and relax. In addition to the elegant food court, Ellie would allow community organizations to hold their events free of charge.

She continued to explain and defend her ideas, including Thursday nights devoted to music, when people could listen to smooth jazz or a string ensemble.

After much debate, she won over the council and began the year-long construction.

Not only was the Stillwell Center artist-friendly,

but it was also dog-friendly and kid-friendly. Well, sometimes kid-friendly, depending on which entitled group of wine-slugging women showed up. Some days a particular group of women came with their undisciplined children—and no nannies—which gave Nathan Belmont, head of security, a run for his money. Literally. One time he chased a five-year-old over three hundred yards through the well-kept gardens. The tipsy mother hadn't noticed her child was missing until Nathan carried him back into the atrium. It wasn't a daily event, and everyone knew who that little group of designer clotheshorses were, so they were prepared when the women and their offspring appeared for a version of Chuck E. Cheese.

While Ellie would never proclaim whose art she preferred, she'd developed a strong bond with Luna Bodhi Bodman, the occupant of The Namaste Café. Luna had once been employed as a social worker in child psychology, but her real passion leaned toward the metaphysical. Ever since childhood, she'd had a way of knowing things. A gift, some would say. She could read people like an open book, and she would do cold psychic readings for customers if they were so inclined. A large easel and drawing pad were her medium. When people came seeking advice, she would stand behind the easel and draw whatever images came to her. It was uncanny, as Ellie discovered when Luna told her things about Richard that no one could have known.

Luna was very low-key when it came to providing insight to customers, even though her reputation was well-known. She never solicited. They had to ask. Luna's bohemian wardrobe, granny glasses, and waist-long hair might have been a clue as to her practice, but then again, it was an art center, and many of its denizens wore unconventional clothing.

Luna's older brother Cullen took the corner spot on the first floor, next to her café. When he'd graduated from college, he was employed in an office doing office-type things. The type of things that weren't fulfilling for him. When their parents retired from their antiques business, Cullen took it over and expanded it to include restoration, then became a master craftsman, resuscitating discarded furniture.

The third person in Ellie's close-knit group was Lebici "Chi-Chi" Stone, a stunning woman whose handcrafted jewelry was an extension of her beauty. Her parents had brought her and her brother to the States when she was nine. Before moving, her father worked in Kano, Nigeria, and was employed making ceremonial bowls. Chi-Chi showed an interest in the craft at an early age. As she grew, so did her fascination with jewelry. She studied metalsmithing after high school, and during her summer breaks, she visited Nigeria and brought gemstones back to incorporate into her work. Now, at thirty-nine, she was renowned for her jewelry, which fetched anywhere from $500 up to thousands of dollars for custom pieces. Chi-Chi and Luna had become best friends, and a romance between Cullen and Chi-Chi began to grow. They often had dinner together, and when Luna's love interest,

Marshal Christopher Gaines, was in town, it was always a cheerful occasion. Unless Luna was on one of her missions to solve a mystery, which usually involved one of the items in Cullen's workshop. Then it became a madcap adventure that drew all of them into Luna's world of mystery.

Visit our website at
KensingtonBooks.com
to sign up for our newsletters, read
more from your favorite authors, see
books by series, view reading group
guides, and more!

BOOK **CLUB**

BETWEEN THE CHAPTERS

Become a Part of Our
Between the Chapters Book Club
Community and Join the Conversation

Betweenthechapters.net